UNCHAINED

BLOOD BOND SAGA: VOLUME ONE
PARTS 1 - 2 - 3

HELEN HARDT

UNCHAINED

BLOOD BOND SAGA: VOLUME ONE
PARTS 1 - 2 - 3

HELEN HARDT

WATERHOUSE PRESS

TABLE OF CONTENTS

Blood Bond: Part 1   7

Blood Bond: Part 2   129

Blood Bond: Part 3   255

For everyone who wants to believe...

BLOOD BOND SAGA

PART 1

DANTE

I used to dream of severed human heads.

They hung above me, their skin gray and pasty as the elixir of life flowed out of them. I inhaled, and the metallic scent of iron infused itself into my cells. It was the iron and other nutrients in blood that our bodies needed, but that wasn't the scent that drew us, the scent we craved.

Humans don't realize they each possess their own scent beyond perspiration and pheromones, a fragrance that comes from their very life force—their blood.

From one neck, a drop of citrusy blond female fell onto my tongue. From another, the leathery and musky flavor of a brown-haired male, this one muscular and full of testosterone. A third fed me with the floral flavor of a female redhead. Redheads were rare, and their blood tasted better than the finest Bordeaux. Redheads with green eyes tasted the best—a lusty concoction laced with essence of lavender yet acidic enough to make a vamp's mouth water for more and more.

Then there were the dark-haired ones with light skin—

those who, somewhere hundreds of generations ago in their family tree, were descended from a vampire. Their blood was the ultimate concoction, the Champagne of plasma. Bold and tannic yet fruity and divine. Peach, plum, blackberry. Leather, coffee, the darkest of chocolate. Tin, zinc, laced with violet and apple and estrogen. Even the men smelled of traces of milky estrogen.

All this plus the one-of-a-kind flavor unique to every human.

I lapped it up, gaining strength, finally able to pull hard enough to release my leather bindings.

I roared, flexing my muscles, ready to bolt—

But before I could escape my prison, my eyes would open. I always awoke.

Those fragrances had been denied me for years, perhaps decades. But I remembered, my memory exaggerating each aroma. The only scents in my enclosed space were the remnants of the two human servants who fed me. Who tortured me.

She would be hovering above me, gazing at me with her cold, evil eyes before she bent down and sank her fangs into my neck.

She never drained me, only took enough so *she* could maintain her control over me and keep up her own strength. The worst days were when *I* had to feed.

She forced me to drink from her. I had no other choice. I needed blood to survive, and hers was my only option.

Feeding from her kept my muscles from atrophying, even though I couldn't move much while in captivity. A good thing. The only good thing.

The dream of sustenance pouring into me and giving me the strength to break free recurred again and again, but escape was always only that—a dream.

    Until the day it wasn't.

ONE

DANTE

Somehow—still, as I crouched in an alleyway, starving for blood, I didn't know how—I'd drawn on all my adrenaline and broken the bonds that had detained me for so long. I'd stumbled a little getting out of the compound, but my muscle memory had now returned.

Unchained.

Finally.

Free from *her*.

I'll find you, Dante. You're mine forever.

Get out of my head!

You are and always will be...mine.

With the last shred of strength I possessed, I forced *her* out of my mind.

My guts churned and my gums itched. Hungry. So fucking hungry. I'd scavenged some scraps from a dumpster to stave off the hunger in my stomach, but they lacked all the nutrients necessary for my diet.

I needed blood.

I'd caught and released not one but five different stray animals since my escape. Their blood would have sustained me, but they were so small that they wouldn't have lived through my feeding.

I would *not* take a life.

Never. I would not violate another living being. Not after the way I'd been violated. I'd survived hell. I could go a few minutes longer to find a source that wouldn't require killing something.

I hid in the shadows, avoiding the all-night commotion of Bourbon Street. The music and voices were muffled in my mind, as my sense of smell and my hunger overrode everything. Humans slid by, each taking the shape of a giant beating heart. I breathed through my mouth so as not to be tempted by the earthy and unique scent each one possessed. But the fact remained.

I had to stop one of them.

I had no choice.

I needed clothes, shoes, money.

Blood.

When I pounced on a homeless man, so ravenous that I was able to glamour him into submission, I promised myself I'd take only his garments and cash.

But the pulsing artery in his neck proved too delicious to resist.

Only a few drops, just enough to get me to a better source. Just enough... The itching in my gums intensified as my canine teeth elongated. I suppressed the growl so as not to draw attention from anyone.

Before I punctured his skin, though, a beaming light shone in my eyes.

"Hey, you there. What's going on here?"

I quickly retracted my teeth and shielded my eyes against the illumination. The man was dressed in jeans and a leather jacket, but he held up a badge.

A cop. A fucking cop. I inhaled. Dark chocolate, blackberry, and copper. Testosterone plus a sliver of milky estrogen. A really good-smelling cop—a cop with a vampire somewhere in his ancestry.

"I asked you a question. I'm Detective Jay Hamilton, NOPD. Is that man okay? Why doesn't he have any clothes on?"

Close your eyes.

The homeless man complied.

"I...don't know, Detective. I found him like this."

"Looks like he's out cold. I'm going to need to ask you a few questions, sir."

Despite the heat of the night, a chill swept over the back of my neck. I suppressed an urge to look behind me.

"Not a good time." I fled past, hoping I was still strong and quick enough to get away and that the cop would stay to help the homeless man.

The detective didn't follow me, thank God, and a block later, I picked up a scent.

A blonde. No, a brunette with dark-blue eyes. A child. Not a child. Couldn't do that. Now an older woman, a bad clotter. Iron and tin. Witch hazel and African violet. Traces of methamphetamine...

The tingles in my gums began again.

Blood. Lots of blood in a cramped space. A hospital or a blood bank was near.

I raced toward the aroma.

I raced toward life.

TWO

Erin

"Female, early thirties, gunshot wound to the abdomen."

"Thanks," I said to the EMT as I took over bagging the patient. "Doc! Gunshot wound."

Dr. Adele Thomas hurried over. "She's a bleeder. Pull three units of O negative."

"Right away."

Shit! Where were all the orderlies? I'd have to do it myself. I scampered down the hall to the small refrigeration unit in the ER. *Red gold,* the docs called it. Other people's blood saved lives every day. I'd seen it perform miracles. As a nurse, I donated as often as I could.

No O neg. Not a huge surprise. O negative was the universal donor. We used a lot of it in the ER when a patient's life was at stake and we didn't have time to do a blood panel. We had O positive, but I couldn't take the chance. What if the patient was Rh negative? I had to go out of the ER to the University Hospital blood bank down the hallway.

The main hospital was just north of the French Quarter and was never quiet at night. I hoped I could get the blood and return quickly.

The door to the refrigerated blood bank was wide open. Not overly unusual, though no one but the ER staff would be grabbing blood in the middle of the night.

I walked in cautiously—

"Aauuhh!"

The high-pitched scream had come from me.

In a flash, a hand was clamped over my mouth.

A bloody hand.

"Easy," a low voice said. "I won't hurt you, but you can't scream again. Do you understand me?"

My heart thundered, and my skin, already chilled from the cool temperature, turned icy. My breath came in rapid pants as blood from his hands oozed between my lips. Metal. *Blech.* I darted my gaze around the large unit. Blood. Everywhere. Bags had been ripped open, and blood dripped from the walls, pooling on the tiled floor.

Fear raced through me. Fear...and something else. Something I couldn't identify. An invisible warmth was trying to relax me, almost like my mother's kiss on my forehead when I was a child.

I fought against it and screamed again, this time muffled against his hand.

He clamped onto me more tightly. "Damn it! Why isn't it working?"

Why wasn't *what* working?

"You can't scream again. I don't want to harm you."

I had no choice but to believe him. I was at his mercy. His strength was apparent as I tried to maneuver against him.

I wasn't going to get away.

He brushed his cheek against my neck and inhaled. "What *are* you? You smell like...truffles. Black truffles. Black coffee. Dark chocolate. Hints of blackberry. Tin. Copper."

"Mmm," I said against his hand. His strange words, any other time, would have made me pause. Now? I was too frightened to give them any credence.

"Okay. I'm going to take my hand away. *Don't scream.*" Slowly he released his hand.

And I screamed.

Back went his hand. "Damn it! Now what are we going to do?" He inhaled again. "Cabernet Sauvignon. Fuck. Fuck, you smell so good."

His hand was lower on my mouth this time, and I bit into the top of it as hard as I could.

"Ouch!" He tore his hand away from me.

I turned to run out the door, but he blocked my exit.

A man. A man with black hair tangled around a face stained with blood. Eyes as dark as strong coffee stared at me. Not in a menacing way. In a pleading way.

"You have to *help* me."

Without meaning to, I reached toward him and touched his cheek. Something pulled at me, forced me to do it, yet I wanted to touch him, wanted to feel him beneath my fingertips.

He whisked my hand away. "Don't," he said. "I won't be able to control myself."

"C-Control yourself?" My hand tingled. Had to touch him.

His stubbly cheeks were covered in blood, some of it already drying into brown, and more of the red fluid rimmed his full lips.

Then, a voice. "Erin, Dr. Thomas needs that O neg!"

I pushed the man behind the door. "Don't move!" I whispered urgently.

I quickly grabbed three bags of the necessary blood and ran out of the bank, handing them to Steve, one of the orderlies. "Here. Sorry."

His eyes nearly popped out of his head. "Shit, Erin, what happened to you?"

"What do you mean?" I asked, willing my voice not to shake.

"Uh...well, you've got blood all over your face and hands."

Crap. *Think fast, Erin.* "A couple bags exploded in the fridge. I need to get custodial down here stat."

"I'll do it. Doc needs you in the ER."

Words forced themselves into my mind. *Can't leave him.*

"Just take the blood to Dr. Thomas, Steve. Please. I'll be there in a sec. I have to wash up, obviously."

"Okay. Sure. I'll get custodial on this as soon as I can." He walked away quickly with the O neg.

I walked cautiously back into the blood bank. The man looked even wilder now. But he didn't frighten me. What had originated as fear had morphed into something else—something I couldn't name. Something that sent prickles all through me but kept me on high alert. Something that warmed my core, made me feel...lusty, yet oddly protective.

"Listen," I said to him. "Someone's coming down to clean up. You need to get out of here."

"Still hungry," he said huskily.

"I'll find you some food, okay? But right now I need you out of here or you're going to get arrested. You broke into our blood bank, and now you're a mess. Did you think you'd find food in here?"

He didn't respond, just glared at me with those gorgeous and expressive dark eyes. How a man whose face was stained with red gold could look so enticing disturbed me more than a little.

"I need to get back up to the ER. We've got a gunshot victim, and the doctor needs me."

I pulled him out of the bank and down the hallway to the restrooms. Not too many people came down here during the night shift, thank God. I opened the door to the men's room and pushed him inside. "Clean up," I said, "and then stay out of sight until I come find you. My shift is over in two hours. I'm Erin, by the way."

I scurried into the ladies' room and faced myself in the mirror.

Lord. I looked like I'd just engaged in some heavy cannibalism. No wonder Steve had freaked. I washed my hands and face as best I could and then went to the locker room for some clean scrubs. I trashed the ones I'd been wearing.

Then I hurried back to the ER.

"Where the hell have you been?" Dr. Thomas demanded.

"Sorry. A problem in the blood bank. Didn't Steve tell you?"

"Yes, but he didn't tell me why you were dealing with that when you should be up here. We've had two new cases come in while you were gone. I've got the surgical chief resident on the gunshot victim. I need you in room eight. A baby with croup. Prepare a nebulizer treatment and get in there."

"Yes, Doctor."

Though she could be harsh at times, I liked Dr. Thomas. She was my favorite of the four ER docs I worked with on the night shift. My least favorite was Dr. Zabrina Bonneville. She was brilliant, but she lacked bedside manner not only with her patients but with staff as well.

I prepared the neb treatment and rushed to room eight. The poor baby was on his mother's lap, barking like a seal. Yup. That was croup. Parents tended to get over-worried about the common cough.

"I'm Erin," I said, holding out my hand.

"Cathy Murphy," the woman said, "and this is Brian."

"Hi there, Brian." I smiled at the cute baby, red in the face from his cough. I turned back to his mother. "I know how worried you must be, but croup is rarely serious. We're going to have him feeling better in no time." I asked Cathy my litany of questions and got the right dosage prepared for Brian. Within ten minutes, he was breathing Albuterol from the oxygen mask.

"I'll be back to check on you in fifteen minutes. In the meantime, if you have any trouble, just push the red button on the intercom and someone will be right with you."

As I left room eight, more EMTs rushed in. "Male, late twenties. Unconscious. Found naked in the street. Possibly homeless. BP a little low, other vitals fine. His eyes are open, but we can't wake him up."

"Let's get him into room four right away," I said. "Looks like an OD to me. We'll need to run a drug panel. I'll get the doc—" I gasped.

The unconscious man on the gurney had grabbed my wrist.

THREE

DANTE

Lust rolled through me. I stood against a sink in the men's room where Erin—her name was Erin—had pushed me, and I glanced in the mirror.

My jaw dropped. I looked like a wild man, my hair in disarray, several days' growth of dark beard on my jawline, blood drying on my cheeks and chin. But that in itself wasn't what astounded me. The last time I'd seen my reflection, an eighteen-year-old high school student had stared back at me. Now I was looking at a man's jaw, a man's profile, a man's beard. The skin around my eyes showed slight signs of age, a few wrinkles here and there. My front teeth no longer had a gap between them. They'd moved together somehow. Maybe when my wisdom teeth had erupted. I remembered the pain when they broke through my gums, pain that had seemed like nothing after what I'd been through.

So long ago now...as if they were only fuzzy memories from a dream. *Or a nightmare.*

Still, I was a mess. I was lucky she hadn't run screaming.

Instead, she was trying to help me. Help I didn't deserve after desecrating her blood bank. Who was she? And why hadn't she responded to my attempt to glamour her?

Her scent had intoxicated me. She was one of *them*— the humans with dark hair and fair skin, whose blood tasted better than the most exotic nectar. Her eyes were a light green, almost as light as a peridot, and they sparkled with fire and ice simultaneously.

My gums began to tingle once more. Just the thought of Erin's blood awakened my urge to feed.

I'd gorged on the bagged blood, enough that I should have been sated. I couldn't go back for more. Someone would have been notified to clean up by now.

More bagged blood wouldn't help anyway. I wanted *her* blood.

I tried to push the hunger from my mind and concentrate on something more important.

I was free.

Unchained from the shackles that had bound me for so many years.

So why did I still feel like I was imprisoned?

I was still in New Orleans. Was my family still here? Dad? Em? River? Uncle Braedon? Grandpa Bill? Bill might be over a hundred years old by now. He could very well be gone.

Even if they *were* still here, I had no idea how to get in touch with them.

Erin. Erin was my only chance.

What if she forgot? Didn't come back for me?

I resisted the urge to lick the dried blood from my face and hands—it wouldn't satisfy me anyway—and furiously scrubbed at them.

Erin.

I needed her blood. I needed *her.*

I'd felt it. She needed something from me as well. I wasn't sure what, but I'd felt the tug. She wanted to touch me. Couldn't stop herself from putting her hand on my skin, even though I must have looked like an animal after a kill with blood streaming from my lips.

I'd brushed her away, for fear I'd lose the last thread of self-control keeping me from lunging toward her, sinking my teeth into her soft flesh, and taking from her the sustenance I craved.

Hunger still clawed at me. Not just for Erin's blood, but for Erin herself. My groin tightened.

Not again.

I willed the erection down. Couldn't go there. Not now. I'd had erections during captivity and no way to release, with my hands always bound. I certainly had no way to release now. How long had I been gone? I had no idea. Only that it had been years. Many, many years.

Erin had told me to stay put, that she'd come back for me. Could I trust her? Why would she want to help me?

I had to get out of here. If I stayed in one place for too long, I risked being tracked by *her.* Vampires had no scent to each other, but we had other ways of keeping tabs. I had no doubt *she* had the ability to find me.

I grasped the edge of the sink, steadying myself.

I pulled against the leather restraints. "Who the hell are you? Why am I here?"

The woman was dazzling...in a terrifying way. She was

masked, except for her icy blue eyes. When she smiled, her fangs were already long and sharp.

"Don't you recognize your queen, Dante?"

She was delusional. We recognized the government of the places we lived. In this case, the United States of America, which didn't have a queen.

My clothes were gone. I lay naked, my wrists and ankles shackled to a table. Or was it a bed?

"So young and beautiful. I can smell the testosterone flowing through you, turning your boy's body into a man's. How old are you? Sixteen? Seventeen?"

I was eighteen. A late bloomer, something I found pretty embarrassing. My cousin, River, who was a month younger than I, had matured before I had. My voice had finally changed two years ago, which was the signal that a male vampire had become fertile.

"You are no queen," I said through clenched teeth. "Let me go."

She laughed. "You will recognize me as your queen soon enough."

"Let me go!" I demanded once more. "My father will come for me. My uncle. My grandfather. They are more powerful than you could ever hope to be."

She snarled, her fangs bared. "They're already on their way, sweet one. Something I was counting on."

A thud pulled me out of the nightmare.

I'd fallen to the hard tile floor.

That horrible night, so long ago, when I'd awakened in her dungeon.

Escape. I needed to flee *now*. Erin had promised to help, but I couldn't wait. Not when *she* could already be on my trail. I left the men's room with my face and hands now clean, but my clothes were a different matter. They were tattered—they'd come from a homeless man, after all—and covered in blood. I sneaked down a hallway until I found a locker room. I traded what I was wearing for a pair of jeans that were slightly small on me and a black hoodie. I didn't like stealing, but I had no choice.

I raced around, looking for the back door where I'd entered.

No! A pull. Erin was mentally tugging me toward something. Something I'd seen before.

I ambled into the emergency room, trying to look inconspicuous, when something tight wrapped around my wrist, and I flinched. I rubbed at it but found only the calluses from the leather bindings I had finally left behind.

Then I saw it.

A man on a gurney had grabbed *Erin's* wrist. The need to protect her hurled into me like a cyclone. I inhaled, yet I smelled only Erin's scent. But I recognized the man.

"Why won't he let go?" Erin asked, pleading.

"I don't know." A woman in a white coat was looking into the man's eyes with a flashlight or something. "Pupils are dilated. We need to take some blood for a drug panel."

I knew what to do. I quickly walked toward the gurney and gazed into the homeless man's eyes, letting go of the glamour that had been holding him since I'd run from the cop earlier. In my hurry to get away, I hadn't released him.

The doctor was too involved in her work to notice me, but when the man closed his eyes and let go of Erin's hand, she looked up.

"You!" she said.

I turned and walked swiftly toward the first door I could find.

FOUR

Erin

He'd cleaned up nicely.

"Whatever was going on seems to be resolved," Dr. Thomas was saying. "Let's get him in an exam room. Erin, we need to get his blood for the panel."

"Yes, Doctor." The words came out of my mouth automatically because the only thing in my thoughts was the man with the dark and fiery eyes now walking out the door.

So I wouldn't see him again. So what? He'd vandalized a blood bank because he hadn't found any food in what he thought was a regular refrigerator. I had better things to do than lust after him, like getting back to the exam room and drawing blood for this poor guy's drug panel.

I assessed him. His teeth looked decent, so probably not meth. Opioids most likely. We were seeing a lot of that lately.

I entered the exam room. He had regained consciousness, and Dr. Thomas was talking to him while she examined him.

"Here's the nurse now. Erin, Mr. Lincoln has agreed to the drug panel."

"Good. It's nice to meet you, Mr. Lincoln. Can you make a fist for me, sir?"

His brown eyes were wide as he looked at me. "Did you see him?"

I tied the rubber banding around his upper arm. "See who?"

"The vampire."

I looked to Dr. Thomas, who shook her head slightly at me. The man was on something, clearly. That was Dr. Thomas's signal for "just go with it."

"I'm afraid I didn't." I tapped at the vein on the inside of his elbow. "You're going to feel a quick prick, okay?"

He nodded. "I'm used to it."

I'll bet he is. I didn't see any tracks on his arm though. I drew two vials of blood and then bandaged the puncture site. "All good, Mr. Lincoln."

Dr. Thomas was looking into his eyes again. "Dilation is gone. Interesting. How's your vision, Mr. Lincoln? Can you see all right?"

"I lost my glasses a year ago," he said.

"I see. We'll have your results soon. In the meantime, we need to keep you here for observation." Dr. Thomas wrote a few notes in his chart and then hung it on the door and smiled. "If you need anything, Erin will see that you get it." She left the room.

He grabbed my wrist again.

I yanked my arm away, and this time he let go.

"I'm not on drugs," he said.

"I understand." I patted his arm. The lab report would tell the truth. "I need to do some rounds. Just push the red button if you need anything."

"I'm not on drugs," he said again.

I sighed and left the room. That's what they all said. It was a continual enigma to me how people who lived on the streets always seemed to find money to get high. I was living paycheck to paycheck. Good thing I wasn't an addict. I wouldn't be able to afford it.

I worked on two more cases before my shift ended at sunrise. I yawned as I retrieved my purse from my locker and changed into my regular clothes. Home, breakfast, and then bed. My routine.

I loved the night shift. I'd always been sort of nocturnal, being more comfortable during the night. I was a classic introvert, and fewer people were around at nighttime, except for all-night partyers, which were plentiful here, but I was not in any shape or form a party girl. Nope, just plain old Erin Hamilton, an ER nurse from Columbus, Ohio, who'd moved to New Orleans for an old boyfriend three years ago. The relationship had ended, but I'd stayed. I liked it here. My brother was here. My best friend, Lucy Cyrus, was here. She was also an ER nurse on the night shift.

I exited the hospital and headed toward the parking lot where my car was—

Someone jerked me backward.

A hand over my mouth muffled my scream.

"Please. You have to help me."

The man. I struggled against his grasp, my heart pounding. "Help!" I yelled, though it came out muffled.

"Please. I won't hurt you. I promise. I need your help." He eased his hand from my lips. "Please don't scream."

Was he kidding? I stepped forward to run, but he grabbed me again. I looked around, hoping someone had seen us.

The parking lot was eerily vacant.

"Please," he said again. "I will *not* hurt you."

I nodded. I had nowhere to run anyway, no one to turn to for help. I'd have to take him at his word. I looked into his eyes. I didn't see anything to fear in them. In fact, they seemed to speak to me. They seemed to say *I need you.* The desire to help him rose again within me.

He eased his hand from my mouth.

"I told you to stay put," I said.

"I know. I would have, but I had...something I'd left unattended."

I drew in a deep breath, attempting to slow my racing pulse. "Do you want me to call someone for you? Do you need a hot meal? There's a soup kitchen not too far from here."

"No!" he said urgently. "I need to get out of the sun. My skin burns easily."

He *was* quite fair-skinned. I hated my own pale skin, but on him it looked good. His hair was in disarray, and he was wearing jeans that were way too small, but there was no denying how attractive he was.

"I hear you. Mine does too. But it looks kind of cloudy today so far."

"Doesn't matter."

"All right." I fumbled in my purse and pulled out a tube of sunscreen. "Try this."

He smeared some onto his face. The rest of his body was covered by clothes. He handed the tube back to me. "Thank you."

"You're welcome." I paused, not sure what to do next. My head said to go to my car and drive home. My legs, though, stayed planted.

"Please. Help me."

"I'll show you where the soup kitchen is, okay?"

"No, I mean—" He jerked his head to the left. "Get me out of here. Please."

"Hey, I don't even know your—"

"Where's your car?"

"Over there"—I gestured—"but—"

He grabbed onto me. "Go!"

I went.

I didn't know why, but my legs seemed to. I walked briskly toward my car in the hospital staff lot.

When he was in the passenger seat of my VW Beetle, I turned on the ignition.

And had no idea where I was going.

FIVE

DANTE

Erin turned to me, her green eyes dazzling. "Where do you need me to take you?"

Good question. I had no idea where my family was, or if they even still existed. *She* had threatened to annihilate them all more than once to keep me in submission. I needed a place to lie low for a while. I needed access to a phone.

Erin would have one.

I stared into her mesmerizing eyes. "Your place."

"My place?" She backed the car out of her parking spot and began driving. "I don't even know your name."

"Dante. Dante Gabriel."

"Huh. That name sounds slightly familiar to me. Where do you live?" Then she shook her head. "I'm sorry."

"Why are you sorry?"

"Because I'm assuming you are..."

"Homeless?" In truth, I might be. I had no idea where home was at this point. Before I showed up on someone's doorstep, I needed to let my family know I was alive.

I was back.

She cleared her throat. "Yeah. We see a lot of you guys in the ER, and—"

"I'm not homeless. At least not in the sense that you think. I have a home. At least I had one."

"Most homeless people had a home at one time," she said. "Do you need...a fix or something?"

What was she talking about? "I'm not on drugs." No, the only substances I needed were food and blood. I wasn't sure how she would react to the second part of that. Even now, as I inhaled her intoxicating scent, the blood lust was rising in me. "Are you a doctor?"

"No. A nurse. I thought about medical school, but I couldn't stomach the idea of ending up six figures in debt."

"I used to want to be a doctor," I said. I hadn't consciously allowed myself to think about that in a long time. I was taken when I was eighteen years old. If I hadn't been—if I'd been allowed to live my life—I might be a doctor by now.

The days had run together. I glanced at Erin's cell phone sitting in the cup holder between our seats, concentrating on the date. She had one of those newfangled smartphones. *She* had shown me hers once.

Fuck. Years. At least a decade, I'd bet. Half of my life had been stolen. I could never be a doctor now. I hadn't even made it to my high school graduation.

I had to figure out what to do about money. My family had lived in New Orleans for generations. We had money. We had history in this city. We were accepted here. My father was probably still in this city somewhere, and so was my grandfather. I just had to find them.

If they were still alive.

"Are you going to answer me, or what?"

I glanced over at Erin. "Sorry. What?"

"So what stopped you?"

"Stopped me from what?"

"From becoming a doctor? Did you zone out or something?"

"Just couldn't get it together, I guess." Major lie. I had been a driven young person. My father and my grandfather had supported me in everything I did. I had no doubt that, but for *her*, I'd be a doctor now.

So fucking unfair.

Erin turned into a complex of townhomes and then into a parking spot.

"Where are we?" I asked.

She turned to me, biting her bottom lip. "My place. I'm not sure what happened. I know you said my place, but I didn't intend to bring you here. Yet here we are."

"Perfect. I need to get inside. Quickly." *She* could be anywhere, searching for me.

"Look. You seem like a nice guy, and I'm sorry for your troubles, but I'm not a moron. I don't invite strange men into my home."

If I had been able to mature naturally, I would be better at glamouring by now. I could only glamour someone when I needed to feed, and even so, I'd failed with Erin earlier. As much as I wanted to get inside her townhome to take cover, I felt a sliver of happiness that I wasn't able to glamour her.

I didn't want to glamour Erin.

I didn't want to violate her in that way. So I resorted to begging.

"I promise you I won't hurt you, but I need you to take me inside. Please."

Erin pulled up her emergency brake. "I must be crazy as a loon. I hope if you were going to harm me, you would have done it by now. Come on." She opened her car door.

I followed her into her townhome. "You live here alone?"

"Yeah. I sank everything I had into this place, and now I'm mortgage poor. But I love it."

It was a modest little abode, and I felt...at home.

"Where do you sleep?"

"Upstairs, master bedroom. And I'm exhausted. But I'm going to make some breakfast first. Are you hungry?"

"Yeah, I could eat." Contrary to myth, vampires were physiologically nearly identical to humans. Our nutritional needs were similar, except we required the added nutrients found in blood.

"Make yourself comfortable, I guess." She set her purse on the table and got to work in the kitchen, frying bacon and eggs.

I inhaled. All I'd had since I'd escaped was crap from my dumpster diving. My stomach growled. I was indeed hungry.

"Do you have a computer?"

"Sure. A desktop and a laptop."

I arched my eyebrows. "You have *two* computers? For one person?"

"Pretty much everyone does." She chuckled.

News to me. My father had one computer. He, my sister, and I had shared it. "Okay. Can I use it?"

"What for?"

"I need to do some research."

"On what?"

"I need to find my family."

"Oh. They live here in town?"

"They used to, but I've been gone for a while."

"Wouldn't they have told you if they'd moved?"

"Not necessarily," I hedged.

She placed two plates of breakfast on the table. "Hope you like bacon and eggs."

"Love them."

"Look. You seem like a decent guy. I'll let you borrow my laptop. It's an old one, anyway, and I'm only a couple dollars away from getting my new one. But you have to take it to a coffeehouse or something to do your research. I need to get some rest. I'm on again tonight."

My skin prickled, and my gums began to tingle. Couldn't leave. Couldn't let this woman out of my sight. "I'm not going anywhere."

Her beautiful green eyes widened. "I assure you that you are."

"I'm not. I promised you I wouldn't harm you, and I won't. But I need to stay here until I can figure out what to do next."

She stood and cleared her plates. Tension flowed off her body.

I hoped she believed I wouldn't hurt her. I could never hurt an innocent person, especially one who was helping me. Not after what had been forced upon me for so long.

I'd need to feed off of her eventually, but right now, my body was reacting in a different way.

My dick hardened.

She was so beautiful. Her hair was falling out of a ponytail, and her eyes showed fatigue. Her clothes were baggy and didn't give me a clue what was under them, but my imagination was vivid. I was attracted to this woman. I felt a pull toward her, the need to be inside her, a need I wasn't entirely comfortable with. Though I hadn't been a virgin when I was taken, my experience was limited to the awkward coupling of two sixteen-year-olds my sophomore year in high school. That was it. Chicks didn't really gravitate toward late bloomers like me.

Erin was not a virgin. I could tell by her scent. She hadn't been with anyone recently, but she was far from untried. A growl lodged in the back of my throat. I didn't want anyone else to touch her.

She turned, regarding me, her eyes heavy-lidded. "All right. For the life of me, I don't know why I'm saying this, but you can stay."

"Where should I sleep?"

She let out a soft sigh. "I have an extra bedroom, but..."

I stood. "But...what?"

Her scent wafted toward me. Was it getting stronger?

She didn't answer, and when I inhaled, I smelled the beginning of her arousal.

I wasn't even close to ready for this, but my body thought otherwise. I strode toward her, wrapped my arms around her, and crushed my lips to hers.

SIX

Erin

His lips were surprisingly soft, in contrast to the hardness of his kiss. He thrust his tongue into my mouth, and I instantly responded. He tasted of the breakfast we just shared, but a tangy different taste, something I didn't recognize.

Whatever it was, it intoxicated me, disoriented me.

He kissed me like an animal devouring its prey, and I reveled in it—the feral, primal nature of it.

I'd had a couple one-night stands, so this wasn't entirely new to me. Still it definitely wasn't my norm. But if Dante was intent on taking me to bed, I wasn't going to stop him.

I slid my hands over his shoulders, up his neck, over his stubbly cheeks—cheeks I'd first seen covered in blood—up into his thick black hair. I threaded his locks through my fingers and pulled on them.

He broke the kiss. "Feels good," he grunted. Then he smashed his mouth to mine again.

His erection pushed into my belly.

This man was so gorgeous. What would his cock look like? Majestic... Just like the rest of him. And substantial, judging from the size of the bulge.

He searched every crevice of my mouth with his tongue, and when he finally pulled back slightly, I pushed my tongue into his mouth.

So sweet and delicious, every part of him. I traced his gum line, the inside of his cheeks, his teeth, and—

"Oh!" I broke the kiss.

A low groan emerged from his throat. "Need you," he growled, his lips barely moving.

I touched my fingertips to my tongue. Blood. The metallic taste meandered over my tongue. Something had nicked me. Something inside his mouth. Did he have a tongue piercing? Not that I had noticed when we were kissing.

"Bedroom," he said.

His dark eyes glowed with electricity. I looked down to his crotch and gulped. It had nearly doubled in size.

I took his hand and led him up to my bedroom. I hadn't made my bed, but I didn't care. Didn't care that everything was in disarray. Only wanted to get my clothes off. His clothes off. Kiss him some more. Taste him some more. Puncture my tongue again. Get that massive dick inside me.

He pushed me toward my bed until my calves hit the mattress, unsteadying me. He grabbed me, gripping my shoulders and keeping me on my feet. He gazed into my eyes. "You're beautiful. So beautiful."

I smiled. "So are you."

He slid one finger over my bottom lip. "That kiss..."

I opened my mouth, but all that came out was a soft sigh. He buried his nose in my neck and inhaled.

"You smell so good. I could exist forever on your scent alone." He inhaled again. "Almost."

Almost? I had no idea what he meant, but at the moment, all I wanted was his mouth on mine again. Though the wet kisses to my neck were pretty awesome, too.

When he made it back to my lips, I parted them for him immediately. He swept his tongue into my mouth, and I nearly collapsed into him, as if I were coming home after being gone far too long, acclimating to something familiar that had been denied me for years. I probed into him, aching for everything he could give me, everything I secretly desired.

And like magic, he deepened the kiss. I met the forceful demand of his mouth with renewed eagerness, a bone-melting fire igniting within the deepest part of me. A hunger coiled inside me, a hunger that only Dante could sate. And when he sated it, I wanted him to consume me.

My nipples hardened, pushing against my bra, yearning for his touch. Between my legs a party had started, the tickle morphing into a pulse of throbbing need.

Our tongues tangled, our lips slid, and when I knew in my soul I'd do whatever he asked of me—

He pulled away.

"Can't," he growled.

My mind was a maze. "What?"

"Can't...do this to you."

"No. It's okay. You *can*."

"Don't want to hurt you..."

"You're not hurting me. I swear. It's okay, Dante. I'm not going to cry date rape."

He cringed. "I would never!"

I reached toward him, but he cowered away.

"I know you wouldn't. Please. Trust me."

"I...do trust you, Erin. I wouldn't have asked for your help otherwise. You could have had me arrested last night, and you didn't. But do you trust *me*?"

Did I? It went against all logic. Why was I drawn to him so completely? Was I just horny? Cory and I had broken up two years ago, and though I was far from promiscuous, I hadn't been celibate since then. No, horniness alone was not the issue. I couldn't deny that I wanted Dante with a raw desire I'd never known, but I also felt something else. A need to be near him, to protect him.

And yes, I trusted him.

"I'm not sure why," I said, "but yes, I do."

"Then trust me when I say I can't take you to bed. Not today. I thought I could. I thought I—" He inhaled deeply. "Your scent. Your arousal. My God..." He inhaled again.

Then—

"No! Not now!"

SEVEN

DANTE

An image swirled in my mind—an image I couldn't forget.

Get out of my head, you abhorrent bitch!

Was I doomed to submit to her even after I'd escaped? Had she somehow made assurances that I could never be with a woman? That I'd always have some memory of her hovering over me? Taking from me? Making me submit?

"No, damn it!" I said aloud, pulling at my hair, inching away from Erin.

"Dante"—she reached toward me, her hand trembling—"what's wrong?"

"Where's your computer?" I demanded.

Her green eyes glazed over a bit.

No. Please don't. Don't cry.

"Did I do something wrong?"

"No."

"Then why—"

"I just can't. I wish I could explain, but...I just really need your computer. Please." My cock was hard as marble inside the too-tight jeans. "Fuck."

"What?"

"These pants are too small. Your computer?"

"It's downstairs."

I tried adjusting the crotch to the jeans to give me some more room. Didn't work.

"I have some money," Erin said, her eyes still laced with sadness. "You can go out and get some clothes that fit. I can't do much more than that for you."

Regret pinched my heart. I'd hurt her. Hurt this sweet, kind woman whose scent had to have been created in heaven. She was offering me money for clothes when she owed me less than nothing. And damn, all I could do was inhale her sweet scent, stare into her beautiful eyes and at her chest, where her nipples were apparent beneath all the layers of her clothing. I wanted her so damned much.

She deserved better than I could give her. Better than an inexperienced vampire who craved her blood.

Her offer of money tempted me, but I couldn't take it. I couldn't go outside anyway. My skin had held up with the sunscreen, but I'd only been in the sun for about ten minutes. Most vampires could handle the sun with adequate sunscreen, but my skin hadn't seen the sun in God only knew how many years. I couldn't risk it. I had to rebuild my resistance to sunlight.

"I can't leave. Not until dark."

"Are you hiding from someone?" she asked timidly.

"Yes." The word tumbled out before I could stop it. It wasn't a lie. *She* would have her goons out looking for me. I'd felt something sinister at the hospital, an odd chill, not unlike what I'd felt when I ran from the detective earlier. That was why I'd nearly forced Erin to take me to her car.

And now...somewhere in this townhome.

Something was lurking.

Something I had to ferret out and eliminate.

"Oh." She closed her eyes for a few seconds and then opened them. "I'm harboring a fugitive."

"God, no!" *Fuck*. "It's nothing like that. I can't explain it any more than I already have."

She crossed her arms over her chest, covering her protruding nipples. "I'm sorry. I really am. But you're going to have to leave."

If only I could glamour her into letting me stay. But again, the thought niggled at me that I didn't want to glamour Erin. I wanted her to obey me of her own free will, though why I wanted her or anyone to obey me made no sense at all. I didn't trust my glamouring power anyway. It hadn't matured the way it was supposed to.

The strong urge to possess her rose within me once more. My body took over my mind, and I grabbed her once more and kissed her with the ferocity of an animal.

Then, pounding on the door downstairs.

"Erin? You here?"

EIGHT

Erin

I reluctantly broke the kiss.

"Sorry," I said to Dante. "That's my brother. I'll see what he wants. Don't go away."

I hastily adjusted my clothes and went downstairs. Jay was helping himself to a bagel from my fridge. "I was going to bed, Jay. I work the night shift too, remember? What do you want?"

"Sorry. I thought you might still be up. Didn't you just get off—"

"Please just tell me what you want," I said, interrupting.

"Okay, okay. Got any coffee?"

"Of course I don't have any coffee. This is my bedtime, remember?"

He sat down at the table and spread cream cheese on a bagel. "A patient is missing from your hospital."

My mind went directly to Mr. Lincoln, the drug addict I had treated several hours earlier. No doubt he had gone out looking for a fix. "I'm afraid I don't know where he is."

"He? The missing patient is a woman."

"Oh. Which one?"

"She came in last night with a gunshot wound to the abdomen. Do you remember her?"

Oh, I remembered her. She was the reason I had been sent down to the blood bank for the O neg—the reason I'd found Dante there.

A fact I had completely forgotten as I'd been launched into the most passionate make-out session of my life.

I had been ready to take him to my bed. Not only that, I hadn't even thought about using protection. I was a nurse, for God's sake. Whatever had gotten into me had to go. Now.

And here was my brother, the detective, sitting at my kitchen table while I was harboring a fugitive. *Good work, Erin.*

"Yeah, I remember her. She went into surgery, but I wasn't on the case."

"That's the thing," Jay said. "She never made it to surgery."

I eyed him as he munched on his bagel. "What?"

"Yeah. The surgical team was waiting, but the patient never made it into the OR."

"Maybe her family came and took her home. Maybe they don't believe in medical care or something."

"Erin, what are you talking about?"

"I don't know." God, I was a mess. My brain was still in a lusty haze.

"Anyway, her name is Cynthia North, twenty-five years old, five feet six inches tall, slim figure, brown hair, brown eyes, fair skin."

"You're talking like a cop."

"I *am* a cop, smartass."

I thought back to my shift. "Are you sure we're talking

about the same woman? I remember the EMT saying she was in her early thirties."

"That was probably their best guess. She may not have had any ID on her when she came in."

"How do you know it's the same woman, then?

"Her significant other told the cop who questioned him. Gave him her name and date of birth."

"How did she get shot?"

"Domestic dispute, apparently. I wasn't on the original call."

"Then I wouldn't put a lot of stock in anything her so-called significant other says. He probably shot her."

"No. He claims he didn't. It was another woman who he was having an affair with. Broke into their home and shot her."

I arched my brow.

"Anyway, the woman disappeared from your hospital, so I thought you might have some information."

"Like I said, I wasn't on the case, other than being sent down to get blood for her. The doc said she was a bleeder. Maybe she bled out before she got to surgery and ended up in the morgue."

"The surgical team would have been notified."

"Yeah, probably. But we're understaffed right now on the night shift. It's possible. Did you look into it?"

"I didn't, but I'm sure someone has. Still, it doesn't hurt to double-check. Let me make a call." He punched in some numbers to his cell phone.

I yawned. It was past my bedtime, and I had the same shift tonight. I needed to get some sleep, but first I had to figure out what to do about Dante, and I couldn't do that with my detective brother in my kitchen.

I stood when someone knocked on the door.

Jay looked up from his phone. "That's probably my new partner. Good guy. He might be wondering what's keeping me."

"Then you might have rethought stealing my bagel." I walked to the door and opened it.

A handsome man with short dark hair and brown eyes stood before me. He looked oddly familiar.

"Hey. I'm looking for Jay?"

"Yeah, come on in. He's making a quick call." I led him into the kitchen. "Sorry I don't have any coffee to offer you. This is nighttime for me."

"Me too. I just got assigned to work with Jay." He held out his hand. "I'm River Gabriel."

NINE

DANTE

After trying, and failing, to make my stolen clothes more comfortable, I walked out of Erin's bedroom and stood at the top of the stairs.

Erin sat at the table in her kitchen with two men. They both had dark hair. I waited.

One of the men looked up, and then his dark eyes turned round. "Oh my God. Who *are* you?"

Erin turned toward me. "Oh, he's a friend of mine. He was just leaving."

The man stood and came toward me.

This time my eyes popped open and my jaw dropped. I knew this man, had last seen him when he was a seventeen-year-old high school student. I'd lain awake so many nights, praying for him to find me. For anyone to find me.

My skin warmed around me as my heart sped up. *Keep it cool, Dante. You don't want questions from Erin.* "River?"

"Yeah. Have we met?" Then he blinked his eyes a few times. "No. It can't be."

I inched forward. "It's me, Riv."

He continued to stare blankly.

"I swear. It's me."

He fell out of his stupor and grabbed me in a bear hug. "Christ, Dante," he whispered in my ear. "Where've you been?"

"I'll tell you what I can," I whispered, "later."

"That's why you look so familiar," Erin said. "You two are related?"

River still held on to me with a vise grip.

I pushed him away gently, even though I never wanted to let him go. "Yeah. River's my cousin."

"Oh, good," Erin said. "Then you have somewhere to go."

The other guy stood quickly and assessed me with a cautious gaze. "Wait a sec. You're the guy I found with that naked homeless man last night."

Then I recognized the detective, though I couldn't smell him anymore, most likely because Erin's scent still pervaded my senses. Jay Hamilton, he'd said his name was. What was he doing here with my cousin?

"I don't think so," I said, hoping he wouldn't push it.

"That's impossible," River said. "Dante hasn't been back here for years. If he were in town last night, I'd have known. Sorry I didn't recognize you, cuz. It's been so long."

He was giving me the alibi I needed. Erin would know it was a lie, but I had to play along for River's sake and hope she wouldn't give us up. "I hardly recognized you either." Then I turned to Jay. "Yeah, I just got into town this morning. I have a friend who used to live in this complex, so I thought I'd crash, but he wasn't home."

Erin's mouth dropped into an oval, but thankfully she didn't say anything.

"Then what are you doing *here*?" Jay asked.

Erin stepped forward then. "He lost his cell phone, and I found him in the parking lot when I was getting home from the night shift. He asked if he could make a call."

"And what was he doing upstairs?"

"Just using the bathroom, Jay," Erin said.

"Don't you have a perfectly good bathroom on this level?"

"The toilet keeps clogging. I have to get a plumber over here."

The story had more holes in it than swiss cheese, and this guy was a cop. Erin was protecting me. I was grateful, but why would she?

"Erin, what is going on here?"

"Nothing. Now stop going all big brother on me, okay? Don't you guys have to get back out on duty?"

"Actually, the shift is over. We're headed back to the station," River said. "Dante, why don't you come along with us, and then we can go over to Bill's together."

"Sure. Sounds like a good plan." But as thrilled as I was to see River, I ached at the thought of leaving Erin.

I looked into her green eyes, trying to convey my thanks, trying to convey just how much these few hours with her had meant to me—her not turning me in, our kisses, the alibi... everything. As River led me out the door, something tugged at me.

Something was telling me to stay with Erin.

I pulled the hoodie over my head to help shield me from the sun and left with my cousin.

My grandfather held on to me for what seemed like forever, and I wasn't complaining. River and my sister, Emilia, had already squeezed me to pieces.

Bill—short for Guillaume; we'd always called him by his first name—finally pulled back. "Let me look at you. You've changed so much, Dante. But I would still know you anywhere."

"I never thought I'd see any of you again," I said, my eyes welling with tears.

"That goes for the rest of us, too," Bill agreed.

"How long have I been gone?"

"You don't know?" Bill massaged his jaw. "Nearly ten years, son."

Ten years? I'd had no idea. "That means I'm twenty-eight years old."

"Yes, you are."

"Over a third of my life. A third of my life was stolen." I plopped onto Bill's brocade couch—the most uncomfortable couch, still—and sank my head into my hands.

"Where have you been?" River asked.

But Bill quieted him. "He'll talk when he's ready."

"He needs to be ready now, Bill. If someone did this to him, took him, we need the facts now to get on the case."

"Stop being a detective for a few minutes," Bill said. "Let him get his bearings."

Ten fucking years. *Her.* As happy as I was to see my family, I knew I wasn't yet free of *her.* *She*'d come after me. I had to leave town as soon as I could.

I stood. River, Em, and Bill. My mother and River's mother had passed away before I'd been taken. But where was my father? My uncle?

"Bill, where's Dad?"

Bill sat down on the sofa and patted the cushion next to him. I sat down again. He hadn't changed much in ten years. He was now one hundred and two years old. His once salt-and-pepper hair glowed silvery white, but very few wrinkles marred his handsome face. He walked without aid, and he still looked as strong as ever.

"Where are Dad and Uncle Brae?" I asked again. "Are they at work or something? This early in the day?"

My grandfather closed his eyes for a moment. When he opened them, he looked to River. "You didn't tell him?"

"No. We were in the car with my partner, and then during the drive here, I just couldn't bring myself to..."

My heart sped up. "To what?"

Emilia sat next to me and grabbed my hand. "You can't blame yourself, Dante."

"How can I blame myself if I don't know what you're talking about?"

Bill let out a long sigh that ended on a groan. "When you disappeared, Braedon and Julian went after you."

"They obviously didn't find me. Where are they now?"

Bill waited a few seconds—which seemed like hours—before speaking. "We don't know. They never returned."

A brick hit me in the gut, and my blood turned to boiling acid. *No. No. No.* "You never found their bodies or anything?"

"No."

They're already on their way, sweet one. Something I was counting on.

Her. All this time, my father and my uncle were probably locked in the same compound I had been locked in. Maybe they weren't.

Red rage consumed me, and I stood, balling my hands into fists.

How dare she take a third of my life?

Take my father's and my uncle's lives?

A big part of me hoped they were dead. Better that than at the mercy of *her*.

I hadn't known whether I'd see any of my family again, and here sat three of them. I should be happy. Ecstatic. But the loss of my father sank inside me, overwhelming me. My father had taught me everything. Taught me what it meant to be a man. He taught me how to be physically and mentally strong, while *his* father, Bill, had taught me wisdom. Or had begun to. I still had so much to learn, things River had known for ten years now.

My father was gone.

And it was my fault.

"Don't blame yourself, son," Bill said, as if he were reading my thoughts. "None of us blame you, like your sister said."

Shudders racked my body.

"You need blood, Dante?" River asked.

It hadn't been too long since I last fed, and I'd tamped down the blood lust after leaving Erin, but this news... "Yeah, I could use some. But how...?"

"Same as you remember. We have a discreet deal with a local butcher. It's cows' and sheep's blood, but it does the job." River stood and walked into Bill's kitchen. He came back with a glass full of warm blood.

I took a deep drink of the thick red liquid. This had come from a steer. Only traces of testosterone and even less estrogen. The flavor was a bit plain, but I wasn't complaining.

I finished the whole glass. No one was talking, and I expected a barrage of questions about where I had been—

questions I wasn't yet ready to answer.

I set the glass on the end table and looked at my grandfather. His eyes were dark like mine, but when I looked into them, knowledge shone in their depths. Knowledge laced with sadness. He'd lost both his sons. I didn't want to tell him what had happened to me. And it was clear that he didn't want to ask, which could only mean one thing.

He didn't want to face it any more than I did. At least not yet. Not in this moment.

Finally River spoke. "I have to ask again. Where have you been? We all thought—"

"You thought I was dead. I don't blame you. Just like you think my father and Uncle Brae are dead. And they may be."

"You don't have to talk about it yet, Dante." Bill said. "But you will have to eventually. The sooner the better, so River can do his job."

Fragmented images broke into my mind.

Yes, my queen.

Sinking my teeth into her neck, strong hands holding me there, forcing me to feed.

Then her teeth sinking into my femoral artery...

Chills skittered through me. If I talked... If I told them... Then I'd have to face the hard truth. This *had* happened. It *hadn't* been a ten-year nightmare.

I couldn't. Not yet.

"I need to sleep first. And some clothes that fit would be nice."

"I keep a couple changes of clothes here," River said. "We've always been about the same size, and from what I can tell by looking at you, that hasn't changed. I'll get them for you."

"Thanks, Riv."

River stood and headed toward the stairs, but then turned around. "How did you meet up with Jay's sister?"

"It's a long story."

"It's bound to be a good story. She lied for you. She lied to her brother, who is a cop."

"You lied for me too, Riv. And from what I can tell, you're also a cop. When did that happen? Last I heard you were headed to business school."

"A lot of things changed," River said. "I suppose it will take a while to get you up to speed on everything. Suffice it to say my priorities evolved."

"Oh, yeah?"

"To quote you, 'it's a long story.'" He headed up the stairs.

Bill turned to my sister. "I think I could use a glass of that blood, Em. Do you mind?"

My dark-haired sister stood. "Of course." She kissed him on the top of his head. "Be right back."

Bill turned to me, his eyes serious. "I understand that you may not want to talk about what happened to you, and you don't have to tell your sister and River if you don't want to. But you're going to need to be honest with *me*, Dante. I can't help you if you're not."

TEN

Erin

I'd stayed up for several hours after Jay and his partner had left, taking Dante with them. I searched "Dante Gabriel" on the internet but couldn't find anything. He clearly wasn't homeless, just a vandal. But something was amiss. River had given him an alibi without even knowing where he had been last night. He was a cop, like Jay. Cops didn't go around giving out alibis. Had they been in contact? Had Dante told River that he had vandalized our blood bank?

Memories of our kisses flooded my mind, making my heart race and my skin tingle. I'd have easily taken him to my bed had he not resisted.

Thank God Jay had shown up. Things were better this way. I didn't know Dante, and I couldn't just keep him at my house.

His cousin, the cop, could handle him.

So I had gone to bed, thrashing around until I finally fell asleep about three hours before I had to be up again, and then I'd woken up early.

Now I was driving into the parking lot for my shift that started at eleven p.m.

Dante hadn't left my mind at all. I kept reliving those kisses we'd shared in the bedroom, how he'd made me feel so alive. I didn't want to give that up.

But I had to. I didn't know anything about him, other than that he made my body throb, and what I did know wasn't exactly positive.

At least I knew he had a place to crash.

I was ten minutes early. Normally I was rushing to get in on time before Dr. Bonneville, who was on tonight, reprimanded me. I supposed I should be thankful I'd woken up early.

I got into the locker room and found Lucy already there and changed into her scrubs. She had her phone in her hands.

"Erin, thank God. I was just texting you. She's on a rampage tonight."

Dr. Zabrina Bonneville was a brilliant physician, able to diagnose and treat rare illnesses that eluded other doctors, but she shouldn't have been allowed to deal with people. The woman should be in a lab somewhere, creating cures for cancer and AIDS. But no, she insisted on being an ER doc on the night shift.

"Really? I guess I got lucky. The only reason I'm here early is because I couldn't sleep last night. I figured why not just get up and come in?"

"Someone was looking out for you."

I hurriedly began to change.

"Hey," Lucy said, "did you hear about that patient that went missing last night?"

"Yeah. Jay stopped by this morning and asked me a few questions about it. I wasn't on the case, but I did see her when she got brought in."

"I heard another woman went missing from the free clinic sometime yesterday as well."

"Which free clinic?"

"The Harry Tompson Center. You know, that one on Gravier Street, where the homeless people hang."

"Hmm." I tugged my scrub slippers on over my shoes. "That's weird."

"I know. It's got me a little freaked, to be honest." She tossed her phone in her locker. "Come on. Let's get up there."

"We've got five minutes."

"Yeah, but I warned you. Dr. Bitchville is in some kind of mental breakdown today. She's yelling at everyone."

"I wonder what got her riled up this time?"

"Steve says the cops were here earlier asking a bunch of questions about the missing patient. She didn't take it well. Kept saying, 'How the hell should I know? I wasn't on duty last night.'"

"Well, there's some truth in that," I said.

"True," Lucy replied. "I expect they'll be around questioning all of us tonight. At least I have the same excuse she does. I was off last night."

But I hadn't been. I had already told Jay everything I knew, but they'd likely have more questions. Unfortunately, I wouldn't be any help. I hoped someone else would be. The thought of a patient disappearing from the hospital was more than a little disturbing.

Lucy and I made our way up to the ER. Dr. Bonneville was already in an exam room on a case. I was almost pissed that she hadn't seen me get on my shift early. It wouldn't have mattered anyway. She would've found something else to be upset about. For now, I enjoyed the reprieve with her being busy.

Steve grabbed me as I walked by. "Can you grab a few pints of B positive for the hag?"

"What's she need it for? I was told she was in an exam room, not in surgery."

"Hell if I know."

"Isn't that *your* job?"

"Nope. Because I'm making her a *latte*." He rolled his eyes. "You know, the important shit."

I rolled my eyes back at him as I turned toward the small refrigeration unit. No B pos. Were we out of everything? Looked like another trip to the blood bank for me. I left the ER.

The blood bank showed no trace of the ruckus from last night. A wave of sadness hit me. This was where I'd met Dante, who I'd most likely never see again.

The place had been scrubbed clean, and the bags were on their requisite shelves. Only problem? No B positive. Not an issue. We had plenty of B neg. I grabbed two units and hightailed it back up to the ER.

Dr. Bonneville was coming out of the exam room when I approached her. "Here's the blood you ordered, Doctor."

She took the bags and frowned. "This is B negative. I ordered B positive."

"I know. There wasn't any B pos in the blood bank. We're out, apparently."

"My patient requires B positive."

"But...you know as well as I do that a B pos patient can take—"

"Yes. Fine." She harrumphed and walked away with the two units, her bleached-blond ponytail swinging in tandem with her hips.

Lucy walked toward me. "Told you. Just stay out of her way today."

"I'm a little confused," I said. "Why was she so adamant about B pos? B neg will work on any B pos patient. That's first-year anatomy."

"She's just being difficult to be difficult," Lucy replied. "As usual. Maybe it's her hormones. How old is she anyway?"

"I don't know. She always looks great. I mean, when she doesn't have a sneer on her face."

Lucy laughed, shaking her blond head of hair. "I can't say I've ever seen her *without* a sneer."

We both jerked our heads as an ambulance pulled up, sirens blaring.

Time to get to work.

ELEVEN

DANTE

*S*he sat above me, her face masked except for her eyes. *"Do you miss your father, Dante? Your sister? Your dead mother?"* She smiled, her fangs elongating.

I closed my eyes, but she forced them back open with her fingers.

"You will look at me when I talk to you, vampire. You will never look away." Her light-blue eyes seemed to slice into me with invisible rays. "I am your queen, and you are my slave. You will never forget that. Your only purpose is to serve me."

Why me? I didn't dare ask the question out loud. Several months earlier, River and I had sneaked out and hitched a ride to Bourbon Street during Mardi Gras. Our fathers had warned us to stay away, that the supernatural activity would be too much for our young vampire libidos to handle.

So what did two young male vampires do?

We ignored our fathers, of course, and went anyway. The risk was an aphrodisiac. We thrived on it.

It was a decision I now regretted. Big time.

River and I were nearly the same age, he the younger by nine months. We had grown up together and were more like brothers than cousins. We could easily pass for brothers. Our fathers were identical male vampire twins, a rarity in our world.

How I wished now that we'd listened to them.

I didn't know where River was, whether he had gotten away.

I fought against the woman on top of me. She'd had me beaten, humiliated, starved. But not recently. Recently I'd been served huge meals of beef and blood. I had no idea why.

I'd been in this lair for weeks now. I had lost track of time.

She liked to grind on top of me, as she did now, forcing me into an erection and leaving me unsated. She seemed to have no interest in fucking me, for which I was grateful, but once, just once, I longed to be set free from my blue-balled prison, even if it was by her treacherous hand.

She bent toward me, snarling. "The vampire testosterone is thick in your blood. You're ready for me. You're ready to give me what I crave." Her tongue slithered along my neck.

I winced.

And then she pierced my flesh.

"Auughh!" Knifing pain, but even worse was the humiliation.

Vampires weren't supposed to feed on each other. I didn't know why, but that fact had been drilled into my head for as long as I could remember. We fed on animals, and in dire need, we could feed on humans, as long as we didn't take too much and glamoured them so they wouldn't remember.

She sucked at my neck, taking my blood into her body.

When she was finally satisfied, she removed her fangs from my neck and gazed at me, her lips and chin crimson with my blood.

"You've just given me a most precious gift, Dante. Now I will give you one as well."

❖

My eyes jerked open.

"Hey, you all right?" River stood over me.

I looked around, for a moment forgetting where I was. I was at Bill's. On the sofa in the living room. I must've fallen asleep.

"You were agitated, thrashing around," River said. "I thought it would be best to wake you."

Then I remembered. *Her.* The first time she'd fed from me. The first time she'd forced me— No. Couldn't relive it.

"I'm okay," I said to River.

"I have to go to work," he said. "But Bill is here."

"Em?"

"She went back to her place."

"My little sister has her own place?"

"Your little sister is twenty-five, cuz. She's had her own place for five years now."

"Does she work?"

"Of course. She's a night manager over at the Cornstalk."

"What time is it now?"

"It's nearing midnight. I need to get to the station. I'm late. Do you need anything before I take off?"

"No. I'm fine." That was a big lie, but I wasn't going to bother my cousin with what was really going on just yet. I needed to talk to Bill first. But what I needed to do and what I could bring myself to do were two separate things.

"All right." He stuck a business card in my palm. "This has

my cell number on it. You call me if you need anything, okay? Seriously, I'll come running."

After River left, I headed into the kitchen and fixed myself a small glass of warm blood and a roast beef sandwich.

Bill walked in as I was finishing up. "I thought I heard something down here."

"I'm sorry to disturb you."

"You didn't disturb me, Dante. You know I prefer the night to the day."

"I'm sorry I fell asleep on you."

"Stop saying that. No need to be sorry. You were exhausted. I can't even imagine what you've been through."

No, he most likely couldn't imagine, and I was damned glad he was spared it.

"Whenever you're ready to talk." He poured himself a glass of blood.

"I have so many questions," I said.

"I'm sure you do. When male vampires reach the age of eighteen, their fathers tell them the history of our people. Julian hadn't told you yet when you disappeared. Then there are the *Texts*..." He closed his eyes for a moment. "There's a lot you don't know."

"If my dad and Uncle Brae have been gone since I've been gone, who told River?"

"I did."

"Then you can tell me."

"I will. At least what I can. After you've had a few more days to acclimate yourself. You have a home here with me, Dante. Always. You know that."

"River and Em don't live here. I'd just be a burden to you."

"River and Em have their own lives now. They have jobs.

They make their own money. Of course they don't live here."

"Did you take care of them after my dad and Uncle Brae disappeared?"

"Yes, they lived here with me until they came of age. And then they went to college."

College. I hadn't even been able to finish high school. What kind of job would I be able to get? Bill wouldn't live forever. Vampire immortality was pure myth.

Again, my grandfather seemed to read my thoughts. "Dante, you know I have plenty of money. You don't need to worry about anything."

Bill had inherited millions from his own father, millions that he'd turned into hundreds of millions with wise investing.

"Everything I have will be yours someday anyway," Bill continued. "Of course you have to share it with River and Emilia, but there's plenty to go around."

"I can't just sit around here spending your money. River and Em don't do that."

"River and Em haven't been through what you've been through. They have their own lives now, just as your father and Braedon did. Just because we were all born rich doesn't mean we sit around and do nothing. I worked until I was seventy, and I still do some consulting and research." He smiled. "But I'm not working now. I'm here, and I'm a good listener."

I wasn't ready to talk to Bill yet. I wasn't sure that day would ever come. How could I tell my strong vampire grandfather what I'd let happen to me?

But I *was* ready to listen.

"Tell me. Don't make me wait. Tell me what you told River when he turned eighteen."

TWELVE

Erin

Three hours after we'd dealt with the two people in the ambulance, Lucy and I finally got to take a break. We sat in the lunch room, when Lucy jerked her head toward the door.

"Your brother's here," she said.

I swore Lucy had a sixth sense sometimes. "How do you know?"

"I can see him, of course. He's out talking to Steve. Who's that hottie with him?"

"Probably his partner." I stood. River Gabriel was indeed a hottie, though not nearly as delectable as his cousin Dante. Just the sound of his name in my mind made my pulse race. *Dante. Dante.* "Let's go see what they want. They're probably here to do more investigation on the patient who disappeared."

Sure enough, Jay and his partner were talking to Steve. Dr. Bonneville didn't seem to be around.

I walked over to them. "Hey, Jay."

"Hey, Sis. You remember River."

"Yeah, since he was just in my house this morning." I shook River's hand and gestured to Lucy. "This is Lucy Cyrus, another nurse, and one of my best friends."

"Charmed," Lucy said, taking River's hand.

"Hey, Luce," Jay said.

"So what are you two doing here?"

"Just more questions about Cynthia North. Thanks for your help, Steve. You can get back to work."

"Oh, joy," Steve said sarcastically, turning and walking away.

"I'm going to go question the other orderlies," Jay said. "Can you take care of the other nurses?"

"Sure," River said.

But once Jay had gone, River eyed me. "We need to talk."

Chills ran through me. "All right."

"In private."

"Hey, three's a crowd," Lucy said jovially. "I'm sure I can find something to do around here. It *is* a hospital after all. Lucky you, Erin."

When Lucy had gone, I led River around a corner.

"You lied for my cousin," he said. "Why?"

"You lied for him too."

"Do you know where he was last night? Other than at your place?"

"I think that's for him to tell you."

"Why did you lie for him?"

"Why did *you*?"

"Because he's my cousin, and I...hadn't seen him in a while."

"Yeah. He told me he'd been gone for a while."

River's eyebrows nearly flew off his forehead. "He *told* you?"

"Well...yeah."

"What exactly did he tell you?"

"That's it. Why are you interrogating me? You just said he's been gone. You obviously already know that."

River looked down, clearing his throat. Then he looked in my eyes. "It was just a surprise to see him. A *great* surprise."

That strange pull tugged at me again. Dante was safe now, so why was I feeling this urge to get to him and protect him? Tingles began in my hand and rushed through my arms into my core. Those kisses. I needed more of them. More of everything Dante.

"I know we don't know each other at all, but believe me when I tell you I have Dante's best interests at heart. Could you please tell me where he was? How you found him?"

Something in his tone made me relent. River was worried.

"There isn't much to tell. He vandalized our blood bank, and for some reason, I protected him." I rubbed a sharp pain that sprang up on my forehead. "I'm still not sure why."

"What do you mean he vandalized your blood bank?"

"I found him there last night. He had blood all over his hands and face, and several bags had been ripped into."

"Did you ask him why he did that?"

"I...didn't." Why hadn't I? "I just assumed he was homeless and hungry. He was wearing tattered old clothes that didn't fit. He went into the fridge looking for food, I guess, and when he didn't find any, he vandalized it instead."

"I see." River twisted his lips. "Why did you lie for him?"

"My brother's a cop. I wasn't going to tell him I was harboring a vandal in my home."

"Why not?"

"I...don't know." And I didn't. I'd only known the urge to

protect Dante. An urge I didn't understand, though I still felt it to the depths of my soul.

"Well, thank you. I appreciate it."

"So why did *you* lie for him? Clearly he wasn't with *you* last night."

"I had my reasons. He's been gone, as I said, but there are things I can't talk about."

"So I tell you what happened, but you don't have to tell me anything?"

"He's my cousin. I need to protect him."

"From me?"

"Maybe. I don't know you."

"You know my brother."

"Jay and I haven't been working together very long. We both just made detective and got paired together."

"Then you at least know he's a good guy. A good cop. And he is. He's a great brother, too."

"Fascinating. I still don't know anything about you."

"Fine." This was getting old. "I need to get back to work. The ER doc on duty tonight is a bitch from hell on crack. Ask my brother anything you want to know about me. I'm an open book." I brushed past him and hurried back into the ER.

Sure enough, Dr. Bonneville was looking for me.

"Erin! Where have you been?"

"I'm sorry, Doctor. I was talking to Detective Gabriel about the pa—"

"Detective Gabriel?" She arched her eyebrows. "Are they still badgering my people about that? Don't they know this is an emergency room, and we have better things to do?"

A patient had disappeared from this very hospital. How could Dr. Bonneville be so callous?

"Well, I—"

"I'm not interested in your opinion on the matter. I need your help on a case. Follow me, please."

THIRTEEN

DANTE

Bill rubbed at his chin, looking pensive. "I'm not sure you're ready to hear it yet, Dante."

"Why?"

"Because I don't know where you've been, what you've been through. You might be scarred, and I don't want to add to your trauma."

He didn't know the half of it. "What you need to tell me is traumatic?"

"No. But it may be for you. I don't know how ready you are. You were barely eighteen when you left."

"Correction. I didn't leave. I was *taken*."

"You and your cousin went to Bourbon Street. After your fathers and I told you not to."

"All kids go to Bourbon Street. It's a rite of passage. You know that as well as I do. And I was eighteen."

"But we warned you about the paranormal activity there, activity that's too much for a young vampire's acute senses. And you went on Mardi Gras, when the veils between the worlds are nearly as thin as on Samhain."

"So you're saying this is really all *my* fault? That I was separated from my family for ten years? You have no idea what I went through!"

"That's right. I don't. And no, it wasn't your fault."

"How did River get back?"

"He didn't. The police found him. The sun had already risen. He was badly burned, though not enough to raise any suspicions."

"At least he got back."

"Yes, and we were thankful for that. But don't for one minute think that we didn't mourn your loss."

"I know that. I don't know why I'm still angry. I don't know why I'm saying half of the things that come out of my mouth." Emotion bubbled through my gut. My anger launched itself toward Bill, though he'd done nothing wrong.

"Your sister suffered the worst," Bill said. "Losing first her brother and then her father."

A spear of regret lanced through me. I had been focused on my own trauma and hadn't thought about how any of this had affected my family. "I'm sorry."

"None of us blame you, Dante. We never did."

All those years I spent in captivity I had tried to remember exactly what had happened that night. But no matter how hard I concentrated, all I had in my head was a jumble of blurry pieces to a puzzle that I could never quite put together. "Does River remember what happened that night?"

Bill shook his head. "No. He doesn't even remember you being taken."

"I don't either. I just remember waking up..."

"*Where* did you wake up, Dante?"

I closed my eyes. Hunger. Hunger and pain. I woke up naked and shackled to a bed.

I couldn't sit here and tell my grandfather, who I admired more than any other person in the world, what had been done to me. How I'd allowed myself to be tortured. He would lose all respect for me, all love for me. How had I not been able to defend myself? How could I have let it happen?

How could I tell him I had been violated? Had my blood stolen?

How could I live with any of this?

No. Couldn't talk yet. Couldn't. But one thing I did have to do.

"You're not safe. They'll come looking for me."

"I assure you this house is safe," Bill said. "I'd stake my own life on it."

"How can you? There are no guarantees." How well I knew that.

"Trust me." He stared into my eyes. "No harm will come to you in this house or anywhere else. Nor will any harm come to Em or River."

"What about their homes?"

"They are safe."

"How? How can—"

"Trust me," he said again, more firmly this time.

A wave of peace drifted over me, accompanied by an odd chill on the back of my neck. I was safe here. Bill said so. Bill was my ultimate protector. He always had been.

But he hadn't protected me that night.

"Now...tell me what happened."

"I don't remember," I said.

"What do you mean? Have you lost the last ten years of your life?"

"Yeah. Pretty much."

How I wished my lie were true. If I could erase the memories, the horrid awful memories, even if it meant having to catch up on ten years, maybe I could live a normal life.

"All right, Dante. That's how we'll leave it. For now." Bill stood. "Don't think I haven't noticed that scarring on your wrists, though."

I looked down. Ten years of chains and leather bindings had left their mark on my wrists, and also on my ankles, though they were covered at the moment. I'd eventually stopped resisting. The marks weren't overly obvious, but my grandfather's acute vision missed nothing.

He didn't believe that I couldn't remember. I could see it in his eyes. I'd never been any good at lying to my grandfather. I used to be able to manipulate my father every once in a while. But Bill? He saw through me every time.

"Aren't you going to tell me all of the coming-of-age crap?"

"Not until you call it something other than crap."

"I'm sorry. I didn't mean anything by that."

"I know you didn't, Dante. But I want you to think about two things first. Think about who you are and where you came from. You're the son of Julian Gabriel, firstborn son of Guillaume Tyrus Gabriel, the oldest living male pure vampire on this planet."

"I know who I am, Bill."

"But you don't, really. You don't know how precious you are."

Precious? I'd spent the last ten years being told I was lower than pig shit, that my only reason for existence was to provide sustenance for *her*. Precious was not a word I'd ever use to describe myself.

"Our kind is rapidly dying out." Bill closed his eyes. "We've been able to continue to exist by lying low, perpetuating myths about vampires so that human memory has forgotten our existence for the last hundred generations. We've all done our part for our own survival. We learned to live among humans, to pass for humans. We send our children to school with human children. We can breed with them, bring children into the world with them. But still our women are rarely fertile compared to humans. And when they do conceive, one in ten don't survive childbirth."

I hadn't thought about that in a long time. My own mother had died giving birth to Emilia. Although River's mother hadn't died in childbirth, she'd died from complications from an ectopic pregnancy when she'd been lucky enough to conceive again. I blinked back tears.

"We're truly dying out?" I'd known humans were plentiful compared to vampires, but I hadn't realized we were an endangered species.

"It is what it is." He shrugged. "We are stronger and faster than humans, but they are so much more fertile. I've come to realize that it's not strength that matters. It's not our superior senses. Fertility has always been a problem for our kind, and evolution hasn't corrected it. We've been dying out for centuries. The world doesn't seem to have a place for us anymore."

"But we still exist. We exist in their DNA. Lots of humans have a vampire high up in their family trees."

"Yes, but they don't know it, and they'll never know it. Those with our blood don't share our nutritional needs. We're just a legend to them now, like King Arthur and his knights, and the way the world is today, it's better that we stay that way."

I couldn't disagree with that assessment after what I'd been through. If a vampire could be as evil as *she* who'd stolen my life, tortured me, reduced me to nothing more than a bag of feed, maybe there *was* no place left for us in this world.

"Take your time, Dante," Bill continued. "You can stay here as long as you need to. It will belong to you someday anyway. When you're ready." He stood and went into his study.

I had already showered and changed into River's clothes. Bill had given me money and a credit card to order some new clothes to be delivered. I could take care of that. Yes, that was what I should do.

But instead, I walked to the door.

FOURTEEN

Erin

After dragging me away, Dr. Bonneville decided she didn't need my assistance after all. The night had gotten quiet. Only the one ambulance had come and gone so far. Other than that, we'd treated some bangs and bruises. Nothing major.

I joined Lucy at the computer station.

"Hey," she said. "What did Dr. Bonneville want you for?"

"Nothing. She changed her mind." A giant yawn split my face. "I got basically no sleep last night. I'm a mess." I logged in to my computer and started working on some records.

"I need to do some rounds," Lucy said. "See you."

I looked at the clock on my computer screen. "Only a couple hours to go, thank God. You want to get some breakfast after work? Camellia Grill opens at eight."

"Sure. I'll meet you down in the locker room, okay?"

I nodded, and she left.

I'd been working for about half an hour when the phone rang. I picked it up. "ER records. This is Erin."

"Hey, Erin, it's Charlene up at the front desk. There's someone here to see you."

That wouldn't go over well with Dr. Bonneville. "Who is it?"

"Can you give me your name, sir?" A pause. "He said his name is Dr. Gabriel."

"Dr. Gabriel?"

"Sorry. I didn't hear him right. He said Dante Gabriel."

My heart lurched. No person in his right mind would come back to the place where he'd committed a crime, even with an ironclad alibi. Either Dante wasn't in his right mind, or he had come back to see me. He was certainly not crazy, not that I could assess—although I wasn't a psychiatric nurse—so it must be the latter. He'd even gotten up in the middle of the night because he knew I worked the night shift.

I smiled.

Dr. Bonneville wouldn't approve, but I didn't care. I ached to see Dante again, to finish what we'd started yesterday morning in my bedroom.

I quickly logged out of my computer, wishing I had time to go to the bathroom to look at my hair. I walked up front toward the waiting room.

There he was. Wearing jeans that looked perfect on his muscular thighs. A lighter denim button-down shirt accentuated his broad shoulders and amazing chest. His hair was even darker than my own and hung in soft waves nearly touching his shoulders. His face was a true creation of beauty—strong jawline, sculpted cheekbones, and a graceful aquiline nose. His dark-brown eyes widened slightly when he saw me.

Did they widen in disappointment? He looked delectable, good enough to eat with a spoon, and here I was in green scrubs, my hair falling out of my ponytail.

"Hello, Erin," he said in a low, husky voice.

"Hi. What can I help you with?"

"You can help me with this." He pulled me into his hard chest and pressed his lips to mine.

Behind me, Charlene gasped. Were there people in the waiting room? I hadn't noticed, and I didn't rightfully care, not when Dante's mouth was on mine. I opened to his kiss, letting my tongue touch his.

I wanted something from this man. Something that went beyond kissing, beyond sex even, though I had no idea what it was. I fell into the embrace, forgetting where I was, why I was here. All that mattered was this man, his lips sliding against mine, his teeth nipping at me. His—

He broke the kiss abruptly with a loud smack and inhaled, pulling me toward the door. "We need to leave."

I yanked my arm away, though I didn't want to. "I can't leave. I'm on duty. I shouldn't even be out here."

"When do you get off?"

I looked at the clock in the waiting area. "Two hours."

"I'll meet you at your place." In a flash, he disappeared into the night.

A few seconds later, Dr. Bonneville came out into the waiting room. "Erin! What the hell are you doing out here?"

"I'm sorry, Doctor. I—"

"She came at my request," Charlene said. "I was having some trouble with my computer, and everyone knows Erin's a tech wiz."

That was a good one. I was a tech idiot. But Dr. Bonneville didn't know that. I sent Charlene a look of gratitude.

"We have a whole department of geeks for that, Charlene."

"None of whom work nights," Charlene retorted. "I had a little bug, but Erin fixed it for me."

Dr. Bonneville scowled at Charlene. "I trust Erin is done here then?"

"Yes, of course," I said.

"Thanks again, Erin," Charlene said, smiling. "You're a lifesaver."

I smiled at her words. She had been the lifesaver, not me. "No problem. Glad I could help." I followed Dr. Bonneville back into the ER.

"You seem distracted, Erin," she said. "Is there anything I can help you with?"

Huh? Had I heard her correctly? Dr. Bonneville was an excellent physician and diagnostician, but never once had she offered to help anyone on staff with anything. As far as she was concerned, we were all there to serve her.

"No, I'm fine."

"Well, if you ever need to talk, please know that I'm here." Then she smiled. Actually smiled! Dr. Bonneville was a very pretty woman, but none of us had ever seen her smile.

"That's very kind of you," I said after I picked my jaw up off the ground. "If you don't need me on any cases, I guess I'll go back to my records."

"You do that." She smiled again. I couldn't decide if the smile was real or fake. After all, I'd never seen it before.

I sat back down at my computer to log the rest of my records, when a certain name caught my eye. The drug panel on Mr. A. Lincoln—only an initial was listed—had come back. He must have been on something strong to make him think he was seeing vampires. But my mouth dropped open. His blood had come back clean. Not even a trace of alcohol or nicotine.

Poor guy was obviously mentally ill. It happened to a lot of people who ended up on the streets. They were often sleep-deprived and malnourished, a sure prescription for hallucinations. I quickly typed the data into his record.

I got through the next two hours of my shift and then drove home quickly, my heart beating like thunder at my anticipation of finding Dante waiting for me.

My phone dinged. A text.

Where are you? I've been waiting for you down here for ten minutes. We were supposed to have breakfast, remember?

Crap. I'd forgotten about Lucy. As much as I hated to text and drive, I rattled off a quickie to her.

Sorry. Something came up. Tomorrow?

Okay. See you tonight at work.

Try as I might, I couldn't feel bad for blowing off Lucy. Images of Dante filled my head, and thoughts of our brief time together twenty-four hours earlier clouded everything else in my brain.

I pulled into my townhome complex and nearly ran to my door. He wasn't here yet. Good. I had time to freshen up.

I opened the door and gasped.

FIFTEEN

DANTE

"How did you get in here?" Erin yelled.

"Easy. Your door was unlocked."

She looked around, her eyes wide. "That's not possible. I never forget to lock my door."

"Well, you did today." I went forward to take her into my arms, but she edged away.

"This has me pretty freaked out."

"You forgot to lock your door. So what? It's probably not the first time."

"I assure you it *is* the first time. Seriously, how did you get in here?"

Did she really think I was lying to her? "I opened the door and walked in. It's that simple."

She looked around again. "Something's off in here. I can't tell what it is, but it's off."

I inhaled. Nothing smelled off to me. But I'd been away from all the scents of the world for so long, I didn't trust my nose quite yet. All I could smell was Erin—lusty, earthy Erin.

She was already getting wet. I inhaled again.

"Did you knock before you broke into my home?"

"Of course I knocked."

"And then, when I didn't answer, you decided to try the doorknob? Who does that?"

"I don't know. It seemed like a normal thing to do."

She brought her hands up to her temples and rubbed. "I'm so stupid. I keep forgetting that I just met you. I keep thinking I can trust you. I *want* to trust you." She closed her eyes and inhaled. "But I can't."

"What are you talking about?"

"I found you vandalizing our blood bank. Have you forgotten already?"

I *had* forgotten. Because it hadn't happened—rather, vandalism hadn't been my intent. I'd had no choice. I was starving. But she had no way of knowing that. "I should explain about that."

But how could I explain? Normal people didn't think vampires existed. If I told her what I truly was, she would run away screaming.

She regarded me, her eyes glazing over as if an opal were clouding a peridot. I'd never seen eyes like hers.

"It's all right. You don't owe me an explanation."

"I don't?"

"No. As long as you tell me you haven't committed any crimes or misdemeanors since I saw you last."

I smiled. "I haven't."

"Good. For the life of me, I can't figure out why I believe you, but I do. So is everything okay with your family?"

"Yeah. Why wouldn't it be?"

She walked into her kitchen and poured a glass of juice.

"Want some?"

"Sure." What I really wanted—*needed*—was surging through her veins, but juice was okay.

"Have a seat." She gestured to her little kitchen table.

Her scent overpowered everything else in the small townhome. I sensed nothing else, not even the citrus fragrance of the orange juice, which was usually a strong aroma for me. I concentrated. There it was. That acidic tang.

"Tell me a little bit about you," she was saying. "What were you doing in the blood bank the other night? I assumed you were looking for food, but since you're not homeless, that's probably not the case."

"I...uh..." What could I say to that? Telling her the truth wasn't an option. I could lie and say the blood bank had already been vandalized when I got there, but I didn't want to lie. I was already being dishonest by not telling her who I truly was. Lying to her seemed profoundly wrong to me. Especially when all I could do was stare at her pink lips, wet from the orange juice. I wanted them wet from my kisses.

"It's okay," she continued. "We can get to that later. Where do you live, anyway?"

Why did she so easily let me off the hook? I'd overthink that later. Right now, all I could think about was her. Erin. Her enticing aroma. That beautiful body that I instinctively knew was hidden under her sweats. "Right now I'm staying with my grandfather. He lives in the Garden District."

"Cool. That's such an amazing place. I get goose bumps whenever I walk around there."

"He lives in an old brick house. It used to be a bed-and-breakfast. The Heartsong B and B."

"The Heartsong? Really?"

"You've heard of it? It's been closed for... Well, over thirty years."

"My friend Lucy told me about it. She's a native. She says it's haunted."

I held back a chuckle. Paranormal activity abounded in the Garden District, but it wasn't from ghosts. It was from all the voodoo practitioners and the cosmic energy they drew down. Ghosts didn't exist. Vampires believed that a person's energy merged with the universe when he died. "It's not."

"It's such a gorgeous house! I envy you. Do you want anything else? Toast or eggs or something?"

About a pint of your blood. Already I knew how sweet she would be, how satisfying. My gums started to itch, but I tamped it down. Couldn't go there. She wouldn't understand.

I should leave. Leave her in peace. Not draw her into my fucked-up world.

But I couldn't. Couldn't get my legs to move. She was so beautiful. Her hair in disarray only made her more so. Her lips were red and plump, her complexion fair and rosy. And that body... I longed to feast my eyes on her flesh for the first time.

"Erin..." I couldn't wait much longer to have her. Just being near her, hearing her heart pump her blood, the heady whoosh as it traveled through her veins.

As much as I ached for it, I could not taste her. Not yet.

But I could have the rest of her. She'd begged me to take her to bed the last time we'd been here. How I'd ached to. I longed to now just as much—even more—but so much of me was still like an untried adolescent.

I'd never been in this situation—wanting a woman so much. It was nothing like the pure sexual urge I knew well. My hormones rose within me, tightening my cock, making my gums tingle. That was familiar. What wasn't was the heady emotion swirling around me, the desire, the passionate ache.

I closed my eyes for a moment.

Erin's soft fingers found my cheek, and I opened my eyes to see her beautiful face staring up at me, her eyes shining. My whole body throbbed with desire, and then something foreign. She was also pulsing with desire. I felt each beat of her heart as if it were my own, felt each prickle of her skin. I reached out and touched her cheek, and it was warm. Tiny pinpricks tore through my fingertips as her capillaries burst—each small pop resonating within me—giving way to an alluring blush that turned her cheeks rosy.

I turned quickly away from her.

My fangs had elongated. I hadn't been able to stop. The raw desire, the primal urge...

It was all too much.

I would not be able to have her until I was able to control this part of me.

I summoned all the strength within me, and when my teeth had retracted and my cock had gone down a bit, I turned back to her.

"Aren't you going to answer me?" she asked.

"I'm sorry. What did you say?"

"I asked you what was wrong three different times. You ignored me. You're starting to scare me, Dante."

"I don't mean to."

"Why didn't you answer me?"

In truth, I hadn't heard her. I'd been forcing all my energy into retracting my teeth and slowing my libido.

I had to face the truth. We could *not* do this. Not yet. Not until I learned to control my urges. No way would I get through sex without taking her blood.

I had no discipline around her. What would happen when I climaxed? My fangs would come out, and my thirst for blood would be too much to handle.

In some ways, I was still that adolescent boy. I hadn't learned to control myself. I hadn't *had* to.

Her skin glowed like fresh strawberries, and when I inhaled, her earthy pheromones infused my senses, and my cock responded once more.

Unfortunately, so did my teeth.

"I'm so sorry. I have to go."

"Dante—"

But I was out the door.

I needed blood.

I needed it now.

SIXTEEN

Erin

"W hat the..." I said aloud.

He had come searching for me. He had asked to meet me here. He had gone in when he found my door unlocked—

Why had my door been unlocked?

At the moment, I didn't care. I was so hyped up, my body so ready to be fucked. My nipples were hard and pushed against my bra.

My panties were already soaked. He hadn't even kissed me, only touched my cheek—yet I was aching for him as if we were right at the brink of consummation.

What had I done wrong?

I wasn't above giving myself an orgasm when I was this needy, but I knew masturbating wouldn't suffice.

No. Only Dante Gabriel.

Dante Gabriel, whom I knew next to nothing about.

But there *was* someone who might be able to help. My brother's partner, Dante's cousin. I sent a quick text to Jay.

Are you guys off duty yet?

His response came about a minute later.

Just about. What do you need?
Want to catch some breakfast?

Yes. That sounds great.
Invite your new partner too.

I'll see if he has any plans. Why?
You got the hots for him?

I rolled my eyes. Men were such pigs.

No. I thought he might be hungry.
Never mind if it's that big a deal.

I'll meet you at Port of Call. Half an hour.

Sounds good.

I pushed my phone into my purse, ran a brush through my hair, redid my ponytail, and left.

"All I know is that he's River's cousin," Jay said, munching on his scrambled eggs. "Though it *is* weird that he showed up at your place yesterday."

I cleared my throat and took a sip of my decaf. "Yeah, that's why I was asking."

Jay could usually tell when I was spewing half-truths at him. Detective's instinct and all. Today, though, he didn't bat an eye.

"I don't know River very well yet," Jay said. "He's a good guy though. A good cop."

"So why didn't you bring him to breakfast?"

"He was busy. Said he had a lot of family stuff to deal with right now."

Classic brush off. Apparently he wasn't interested in getting to know his new partner or his sister any better. Today wasn't the day I would find out anything more about Dante Gabriel.

I could deal. Not that I had a choice.

"You have any more information on the woman who disappeared from the ER the other night?" I asked.

He shook his head. "It's like she vanished into thin air. And then we have another missing patient from the clinic on Gravier Street."

"Lucy told me."

"How did *she* know?"

"I have no idea. I just assumed you or some other cop had told her."

"Not that I know of."

That didn't particularly surprise me. Lucy always seemed to know things before other people did. She would laugh it off, saying she came from a long line of really intuitive women. Said she didn't believe in any of the psychic bullshit that flooded New Orleans.

I didn't believe in that stuff either, but sometimes Lucy made me wonder.

Jay rubbed at his neck. That was the third time I'd noticed him doing so since we started breakfast.

"You all right?" I asked. "Stiff neck or something?"

"No. I've just got this itchy spot."

"Let me take a look."

"What for?"

"Because I'm a nurse, dumbass. I might be able to tell you what it is."

"All right."

I got up and walked over to his side of the table. "You've been scratching it a lot. It's all swollen and red."

"Erin, that's what I do when something itches."

"We've had this talk a million times, Jay. You have to resist the urge to scratch it, or you just make it worse. It's all so red now that I can't even see what's going on." I examined his neck, palpating the tissue. The skin was mostly smooth, except for a couple of tiny raised welts about an inch and a half apart.

"Looks like something bit you," I said. "Maybe a mosquito."

"Not that I recall, but it itches like crazy."

"Could be a spider. Probably happened while you were asleep. Get some hydrocortisone cream from the drugstore. That will help the itching. It should go away on its own, but if those bumps aren't gone in a week, let me know. I'll take another look."

"Yes, Doctor," he said jovially.

My brother was a good guy. He didn't ever mean to upset me, but he did know I had become a nurse because I didn't want to go into six-figure debt going to medical school.

"Jay…"

"Oh. Sorry, Sis."

"It's all right."

"No, it's not. You made the right choice. I wouldn't want to be up to my eyeballs in debt either. I'm sorry Mom and Dad didn't have more resources."

"It's not their fault, either."

"Yeah, I know." He finished up his eggs. "I'm beat. It's home and to bed for me."

I yawned. "Yeah, me too." I got some bills out of my purse and placed them on the table next to the few he had thrown out. "We're good with a decent tip."

"Okay. See you, Sis."

As I drove home, med school invaded my mind. I'd dreamed about it since I was a kid and had gotten my first toy stethoscope for Christmas. But Jay and I were the children of a construction worker and a cashier. They worked hard, but they didn't have the money to put me through med school. Or college for that matter. I was paying off student loans for my RN and would be for the next several years.

I was nearly home, when something compelled me to turn down a different road.

SEVENTEEN

DANTE

I no longer knew night from day. The room had no windows. Sometimes fluorescent lights nearly blinded me, but more often I was left in the dark. A servant came three times a day to release me so I could go to the bathroom and eat my meal. Meals were usually some kind of chicken or beef, potatoes, a vegetable, and a quart of water.

"The queen wants you to stay hydrated."

Staying hydrated only made me have to piss, which I ended up having to hold until they let me go to the bathroom. If the servant got lazy and took his eyes off me, which he rarely did, I would dispose of some of the water down the toilet instead of drinking it.

Until she *found out.*

She *never told me her name. But* she *knew mine.*

"I hear you haven't been drinking all of your water, Dante. Have I not told you to eat and drink everything that is brought to you?"

"Yes."

"Yes what?"

"Yes, my queen," I said through gritted teeth.

"When you don't drink enough water, you don't produce enough blood. You wouldn't want me to drain you, would you?"

If she drained me, I would die.

Sometimes I wished for death. Other times I yearned for survival so badly that I knew I would do anything to save my own life.

What I yearned for mostly was escape. To be unchained.

How long had I been here?

I had no idea. Days had morphed into months and months into years. My facial hair had thickened. A servant shaved me every day—not only my face but my groin. The queen liked it that way, he said, didn't want anything hampering her access to my femoral artery.

"Answer me, damn it!"

"No, my queen. I don't want you to drain me."

"You need to be more careful, Dante," Bill said, handing me a bottle of aloe lotion. "Your skin apparently isn't used to the sun. It's even more sensitive than normal."

I squirted some of the lotion into my hands and rubbed it on my neck and face.

"You're pretty red."

"I know. I can feel it." The aloe cooled it a little, but it still hurt. I'd come home and gorged on a pint of blood from the refrigerator. Being with Erin had made me ravenous in a way I wasn't sure I'd ever be able to sate.

Bill had found me in the kitchen wiping my mouth.

"You're not blistering, so that's good. What were you doing out after sunrise without sunscreen on?"

"I wasn't thinking."

"I suppose you weren't thinking about *that*, anyway." Then he arched his brow. "You were kept somewhere away from the sun, weren't you?"

"I'm not ready to talk yet, Bill."

"I understand."

But he didn't. No one would. And he was right. I *hadn't* been thinking about sunscreen.

I'd been thinking about—had been *consumed* with—getting to Erin. I hadn't given a damn about what the sun might do to my skin.

"Where did you go anyway?" Bill asked.

"Just to get a cup of coffee," I lied.

"You do know that I have a coffeemaker here."

"Yeah, but I don't understand it. It doesn't look like the old one I remember."

"It's a single-serve machine. You use little cups or pods. Come on. I'll show you how to use it. It's simple. You can make a cup for your sister. She's coming over after work for coffee. In fact, she should be here by now."

After a quick lesson on Bill's newfangled coffee machine, I had a cup of coffee that I didn't particularly want. It was nice and strong, though. Strong coffee was a decent substitute for blood when necessary. We couldn't go longer than a week without real blood, but coffee helped ease the withdrawal symptoms that popped up if we went longer than twenty-four hours.

Since I'd just had a pint of blood, I didn't need the coffee for that reason. I drank it anyway.

"You know," Bill said, "we can get you some help. I can find you a therapist."

I laughed. "After hearing my story, any therapist worth his degree would have me put away."

"*I* won't put you away, Dante. If you tell me, maybe I can help."

I shook my head. "No one can help me."

"That's not true."

"I get it," I said. "I'm not trying to be rude or unappreciative." *I was held against my will for ten years. Unspeakable things were done to me. And I finally escape and find that my father and my uncle went after me and never returned. How am I supposed to deal with any of that? No one could.*

"People deal with things every day that none of us can imagine," Bill said.

Had he been reading my mind again? Telepathy wasn't a common trait among vampires, and I'd never known Bill to have it. Could he have developed it in the last ten years? Or was he just intuitive, having lived so long?

I stood, trying to tamp down the rage that began to boil inside me. "Yeah? Well, I'm not really concerned about those people right now. Maybe that makes me a selfish bastard. I don't fucking care."

"Calm down. I was trying to get you to open up your perspective a little. That's all. You're not ready for that yet, and that's okay too. Sit back down, Dante. Please. Let me help you."

I sat. I always did what Bill requested. It had been drummed into me since I was able to think for myself. He was the oldest living male pureblood vampire, and he deserved the respect of his kind.

Then something popped into my head. "If you're the oldest

living male vampire, who is the oldest living female vampire?"

He sighed. "I don't know. Pure vampire females are much rarer than males."

"Why?"

"In the beginning, it was because childbirth was very difficult for them. Now, I don't know."

"My mother died giving birth to Em."

"Yes, she did. We've come a long way with medical technology, but childbirth still isn't easy for our women. And those who do live through it produce a male child eighty percent of the time."

"Why is that?"

"No one knows. We've had our best scientists studying it for decades, with no reliable outcome. I've discussed it with the other elders. It seems the universe has decided it's done with us. There is no other explanation. We're a dying species, Dante. You know that as well as I do."

"It still doesn't make sense. We're superior in many ways."

"Back to childbirth. Fertility. You know that vampire females only go into estrus once every two to three years. With human females being fertile once a month, our demise was inevitable."

He was right. When we were gone, no one would miss us. No one even knew we still existed.

Emilia burst through the door.

"You're late," Bill said. "Did they keep you longer than normal?"

"No. I just went to the pharmacy for a few things after my shift ended." She held up a bag and walked toward me, sniffing. "You smell... There's something strange about how you smell."

"What do you mean?"

"There's something different about your scent. Something kind of... earthy. Like truffles."

Erin. I wasn't ready to talk about that either.

"I was out this morning," I said.

She sniffed again. "It smells...familiar to me. I can't place it..." Then she clamped her hand over her mouth and ran from the room.

"Emilia, what's wrong?" Bill yelled to her.

Her retching sounds echoed from the bathroom.

"Poor thing must have picked up a bug," Bill said.

Either that or the smell of Erin on me made her sick. I hoped that wasn't the case, because I planned to smell a lot more like Erin in the future. As soon as I figured out how to control my blood lust.

"Bill—"

But a knock on the door interrupted me.

EIGHTEEN

Erin

The home that had once housed the iconic Heartsong B and B was huge and gorgeous. It was painted canary yellow with navy-blue shutters. White columns held up a balcony outside the second-floor windows, and two additional wings stood adjacent to the main part of the house. I slowly opened the wrought iron gate and strode forward until I stood in front of the cherry wood door that featured an antique brass door knocker.

Goosebumps erupted on my flesh. Why had I come here?

The compulsion had frightened me. Something had taken over me as I turned down Prytania Street, the street that would lead me toward Heartsong. Lead me to Dante.

He'd run out on me only hours before, and though I should be in bed right now, I hadn't been able to control my desire to come here.

To see him.

I pulled the heavy ornate door knocker toward me and let it go.

I was all in now.

The door opened, and Dante stood there. "Erin. Hi."

"Hi," I said, warmth flooding my cheeks. "I'm not sure why I'm here. I—"

"That's okay. Uh...I'd invite you in, but my sister's really sick."

What a moron I am. Needy much, Erin?

"I'm sorry. I honestly don't know why I'm here." I regarded his face. "That's quite a sunburn. What happened?"

"Oh. Yeah. I told you my skin is really sensitive. This is what I get for going without sunblock."

"Right." Seemed pretty harsh for only being out for a little while. He hadn't been red at all when I'd seen him at my apartment earlier. "So...I should go."

"Dante, who's at the door?" A pretty young woman with short dark hair and brown eyes approached.

Must be his sister. His sister who didn't look sick at all. If only a hole would open on the porch and swallow me up.

"This is Erin. She's a nurse. Erin, this is my sister, Emilia."

She stuck out her hand. "Nice to meet you. Why are you standing out there? Come on in."

"Well, I..."

"Don't be silly. Can I get you anything? Coffee? Sweet tea?"

"No, please. I'm fine." I walked into the hardwood foyer.

The inside of the old house had been modernized, and all the beautiful antique furniture that I'd seen in old photos of the Heartsong was gone. Still, the house definitely had an old feel to it—as if it knew things, was keeping secrets.

I had only lived in New Orleans for a few years, but even in that short time, I'd come to realize it was a very special place.

I didn't believe in ghosts, but I'd met some otherwise rational and logical people who did, who actually believed many of the places in our fair city were haunted.

Including this house.

Dante had said it wasn't, but as I stood in the elegant foyer, I wasn't so sure.

I went no farther than a few feet. Why was I here? Embarrassment cloaked me, making my skin tighten around my body.

I needed to leave.

I opened my mouth to say as much, only to find Emilia staring at me, one eyebrow raised.

"Have we met before?" she asked.

"I don't think so. I work the night shift at the ER."

"I haven't been to the ER in about... Well, never." She laughed. "But something about you is very familiar." She inhaled and let out a breath slowly.

"Are you feeling better, Em?" Dante asked.

"Yeah. I don't know what came over me. Just a sudden attack of nausea."

I felt a slight sense of relief. At least Dante hadn't been lying to me about Emilia being sick.

"Maybe I can help. Do you have any other symptoms?"

"Not really. Well, there is one thing, but I don't want to be rude."

"I'm an ER nurse," I said. "Believe me, I've heard it all."

"Would it help if I left the room for a minute?" Dante asked.

Emilia laughed. "I have no secrets. It's just that Erin and I just met."

"Like I said, I'm a nurse. But if you don't want to talk about it, that's fine."

Her fair cheeks pinked, but just a little. More from her laughter than embarrassment, it seemed. "Well...it's just that... I've had to pee a lot."

"Sounds like a urinary tract infection. All you need is some antibiotics, and it will go away in a few days. If you're having any pain, you can go to the drugstore and get some OTC meds that will help."

"Can you give me the antibiotics?"

"Sorry, I can't. If I had some samples on me, I'd give them to you, but I shouldn't even do that. I'm not a doctor."

"Some nurses give out prescriptions."

"Nurse practitioners can, but only under the direct supervision of a doctor. Unfortunately, that's not me."

"I understand," she said. "Just would've made it easier. When the heck am I supposed to find time to go to the doctor?"

"For God's sake, Em," Dante said. "If you're uncomfortable, go to the doctor. You have insurance."

"He's right," I said. "UTIs are really common and rarely serious, but if they aren't treated, they can turn into a kidney infection, and you don't want that. It's best to get it taken care of as soon as possible."

"Listen to the nurse, Em." Dante smiled.

And I almost melted. That smile. It seemed made for me. He was the best-looking man I had ever laid eyes on.

Emilia yawned. "I should get going. I'm beat."

"Em works a night shift too," Dante said.

"Oh, yeah? What do you do?"

"I'm a night manager at the Cornstalk Hotel."

"Such a small world. My brother works nights too. In fact, he works with your cousin River."

"Really? You're Jay's sister?" She inhaled. "No wonder you look so familiar."

"You know Jay?" I said.

"Not well," she said, color rising to her cheeks. "He came in to the hotel one night asking questions on a case. Riv really likes him."

"He's a great guy. A great brother."

"Then how do you know Dante?" Emilia asked.

Dante and I looked at each other, both saying nothing.

After what seemed like an eternity passed, I decided to go with the lie River had told Jay. But before I could, music blared from Emilia's purse.

She pulled out her cell phone. "Sorry, I have to take this. I'll see you all later." She walked out the door.

I silently thanked whoever had called her.

"She seems...nice," I said.

"Em's great." He smiled. "A little nosy, but great."

"Sorry about the UTI talk," I said.

"Don't be. I'm glad you were here for her. And Em doesn't know the meaning of the word embarrassed."

I let out a nervous laugh. "I like her. I like people who know who they are."

Silence for a moment.

Then, "So why are you here?" he asked.

I shook my head. "I wish I knew." I could tell him how attractive I found him, how his kisses were unlike anything I'd ever experienced. How I wanted more than my next breath to finish what we'd started in my bedroom a day ago. How he was always on my mind. How I didn't seem to care that I'd found him covered in blood, and how the fact that I didn't care disturbed yet aroused me. How I'd forgotten all about safe sex when I'd been ready to bed him. How I was wet just being in his presence.

But those words wouldn't form.

"It's okay if you just wanted to see me," he said.

"I don't want you to think I'm the kind of woman who chases men. I'm really not." God's honest truth there.

"Then I'm flattered."

"I mean really. I had no intention of chasing you. I just wanted..." God, I sounded like a complete idiot.

He trailed a finger down my cheek. "What did you want?"

"To see you." I let out a breath. "To...just *see* you."

"That's not so bad. I want to see you too."

"Then why did you run away this morning? You came to me. Wanted to meet me at my place. Then you just left."

He smiled. "Believe it or not, I'm not the kind to chase women either."

"Then why?"

"I don't know. There's something about you. You're beautiful, of course, but it goes deeper than that. You didn't turn me in when you found me in the hospital. That means a lot."

"I'm still not sure why I didn't." Again, God's honest truth.

"I'm not sure why you didn't either, but I'm beyond grateful. And I'm sorry about this morning."

"It's okay. If you're not interested—"

He sighed. "I *am* interested. It's just that I'm not in a position to get into a relationship right now."

"So you just want sex?" I could live with that. For a little while, anyway.

"I want *you*. I want sex with you, yes. I even might want a relationship with you. I just can't right now. Not until I can contr— I mean, I just can't right now."

"Dante, we've known each other for about five minutes.

We don't need to talk about relationships quite yet."

He laughed. "That's true."

"Then what? Do I leave? Do we never see each other again?"

"God, that's not what I want at all. I don't know how to do this, Erin. I'm not all that...experienced."

"How is that possible? Have you looked at yourself lately?"

"For the first time in a long time, actually." He looked to the ceiling. "It's complicated."

How well I knew to stay away from a man who said anything was "complicated." That meant baggage. Not just regular baggage, but tonnage. Like another wife somewhere, or it got blown off in the war.

Of course I already knew the latter wasn't true. The erection under his jeans had been substantial.

Run away, my mind said. *Run away and never look back.*

But my body and heart didn't agree.

"It doesn't have to be," I said, stepping forward. "It can be very, very *un*complicated." I wrapped my arms around his neck and pulled his lips toward mine.

NINETEEN

DANTE

At least I'd had some blood this morning. Still, though, my gums began tingling. If only I could surrender to Erin's kiss, to kiss her back the way I longed to without being afraid of what might happen.

She'd already nicked her tongue on my tooth once. If it happened again, she wouldn't be able to explain it away for long.

And God knew I wouldn't be able to stop if I had even the tiniest taste of her blood again.

I didn't pull away, not at first. I relished the warmth of her lips, how they swelled as the blood rushed into them, the muffled snap of her tiny vessels bursting, painting color into her skin...

My left cuspid began to descend.

As much as it pained me, I broke the kiss and pulled away from her warm body.

"You have to go," I said.

She bit her lip, clearly struggling for composure. As

beautiful and captivating as she was, she probably wasn't used to being turned away. I ached for what she was feeling, for what I was making her feel.

If only she knew how much I truly wanted her in every way. Ways she could never imagine.

"I'm sorry, but I—"

"I said leave!" My voice came out harsher than I'd meant it to. But she *did* have to leave. Now. Or I couldn't be sure I wouldn't harm her.

"I'm really sorry about this," she said. "I won't bother you again." She turned and walked out the door.

My chest tightened with a sharp pain. Was this what heartache felt like? Pure heartache? What if I never saw her again? Could I live with that?

No. I couldn't.

I had to figure out how to deal with this.

Bill had gone into his study. We weren't supposed to disturb him while he was working, but this was an emergency as far as I was concerned.

He'd been wanting me to talk. Now I was ready to talk, although not about what he wanted to know.

I knocked hesitantly on his door.

"Come in," he said.

I opened it and walked in.

"Who was at the door, Dante?"

"A woman," I said.

"Oh? What did she want?"

"She came to see me."

"You've been back two days. Who would come to see you?"

"She's a nurse. I met her the night I... She helped me."

"And...?" The glint in his eye indicated he knew where I

was going with this.

"I'm...interested in her. Sexually."

"I see."

"I...only did this once before. And I wasn't all the way... mature. I don't know how to..." God, how would I get through this uncomfortable but necessary conversation?

"Yes. How to control yourself when you mate with a human woman."

"Mate? I'm not planning to mate. I just want to..." Fuck her senseless, smell her all day, never leave her presence. "I... I'm not a virgin, but for all intents and purposes, I have no experience."

"Dante, I don't mean to sound patronizing, but have you considered that maybe you're not ready to become involved with a woman yet? You need to work through what happened to you. If you don't want to talk to me, you have to talk to someone else."

Impatience tugged at me. Bill meant well, but he didn't understand the urge overtaking me.

Did he?

He'd been my age once. Of course he hadn't been held against his will for ten years.

Damn *her*! What more was *she* going to steal from me?

I stood. "You don't understand, damn it. No one will ever, *ever* understand!"

He was at the door, blocking my exit, in a flash.

"Help me understand, son. I want to help you. We *all* want to help you."

No. No. Couldn't say the words. Couldn't even bring myself to *think* the words.

My vision blurred, a red hue overtaking everything. My

fingers curled into a fist, a fist that landed on Bill's left cheek. He slammed against the wall, his eyes bulging.

I'd hit my grandfather. Punched him like a thug. Hadn't felt it at all. What was happening to me?

"Bill, I—"

"Leave this study," he said calmly. "And leave this house. Do not come back until you're ready to accept my help."

TWENTY

Erin

I went home and sank into my bed, covering my head with my blankets. I'd just made a ridiculous fool of myself. I'd never be able to look at Dante again.

What did I want with a fling anyway? I could do better. A young resident in the ER had shown interest in me. Logan Crown, MD. He was handsome in an understated way. Kind of a sexy geek with tortoiseshell glasses and a lean build. He had amazing green eyes, much darker than my own.

My interest had never been sparked. He'd pursued me for several weeks, but I couldn't get behind the idea. Even if I could, I tried to never mix work with pleasure, though sometimes the handsome residents had made it difficult. Lucy and I argued about my stance all the time. She thought I was being overly rigid.

Finally, Dr. Crown had asked Lucy out, and she'd accepted. They only went out once—"What a bore!" she'd complained—and now it was just too weird to date a guy who'd been out with my best friend. Lucy had probably screwed him, no matter how boring he was. The woman had the sex drive of a teenage boy.

Even if I *was* willing to bend my rule, our chief resident was a woman. Our nurses were all women. Our orderlies were all women except for Steve, who, though he was gorgeous and I loved him, had no interest in me for obvious reasons. He and his boyfriend had been together for almost a year now. Two of our ER docs were men, but they were both married.

Even my former boyfriend, Cory, whom I'd followed to New Orleans, had never sparked the feelings in me that Dante Gabriel did. And I'd been in love with him. Or so I thought, anyway.

Dante Gabriel—a virtual stranger. And frankly...an asshole.

He'd rebuffed me, after pursuing me in the first place.

What had I done wrong? Was it too presumptuous that I'd gone to his place without asking?

It was so not like me. I'd never been so forward in my life, not even with Cory. He'd *asked* me to move here with him. If he hadn't, I probably wouldn't have. Being forward was not exactly my style.

So what was different about Dante Gabriel?

Even thinking his name ignited sparks within me.

His rejection stung like a scorpion's bite. I hardly knew the man, yet I felt like we'd been together a lifetime and he was ending it for no apparent reason.

I squeezed my eyes closed, willing sleep to come.

I went to him in the night, clad only in a translucent white robe. How I had gotten there I didn't know. Perhaps I'd floated on a

cloud. *My nipples protruded through the material, dark pink buttons against the silky fabric.*

He lay in a large bed covered in dark red silk. He was naked, his dark hair fanned out on the pillow.

"I've been waiting for you," he said, his voice raspy with desire.

"I heard you calling. Not in words. I heard something else."

"My blood. My blood calls for your blood, and your blood has answered."

His words made no sense to me, but something within me responded, and I walked forward.

"Remove the robe," he commanded. "Present yourself to me."

I dropped the white gauzy garment to the floor and stood before him naked, my nipples puckered and hard, the rest of me tingling.

Something would happen tonight. Something I would learn to understand.

His cock was erect and jutted out magnificently from his black curls.

"Come to me. Sit on my cock and ride me."

I sank down onto his magnificence, and he filled me so completely.

"That's it. Ride me. Make love to me. Show me how much you want me."

"I do want you. I want nothing but you. You're all I think about."

"As it should be."

I undulated over him, moaning, embracing the completeness of our joining, until the tickle between my legs magnified and my orgasm exploded through me.

He pulled me toward him.
"Come, my love, and I will bring you to true completion."

My eyes shot open.

Dante.

I hadn't called him by name, and he hadn't called me by name. Our faces had been colorless blurs, but it had been him.

I'd dreamed of going to him, making love to him.

It had seemed so real!

It had been dark, a little twisted, but it had been amazing. Wonderful. He'd commanded me, and I'd obeyed. I hadn't even thought about it. I was far from submissive, but disobeying him hadn't entered my mind.

And when I'd climbed on top of him, sunk down on that beautiful cock...

It wouldn't happen. I had to accept that.

Why couldn't I get this man out of my mind? It was crazy. I barely knew him.

Time to go to work. At least I'd gotten some sleep, infested though it had been with dreams of Dante, but it was more than I'd had the previous day.

Driving in, I stared at the full moon in the clear night sky. I'd always loved the nighttime. I'd been a night owl all my life. When I became a nurse, I had been one of the few people who actually requested the night shift. Lucy, I found out later, also preferred the night shift, which surprised me, given how sexually active she was. She thought nothing of having a one-night stand and then never seeing the guy again. She was my best friend, and I certainly didn't judge her, but that wasn't the life I wanted.

Or was it? I hadn't been able to get Dante Gabriel out of my mind. Maybe what I needed was an old-fashioned fuck. It had been a while. I also needed some girl talk with Lucy.

But she was nowhere to be found once I left the locker room and went up to the ER. I grabbed Steve. "Hey, where's Lucy?"

"She called in sick earlier. Said she has food poisoning or something."

"Crap. I want to talk to her."

"Talk to me instead." Steve smiled. "At least the hag isn't working tonight. It's Dr. Thomas and that resident who has the hots for you."

"Dr. Crown?" I shook my head. "He's over me."

"I doubt that, Erin, since he just asked me a few minutes ago if you were working tonight."

"Really? I just figured, after he went out with Lucy..."

"They didn't click, according to both of them," Steve said.

"How do you know that?"

"Girlfriend, do you think there's anything that goes on in the hospital I don't know? I'm the Perez Hilton of this place."

"True." I laughed. "But Lucy never even told me whether they slept together."

"Did you ask?"

"Well...no. But Lucy usually volunteers information with me."

"Yes, and she usually fucks every man she goes out with. But not Dr. Crown. Said she wasn't feeling it and neither was he. So I'd say the door's wide open if you want to go through. He's still hot for you."

"Are you sure?" Normally I wasn't so insecure, but after being thrown out of Dante's home this morning, I was feeling a little low on the self-esteem meter. I sure as heck wasn't going to open myself up for more rejection.

"I'm sure, Erin. Haven't you noticed that his eyes never leave you if you're in the same room?"

"No."

"Well, they don't. Are you interested in him? I mean, he's hot in a sexy nerd kind of way, but I never got that vibe from you."

"That's because there was never a vibe to get. And I don't like to screw where I eat. But I think I might be changing my tune." I had to do something to ease the ache between my legs.

"That will make young Dr. Crown very happy." Steve winked at me. "And speaking of him, I have to run. He asked me to grab some stuff from the supply room."

What the heck? If a fuck was what I needed, Logan Crown would suffice. Especially now that I knew Lucy hadn't gone there.

Before I could find him, though, two ambulances screeched up to the ER. I was busy for the next four hours assisting on cases. It was a rough night. A young mother and her infant child came in dead on arrival from a car accident. The father and an older son were in critical condition. A teenage daughter had minor scrapes and had been released to social services. Her name was Ashley, and she had cried in my arms for a few minutes before I had to let her go so I could assist on yet more cases.

Sometimes I felt so useless in my profession. I often wondered why things happened the way they did. Nursing was so rewarding most of the time, but nights like these nearly sucked the life out of me.

So, after I had showered and changed back into my street

clothes, ready to go home, when Dr. Crown came up to me and asked me to have breakfast with him—Steve must have filled him in on my possible interest—I said yes.

Maybe he wasn't the man of my dreams. After such a lousy shift, I didn't want to be alone, even if it was only an hour to share a meal.

"Tell me about yourself," Dr. Crown said after we had ordered our breakfast.

"Not much to tell. I have a brother. He's a detective with the NOPD. He works the night shift like I do."

"That's interesting. Both of you working the night shift and all."

"We both prefer it. Our family has always been a little nocturnal."

"These shifts kill me," he said. "But as you know, the residents go where we're told. I'm glad I got the shift, because otherwise I probably wouldn't have met you."

I smiled and took a bite of my egg and bacon sandwich. I had no idea what to say anyway.

"How come you finally agreed to go out with me?"

Nothing like being put right on the spot. I certainly couldn't tell him the real answer—that I was hoping for a good quick fuck.

"I don't know. I guess I'm just in a different place now."

"Different than you were a few months ago?"

"Yeah. I didn't want to start anything up then."

"Why?"

What was with all the questions? "Some family issues," I lied. "But everything's been resolved now."

"I get it. You don't want to talk about it."

"No, not really."

"Then what *do* you want to talk about?"

"Honestly? I don't want to talk about anything, Dr. Crown. I want to go back to my place, take you up to my bedroom, and fuck the daylights out of you."

I clamped my hand over my mouth. What had I been thinking? After yesterday morning's rejection by Dante, I had just set myself up for another one.

But a broad grin split his face. "Then I think you'd better start calling me Logan."

TWENTY-ONE

DANTE

I'd spent the day at River's. He'd slept, since he worked the night shift, so I'd tried to sleep as well. Hadn't worked. I'd ended up pacing most of the day, and then, when Riv left for work in the evening, I paced some more.

Now the sun was rising.

I was sleep-deprived and blood-deprived. River had the same animal blood in his refrigerator as Bill. I drank two cups but was still not sated.

I knew what I needed.

I needed Erin's blood.

Erin, whom I had rejected for her own well-being.

Erin, whom I couldn't trust myself with—again for her own well-being.

Erin...who hadn't turned me in that first night when she'd had every right to.

Erin...who never left my mind.

I wasn't in love with her. Was I? I couldn't be. I didn't even know what love was or whether I was capable of the emotion.

But something about her drew me, pulled me...

Her scent, the sweet sound of her blood flowing through her veins to her heart, and then the higher-pitched whoosh of it flowing out into her body through her arteries.

Yes, human arteries. The pipeline to life for a vampire.

I'd had a slight taste of her when she nicked her tongue on my fang that first time. The memory flooded back into my mind. An earthy ambrosia that bubbled over my taste buds and then flowed into every cell of my body, making my fingers and toes tingle.

Perhaps my lust for her was purely blood lust.

And blood lust could be sated elsewhere.

But not with bagged animal blood that was days old.

I needed fresh blood.

Fresh...from a human. A female human.

I'd been brought up not to feed on humans. Some vampires did, Bill said, but those who had evolved found it distasteful.

Morally distasteful, that was.

Physically, it was not distasteful at all. In fact, he warned, do not ever do it, or you might not be able to stop. It would become an addiction.

I'd learned that lesson when I was old enough to recognize the urge for blood. I'd been only five years old, but in truth, I'd known the urge for much longer, after I'd been weaned from my mother's breast. I just hadn't been able to put it into words.

Bill had drummed that truth into Em even more so than me. Because our mother had died birthing her, she didn't have the benefit of mother's milk to lessen her urge for blood. She was only a toddler when she fed on a neighbor's cat.

Luckily, Bill had stopped her from killing the animal, and our neighbor saw her pet safely returned.

But now I understood more than ever how Em had felt.

An uncontrollable urge.

I hadn't had the last ten years to learn to control the combined blood and sexual urges that came with adulthood. Em had experienced only the blood lust of a toddler who hadn't had the benefit of mother's milk.

What I was feeling went so far beyond that.

I lusted for Erin's blood, God yes, but I also lusted for her body. To embed myself so far within her that Dante didn't exist anymore, to join our souls.

I needed to be saved—saved from the horrors of my past, saved from the uncontrollable lusts kaleidoscoping through my body.

Being with Erin would save me. I didn't know how, but I knew it with every molecule within me.

I needed her.

I'd suppress my blood lust with her. I had to find a way. Because not having her was no longer an option.

I left River's home and began walking. I had no idea how to get to Erin's place, but somehow I found it. Some inner drive propelled me to where she was. Her scent was a part of me now. All I needed to do was follow the path laid out for me.

I knocked on her door. When no one answered, I threw it open.

Unlocked again, thank God.

"Erin!" I yelled. "Erin. Come to me!"

I sniffed. Yes, she was here. Upstairs. Along with...

The back of my neck prickled as my fangs descended.

Someone was with her.

I couldn't pick up his scent, oddly, but I picked up hers, heavy with oxytocin. She was aroused, and not by her own hand.

I raced up the stairs.

Erin came running out of her bedroom clad in jeans and a shirt. A shirt that was unbuttoned, exposing her bra and her breasts bursting to tumble free.

I snarled low in my throat.

"Dante! What are you doing here? How did you get in?"

I willed my fangs to retract. It took more effort than usual. "Your door was unlocked. Again."

"That can't be. I remember..." She glanced over her shoulder. "You need to leave."

"I'm not going anywhere." My veins turned to boiling rivers beneath my skin. The itching in my gums grew unbearable, and a growl rumbled low in my throat.

She advanced toward me. "You kicked me out of your place twenty-four hours ago. Now I'm returning the favor. Get. Out."

I inhaled. She was ripe. Whoever was here intended to get inside her.

He would not.

I brushed past Erin and headed to her bedroom.

He was there, standing by her bed, his face shiny with perspiration, an erection apparent beneath his pants.

He was tall, but I was bigger. Stronger.

And mad as hell.

I held my blood lust in check, keeping my fangs from protruding. "Get out!" I growled.

"You! Wh-Who are you?"

Erin came running back in. "Dante! You can't break into my home and go running into my bedroom like a lunatic. I won't have it!"

"Try to stop me, Erin," I said. "Just try. You won't be able to."

"Don't you threaten her," the man said, his voice cracking slightly. "You heard her. Get out of here."

I laughed maniacally. I could take him out with a hard look, and right now, his blood was filled with testosterone. I could bite him, drink from him, and make myself even stronger.

My gums itched.

Yes. All that testosterone from a male on the cusp of becoming a man. It's intoxicating.

"Get out of my head, you bitch!"

"Call her that again, and I'll—"

I hadn't been talking to Erin, but still I pushed the man against the wall, my hands gripping his shoulders. "And you'll *what*?"

I inhaled. His testosterone had fled, replaced by the sharp scent of adrenaline.

"Look," he said, "whatever is going on, it's a misunderstanding."

"You will leave this bedroom," I said. "*Now*."

Erin

"No, Dante," I said, harnessing my anger as I entered my bedroom. "*You* will leave. And if you don't, I'm calling the cops. I'm sure my brother will be happy to come over and arrest you."

I didn't threaten him with his vandalism of the hospital several nights ago. For some reason, I still wanted to protect him from that, though I had no idea why.

"It's okay, Erin," Logan said. "Tell him to let me go, and *I'll* leave."

"What? Are you kidding me? No way." Dante had to leave. I had to tell him again. But my heart wasn't in it. All I wanted to tell him was to get in my bed.

"It's okay," Logan said. "Breakfast was fun, but clearly this wasn't meant to be."

"You heard the man, Erin." Dante released Logan. "Get the hell out of here."

Logan straightened his collar and left my room in a flurry.

I advanced on Dante, fuming. "What the hell was—"

He grabbed me and pulled me into his body as his lips came down on mine. My knees weakened when his erection pushed into my belly.

I responded to his kiss despite myself, despite what he'd just done. Despite...everything.

Then I stopped thinking. Only pure emotion coursed through me as I responded to his kiss, let my tongue wander into his mouth, groaned when he took it between his lips and sucked.

No one had ever kissed me the way Dante kissed me.

I wanted more of it.

So much more.

He brushed my shirt forcefully from my shoulders down to my waist and then broke the kiss. "You kissed him," he said through gritted teeth.

"Y-Yes."

"You were going to fuck him." Not a question. A statement. An angry statement.

I forced myself not to stammer this time. "Yes," I said on a gulp.

"You will *not* fuck him."

"Well...not right now. You scared him away." I bit my trembling lip. "But I—"

"Ever. You will not fuck him...*ever.*"

"Now you wait a—"

He slammed his lips down on mine once more, crushing our bodies together. Without thinking, I slid my hands up his muscular arms to his shoulders clad in black cotton.

So hard beneath my fingertips, so perfect.

He swept me into his arms and placed me on my bed.

"Mine," he growled. "These lips are mine." He ripped my bra open at the middle. "These breasts are mine. That treasure between your legs is mine." He licked his lips, his eyes dark with desire. "*You* are mine."

"But yesterday," I whimpered. "You didn't want—"

"Forget yesterday. I want you now. And I will have what's mine." He inhaled. "I can smell you. I can smell how much you want me."

I could smell it too. My lust was thick in the room, and it hadn't been there with Logan. Dante had brought it out in me.

Dante, who I hardly knew.

Dante, who was rude as hell.

Dante, who had broken into my home.

Dante, who I'd found vandalizing the blood bank.

Dante...who I wanted more than my next breath of air.

Couldn't think. Couldn't form words. All I wanted was his mouth on me. Everywhere.

He tugged off my shoes, then my jeans and panties. He spread my legs and closed his eyes. "Your musk is the sweetest thing I've ever scented."

Scented? Odd use of the word. But then he lowered his head, slithered his tongue over his bottom lip...

Opened his eyes...

And then his mouth, his eyes ablaze with rage.

"What the hell is *that*?"

THE QUEEN

You've made me stronger than ever, Dante, and I won't give you up that easily. Your blood has given me more power than I thought possible. Still I feel its magnificence in my body. I am life itself. Death no longer exists.

I will miss you, miss what we've been to each other. But I have a suitable substitute, someone whose blood is nearly as potent as yours. So for now, go. Spread your wings and learn. Your experience will only enrich me, make you a better blood slave when we are reunited.

But I'll be watching you.

Always watching you.

And never forget...

You did *not* escape.

I unchained you.

You are and always will be...mine.

BLOOD BOND SAGA

PART 2

PROLOGUE

Erin

He swept me into his arms and placed me on my bed. "Mine," he growled. "These lips are mine." He ripped my bra open at the middle. "These breasts are mine. That treasure between your legs is mine." He licked his lips, his eyes dark with desire. "*You* are mine."

"But yesterday," I whimpered. "You didn't want—"

"Forget yesterday. I want you now. And I will have what's mine." He inhaled. "I can smell you. I can smell how much you want me."

I could smell it too. My lust was thick in the room, and it hadn't been there with Logan. Dante had brought it out in me.

Dante, who I hardly know.

Dante, who was rude as hell.

Dante, who had broken into my home.

Dante, who I'd found vandalizing the blood bank.

Dante...who I wanted more than my next breath of air.

Couldn't think. Couldn't form words. All I wanted was his mouth on me. Everywhere.

He tugged off my shoes, then my jeans and panties. He spread my legs and closed his eyes. "Your musk is the sweetest thing I've ever scented."

Scented? Odd use of the word. But then he lowered his head, slithered his tongue over his bottom lip...

Opened his eyes...

And then his mouth, his eyes ablaze with rage.

"What the hell is *that*?"

ONE

DANTE

She didn't respond, just stared at me, her peridot eyes wide.

Anger inched along my skin as it tightened around my body. The tingling in my gums. I'd already let my fangs out once without meaning to, during our first kiss. She'd nicked her tongue, and I'd gotten a brief taste of her essence—a flavor so intense and intoxicating...

And I'd had to have her.

Her pussy smelled like fresh flowers and fruit, but when I opened my eyes...

Two puncture wounds on the inside of her left thigh.

A vampire bite. I'd recognize the lesion anywhere. A vampire had fed from her femoral artery.

Someone had tasted what was *mine*. The need to possess rose within me, while the wild urge to punish whirled through my veins.

This had happened recently. Though the wounds were healing, they were near fresh.

"Who tasted you?" I demanded in a snarling voice.

She met my angry gaze. "Wh-What?"

Rage overtook me. I looked away, squeezing my eyes tightly shut. Couldn't look at her right now. If I looked, I might... Damn! I opened my eyes and turned back to her, her own eyes frightened and confused.

"You let someone—"

I stopped abruptly. She'd most likely been glamoured and didn't even know she'd been fed from. I closed my eyes again and drew in a deep breath. Control eluded me, but I had to find it from somewhere. I dived deep within myself, the self I'd been before I was taken.

As angry as I was that someone had fed from her, this wasn't her fault. She hadn't known.

But *I* needed to feed. Needed to mark my territory.

Can't. Can't do it... She doesn't know what I am.

I gathered all my strength, moved away from her, and opened my eyes.

My dick was still hard. I'd been running on instinct with Erin. For all intents and purposes, I was still a virgin, though not in the technical sense.

Would I even know what to do with a woman? I'd known how to kiss her. I knew I wanted her mouth on my cock, wanted to taste the sweet nectar of her pussy.

No instruction manual necessary, apparently.

Erin.

I yearned for her, needed her, wanted to drown inside her.

But I couldn't. Not when someone else had fed from her. Someone had violated the woman who was mine. I suppressed the growl that rose in my throat. I'd find out who it was, and I'd make sure he never came near her again.

She sat up in bed. "I don't understand. What's wrong?"

I couldn't begin to explain the horrors running through my head. Yet something overpowered the horrors. Another urge—the urge to protect her. To protect what was mine.

I hadn't protected her from whomever had violated her. How could I live with that?

The hiss of my own blood in my veins thrummed in my ears, creating white noise.

What's wrong, Dante? Please, tell me what's wrong.

Her voice was sluggish and thick, as if she were speaking through a murky cloud of fog.

No. It wasn't her voice that had the problem. My hearing wasn't right somehow.

I pulled her up from the bed and into my arms. This wasn't her fault. I had to believe that she had no idea what had happened to her. I sank my nose into her dark hair and inhaled. Her sweet fragrance invaded my senses.

I'll never let you go, Erin. I'll find out who did this to you, who took what belongs to me. And they'll never touch you again.

"Dante?"

I grabbed two fistfuls of her hair and inhaled again.

"Dante?" Her voice was timid, fearful.

I pulled back and gazed into her green eyes. "I'm sorry, Erin. I'm sorry I couldn't protect you."

"What are you talking about?"

"I need to protect you, Erin. I *need* to."

"I'm a grown woman, Dante. You just looked between my legs and... I can't even." She rubbed at her forehead.

I curled my hands into fists, rage surging through me like a black tornado. Violence. Brutality. Bloodshed.

The urge to protect what was mine—to erase whoever had

done this to her from existence—throttled me. I ached to mark her, to take her blood and mark what was mine.

Not yet, though. She wouldn't understand, and I had to protect her. From everything.

"You're beautiful. Every part of you." I turned and sped out of her bedroom, down the stairs, and out of her home.

And I grabbed the first person I encountered, my cuspids ready to puncture flesh.

The man screamed and struggled in my grasp.

Don't do it, Dante. This isn't who you are.

Erin's voice.

Why was she in my head?

No, do it. Give in to what you are, what you can become.

Another voice. *She* who'd abused me, held me captive, taken my blood against my will.

Stolen my life.

She'd said those words to me many times while I was imprisoned, and I'd fought them with everything I had.

I needed to fight them now, fight the animalistic urge that demanded control over me.

I loosened my grip on the man. "I'm sorry." I cleared my throat. "I thought you were someone else."

"Whatever, man." He looked around, his eyes twitching. "I'm outta here."

I inhaled and exhaled slowly, trying to calm myself.

I'd succeeded. I'd controlled the violent compulsion. But not before I'd scared an innocent man into peeing himself.

The thirst for blood consumed me.

I turned, heading toward River's.

I'd find sustenance there.

But I wouldn't find what I needed.

I'd never have what I needed, what I desired more than life itself.

I'd never have Erin.

I had to protect her, at all costs, from whoever had been feeding on her.

I also had to protect her from *me*.

TWO

Erin

*W*hat the hell is *that?*

That was my vagina. *That treasure between my legs,* as he'd called it. Something down there had triggered him. Afterward, he'd said every part of me was beautiful, but still, the look in Dante's eyes had been something beyond anger, beyond even rage.

I'd seen that look before in certain patients— schizophrenics who'd gone off their meds.

Madness.

Pure madness.

I needed to face something that I'd been blocking out, for some reason.

Dante Gabriel was dangerous. Mad.

As much as I was drawn to him, I needed to stay away from him. Far away from him. It wouldn't be easy, considering the magnetic pull that seemed to force me toward him. What was happening? Maybe this was something more, something I'd never experienced.

I'd thought I was in love with Cory. Maybe I hadn't been. Maybe *this* was love. This all-consuming, almost frightening craving for someone.

No, couldn't be love. More like obsession—an obsession I needed to fight with everything in me before I found myself as mad as Dante.

Sleep eluded me for most of the day, and at dusk I rose to shower and get ready for work. I wasn't looking forward to seeing Dr. Crown—well, since he'd unbuttoned my shirt, Logan—at the hospital. Maybe he wouldn't be in tonight.

But once I got to work, there he was. He didn't meet my gaze when I said a soft hello.

Not that I blamed him. I'd brought him to my place with the intention of fucking him, and he'd been chased away by a crazy man.

A crazy man I couldn't get out of my mind.

"Hey, chick." Lucy walked toward me.

"You feeling better?"

"What?" She arched her brow.

"Your food poisoning."

"Oh, right. Yeah, much better. Thanks. So I heard you went out with Dr. Hottie Nerd."

I rolled my eyes. "Good news sure travels fast."

"It does when Steve's around."

I shot Steve a heated look, but he only laughed and continued his work.

"So how'd it go?" Lucy continued.

"It didn't. We had breakfast. That's it."

Lucy stared at me, her blue eyes wide. "Erin, when was the last time you got laid?"

I looked around quickly. "Could you have said that any louder?"

"Don't be ridiculous. I wasn't loud. You're just uncomfortable with the words." She put on a pair of rubber gloves. "I'm serious. When?"

"Not long ago."

"Bullshit. You haven't been with anyone since Cory, have you?"

Actually, I had. A couple one-nighters, and a guy I'd dated a few times. Funny that I hadn't told Lucy. I didn't usually withhold information from her, but one-nighters weren't my thing. They were Lucy's thing.

"Not true. I've had a few flings."

"Yeah? Without telling me?"

"I don't tell you everything, Luce."

"Why not? I tell *you* everything."

"I know." Lucy's exploits were legendary. She was the horniest woman on the planet—"a horny little bitch," she called herself, though I didn't care for that epithet.

"So...?"

"So...how can I compete with *your* sex life?"

"Erin, Erin. It's not about competition." She smiled, mischief in her eyes. "And you can't."

Lucy was beautiful in a girl-next-door kind of way—honey-blond hair and blue eyes, a slightly curvy figure, and a bubbly personality. Men flocked to her. I'd been truly surprised to find out she hadn't slept with Logan.

"Trust me, Luce, I'd never try." I couldn't help a laugh.

"So go over and talk to the good doctor," she said. "Next time make breakfast into a sleepover."

Ha! She had no idea how I'd tried. I couldn't relay to her the horrible story of this morning. She'd never believe it anyway. Plus, I was embarrassed. Dante had walked out on me after he'd interrupted my "date" with Logan.

What the hell is that?

Just what every woman wants to hear when a man looks between her legs.

"I don't think so," I said.

"Okay, fine. So he's not your cup of tea. I get that. He's not mine, either. Tell you what. You need a night on the town. We're both off tomorrow night. Let's go out."

I so wasn't the party-all-night type, but I'd be up all night anyway. Why not? "Okay, Luce. You've got yourself a date."

"Great." She sniffed and twirled around. "Dr. Bitchville is here. Shit. Look busy."

Looking busy was difficult on a slow night in the ER. However, the EMTs arrived a few minutes later with a heart attack victim. I rushed toward the gurney.

"Male, mid-fifties. About two hundred and fifty pounds," the EMT said. "Pulse is at 101, BP ninety over forty. We're losing him."

"Doctor!" I called.

Dr. Bonneville arrived swiftly. We got him situated, and I hooked him up to the EKG and started an IV.

"We've got elevation of the ST segment," I said.

"Current of injury," Dr. Bonneville concurred. "Here come the T wave inversions. Let's save this heart. Five thousand units of Heparin, Erin. Forty milligrams Tenecteplase."

I administered the medications while Dr. Bonneville monitored the patient. "Come on, now. Fight for me. Fight, damn it!"

Then the telltale buzz.

"He's flatlining," I said.

"Damn it!" Dr. Bonneville began cardiopulmonary

resuscitation. "Prepare the paddles, Erin."

I'd been working as an ER nurse for five years, and never had I gotten used to watching a doctor try to shock life back into a patient. Sometimes it worked. Sometimes it didn't.

Tonight it didn't.

Dr. Bonneville closed her eyes and sighed. "Time of death, twelve thirty-five a.m."

I made the notation.

We didn't even know the patient's name. No one had come in with him. He must have lived alone and called 911 when he began having pains.

We'd establish his identity. We always did. Didn't make the whole thing any easier though.

Dr. Bonneville didn't like losing patients. No doctor or nurse did, but she took it harder than most, which always stunned me, given her normal attitude and willingness to treat her coworkers like yesterday's trash. I'd tried comforting her once.

Once.

I knew better now.

She needed to be left alone...which was why I dropped my mouth open when she asked me to have a cup of coffee with her.

It wasn't break time, and Bonneville wasn't one for taking time off that wasn't scheduled. But she was the boss.

THREE

DANTE

"*N*ow I will give you *a gift.*"

She ripped the skin on her wrist open with her fangs and presented it to me.

"*Drink of me, as I have drunk from you.*"

Not supposed to feed off each other. Dad and Bill had warned of severe side effects, but they'd never elucidated.

I turned away, squeezing my eyes shut.

Whomp!

A punch landed on my exposed cheek. My eyes were forced open by one of her goons.

"*You dare refuse such a precious gift?*" Blood dripped from her cut wrist onto my closed lips. "*Drink, Dante. Drink from me.*"

This time another goon pried my lips apart, and a drop of her blood trickled across my tongue, leaving a trail of flame in its wake.

My mind went fuzzy.

I spent the next night and day lounging at River's apartment, fighting a duel with myself. How could I protect Erin from everything, including me, when she—and the desire I had for her—never left my mind? After I'd downed a quart of steer's blood and was able to think clearly, I fell asleep. At dusk I rose and left River's. I had to see Bill. Only he could give me answers, though I wasn't looking forward to returning.

I still couldn't believe I'd slugged him. What had come over me? He'd been pushing—pushing for me to talk. He'd said not to return until I was ready to accept his help.

I *was* ready to accept help. I just wasn't ready to tell him everything. Somehow, I'd have to make him understand that and agree to help me anyway.

I found Bill in his office, his gaze locked on his computer screen. I stood in the open doorway. He looked up at me, his cheek bruised from my punch.

"Dante," he said calmly.

I should apologize. Beg his forgiveness. But the thought of begging for anything tasted like bile in my mouth. For ten years, I'd forced myself not to beg for mercy. I wasn't sure I could ever beg for anything again, even for forgiveness from my one-hundred-and-two-year-old grandfather who hadn't deserved my wrath. I opened my mouth, ready to force out the words, when he spoke.

"Are you ready to accept my help?"

"I've always been ready to accept your help. I *need* your help." I cleared my throat. "What are you doing?"

"Research," he said, his gaze back to his computer monitor.

"On what?"

He slid his chair around and looked straight into my eyes. "I can't talk about it now. Is there something you need?"

"What do you mean you 'can't talk about it'?"

"I mean I can't talk about it." His voice was steady, firm, and commanding.

I remembered the tone from when I was a teenager. My father had spoken in a similar pitch when he didn't want to be interrogated. I'd never pushed my father or my grandfather.

But I was no longer a teenager.

"Why are you keeping secrets?"

Bill stood and removed his glasses. "Why are *you* keeping secrets, Dante?"

"I'm not. I just can't..." I bit my lower lip. "Try to understand."

"I *do* understand."

"But you don't. You can't possibly."

"I'd lived nearly eighty years before you came into the world. You have no idea what I've seen, what I've been through."

I wasn't buying it. My grandfather hadn't been held captive and violated for ten years. If he had, I'd know about it.

He continued, "My ability to help you will be limited if I don't know what you went through. As for what I'm doing, I'm not keeping secrets. I'm saying this is none of your business. I will not talk about it, not until I can. If you can't respect that, you can leave this house at any time."

That was the second time he'd told me I could leave his house.

"You told me I'd always have a home here."

"Having a home here doesn't mean you get to know everything I'm doing. It also doesn't give you license to exercise violence toward me."

I couldn't argue, but I'd never known Bill to be secretive about anything. Then again, I'd been gone for a long time. Things had clearly changed in the last ten years.

I turned when I heard bustling outside Bill's office.

"It's River," Bill said. "He's off tonight."

Perfect. If I couldn't get any answers from Bill, maybe I could get some from my cousin. I left the office.

"Hey, Riv." I walked toward him.

"Dante. Hey. I woke up and you were gone. I figured you'd come back here. You and Bill good now?"

Were we? I had no idea. Seemed I didn't know my grandfather at all anymore. "I guess so."

River had also been different since I'd returned. He wasn't distant, as Bill appeared to be, but he seemed obsessed with moving forward on "my case" and getting whomever had taken me behind bars. I wanted that as well, but I wasn't ready to cooperate yet. Memories tugged at me, and I'd spent so much time out of it that I wasn't sure which ones were true and which weren't.

Only one thing was constant.

Her.

She who called herself the queen.

"Can we talk?" I asked.

"Yeah. Sure. Just let me get a drink." He went into the kitchen and came back with two goblets full of blood. He handed one to me.

I wasn't thirsty, but I took it anyway.

"Where's Bill?" he asked.

"In his office. He's not in a talkative mood."

"Yeah. He's working on some stuff."

"Do you know what it is?"

River shook his head. "He won't tell me. Won't tell anyone. Not even Em, who usually has him wrapped around her little finger."

"Can we talk in private?" I asked.

River drained his glass. "Sure. You want to go out to a bar or something? We can hit Bourbon Street."

Bourbon Street. The last time I'd hit Bourbon Street, I'd never returned. I stiffened.

"Hey. Sorry. I wasn't thinking."

"No." I gripped the stem of my goblet, my knuckles whitening. "I can't hide forever. I have to figure out what happened to me and why. Maybe Bourbon Street is the key."

"Lots of shit happens on Bourbon Street, cuz," River said. "It's a haven of supernatural activity. You know that."

"Yeah. Let's go." I downed the liquid in my glass.

River ordered a high-end bourbon for both of us. I hadn't had a drink—that I knew of—in ten years.

"Go slow," River cautioned. "This stuff is lethal. But damn, it's good."

I picked up the heavy lead crystal glass and took a sip. Woodsy and a touch of maple. Delicious. Though it did burn my throat going down.

"What did you need to talk about, Dante?"

I took another sip and then cleared my throat. "It's a woman, actually."

"Yeah? Jay's sister, right?"

"Right. How did you know?"

"How could I *not* know? She smells amazing."

Ice chilled my neck as I gripped my glass on the walnut bar, jealousy spearing through me. In an instant, it shattered.

"Shit!" River grabbed a napkin and sopped up the bourbon. "Did you cut yourself?"

The bartender hurried over and swept away the shards of glass. "I'll get you another, sir."

A drop of blood trickled from the space between my thumb and forefinger. I pinched the area to stop the bleeding.

"What the hell happened?" River said.

Vampires were stronger than humans. Not hugely stronger, but enough to make a difference. River had no doubt learned to hide his strength—another of those lifelong lessons I'd missed while the power of my muscles increased during early adulthood.

In truth, the thought of River scenting Erin had enraged me.

Mine.

The thought had consumed me. Still consumed me.

Erin is mine.

"Earth to Dante," River said.

The bartender set another glass of bourbon in front of me. I mumbled a quick thanks.

"Easy, now." River eyed me. "What's going on?"

"How the fuck should I know? I didn't know I could shatter thick lead crystal with my hand."

"You can do a lot more than that," River said. "Be careful, okay?"

Sure. I'd be careful. I'd do my best anyway. What else was I capable of? I had no idea.

"About Erin," I said.

"Yeah. What about her?"

"I'm...*drawn* to her."

"What do you mean?"

"I'm not sure. It's like I can't stay away from her. Like we're destined to be together or something."

"Not possible."

"Why not?"

"Because it's bullshit. That's why. Vampires don't have fated mates. Neither do humans. Only the shifters."

"Shifters?" Fuck. How much did I not know?

"Werewolves. Werecats. Yeah."

"Werelions, weretigers, and werebears? Oh my?" I couldn't help myself. He was off his rocker.

"What? Of course not. Everyone knows there's only—" He set his drink down with a thud. "That's right. Your dad never... You really don't know, do you?"

"I could fill a fucking warehouse with everything I don't know. You need to help me, River. Bill won't."

"Bill's just being cautious. He doesn't know what happened to you. He's not sure you're ready—"

I thumped my fist on the bar, startling the other customers.

"Sorry," I said to them. Then, to River, I spoke low. "It doesn't matter what happened to me. I need to know how to exist in the world I'm in *now*. How am I supposed to get along without all the knowledge I was supposed to get from my dad after high school?"

"But depending on what—"

"God, River, are you hearing me? I need your help! You're telling me that werewolves are a real thing. Do you know how that fucks with my mind?"

River eased my glass of bourbon out of my hand.

"Don't treat me like a child," I demanded.

"We can talk about shifters later. They're nearly extinct anyway, even more so than we are. You said this had to do with Jay's sister. That you're drawn to her. And I'm telling you that it's just her fragrance. You haven't been around. You haven't become accustomed to the scents around you. Our senses of smell increase tenfold during early adulthood, but you've been gone since then."

"Look. I know all about her scent. She has the dark hair and fair complexion of a human who is descended from a vampire somewhere up in her line. It's an intoxicating smell."

"It is. Her brother has it too. Sitting in an unmarked car with him for eight hours a day isn't the easiest thing in the world. But you *can* control yourself, Dante. You just need to learn how."

"You're not hearing me, Riv. It's more than her scent. I fucking *ache* for her."

"Maybe you just need to get laid."

I curled my fingers into a fist. River hadn't meant to upset me. He didn't know how I'd been aroused and left to stagnate for the last ten years, and that getting into Erin's pants wasn't what I *needed*, even though I *wanted* it more than anything. If all I needed was a lay, I could get that anywhere.

"It's more than that. You don't understand."

"You think I don't understand the need to get laid?" He laughed. "It's been a while for me too."

"No. I don't need to get laid. I need Erin. I need her body, her blood, her soul."

"You said it yourself. The key word is 'blood.' It's her blood, Dante. You'll get used to it."

"You're not hearing me!"

"That's the third time you've said that to me, and I assure

you I *am* hearing you. You *will* get used to the different scents. Some will be more enticing than others, but you'll learn to control the urge. We all do."

Still, he wasn't getting it. It was more than Erin's fragrant blood, more than her beautiful body. Something about her pulled at me, something I couldn't put into words.

"I was eighteen, Riv. Adulthood had begun, and I already understood the power of the scent of blood. I already knew that vampire DNA coupled with dark hair and fair skin produced a fragrance no vamp could resist. I had smelled it before. I'm telling you. This is something more."

"I don't want to pry, but were you...exposed to a lot of human scents while you were gone?"

Only two. Her goons, both human. They'd smelled like garbage after a while, their natural scents tainted by my hatred.

I didn't respond. Was it possible he was right? That I just wasn't used to all the various scents?

No. Even now, all of Erin—not just her fragrant aroma— invaded my mind. Her eyes, her body, the sweet sound of her voice... What I felt toward Erin was so much more than being attracted to her scent.

"You've obviously never experienced what I'm talking about," I said.

He regarded me, his right eyebrow raised. He didn't believe me. "I'm sure I have. I just recognized it for what it was."

"You haven't outgrown that stubborn streak." I took a sip of bourbon, draining the glass. I signaled the bartender for another.

My mind was starting to fuzz up a little. How many years had gone by since I'd had alcohol? Ten, most likely, unless *she* had given it to me without my knowledge.

Ten years. *That* night.

I took a quick sip from my refilled glass and turned back to River. "Maybe you're right. Maybe it's just the scent of her blood."

The lie didn't taste so bad in the wake of the bourbon. River didn't get it, so he hadn't experienced it. I'd have to ask Bill, and if he wouldn't talk to me, I'd figure it out on my own.

I had to stop the craving. The ache. Because if I didn't, I wouldn't stay away from her.

And I had to keep Erin safe.

FOUR

Erin

Bourbon Street. The street where sleep didn't exist. Lucy dragged me into a club, and I found myself smashed between two Adonises—one blond and one dark, both gorgeous.

Didn't do a thing for me.

When I was danced out, I hauled Lucy outside the club.

"What's the matter with you?" Lucy demanded. "They were totally into you. You probably could have had them both at the same time, which, let me tell you, is amazing."

"You've had a threesome?" I asked, surprised. But why would this surprise me? Lucy had probably tried everything.

"Several. I had a foursome once too. And a fivesome, although one of them was another woman. But you're changing the subject. Didn't you think they were good-looking? And if you didn't, we need to talk."

I tried to erase the visual of Lucy with three men and a woman. "They were magnificent, and nothing like Logan."

"No shit. They were both the anti-Logan. I thought that was a good thing."

"It is."

"Then what's your problem?"

"Just not in the mood, I guess."

"You're nuts. What am I going to do with you?"

"Luce, why don't you go back in and have fun? I'll be fine out here. I'll find a table at a nice quiet café."

"Quiet? This is Bourbon Street, Erin."

True enough. "Maybe I'll just go home."

"No, you won't. I know a good place where there are always a couple spots at the bar." She tugged on my arm. "Come on."

We walked to a hole in the wall called Moulin Blanche. I'd never heard of it, but Lucy was right. It was nicely crowded, and sure enough, three stools were available.

"Come on." Lucy pulled me toward the empty spots.

And my heart lurched.

Dante and River sat at the bar.

He turned around, his dark eyes wide.

"Uh...hi there," I said, willing myself not to stammer.

"What are you doing here?"

"Having a drink. This is my friend Lucy. Lucy, Dante Gabriel."

Lucy turned on the charm. "Thrilled to meet you." She turned to River. "And you I remember. You're Jay's partner."

"Guilty." River's lips formed a crooked smile. "Nice to see you again."

Lucy went into full flirtation mode. Yeah, she'd be going home with Dante's cousin tonight. So where did that leave me?

The last time I'd seen Dante, he'd looked between my legs, held me for a minute, and then went running.

Maybe, if I closed my eyes, I could harness some of that alleged paranormal activity and conjure up a hole in the wood floor to escape into.

"Sit down, Erin."

My eyes shot open.

"Are you sure?"

Lucy and River were already deep in conversation. She had edged Dante out of his seat so she could sit next to his cousin.

"Yes. Please. Sit."

I sat. Didn't think about it again. I'd been compelled to sit as soon as he told me to, but given our short history, I couldn't help asking if he was sure.

An empty glass sat in front of him. He signaled to the bartender. "Another, please. And whatever the lady wants."

"I'll have a martini, dry, extra olives." Might as well go for something strong. Dante appeared to be drinking straight bourbon or scotch. Something brown, anyway.

His thick dark hair was in disarray, as if he'd been messing with it, and gray circles marred the fair skin under his gorgeous dark eyes. Something was bothering him.

That something was probably me.

The bartender set my drink in front of me, and I took a long sip. Whoa! Martinis were strong, and I hadn't specified vodka. This was gin.

Perfect.

I took another sip. Then another. Anything to keep from having to talk. The silence could fill an amphitheater.

Until he said, "I owe you an apology."

"For running away at the sight of me?" I shook my head and took another drink. "Think nothing of it."

HELEN HARDT

"It wasn't you."

"Oh, of course not." I took a huge swig of my martini for courage. "Just my ugly pussy."

Yes, I'd just said those words to a man who'd taken over my mind and heart. God help me.

He widened his dark eyes but said nothing.

"Yes, you heard me."

"There's nothing ugly about any part of you, Erin. None of what happened was about you."

One more long drink, draining the martini glass. Yes, liquid courage. Nothing like it. "You threw my date out of my home, and then you yourself went running out after looking at me...down there. If it wasn't me, what the hell was it?"

No response. He just took a sip of his own drink.

I looked toward Lucy, who was sliding her hand across River's forearm. Seemed crystal clear where they were headed.

Not so clear for me.

I tapped my glass and signaled the barkeep. "Another here, please." Heck, Lucy had wanted to party. I was ready to party. I'd downed the first so quickly that I was already feeling a little buzz.

"So tell me," I said to Dante. "What the hell is wrong with you, anyway?"

FIVE

DANTE

What a loaded question.

So much was wrong with me that I couldn't even begin to respond. I didn't even *know* half of what was wrong. I'd lost so much time, and so many of my memories were clouded that I wasn't sure which ones were dreams—rather, nightmares—and which were real.

She still thought I was a vandal, and why she hadn't turned me in still puzzled me. She'd gone along with River's lie that first morning. I longed to interrogate her about that, but I didn't dare. What if she changed her mind and decided to turn me in? Riv might be able to pull some strings, but I didn't want to put him in that position.

No, I needed to stay quiet about that and not remind her.

Her scent hung thick in the air around me, negating all other aromas in the room. Riv had said I'd get used to it, learn to control my impulses, but her fragrance was so enticing. Did it affect him as well? I looked toward him for a moment, but he looked anything but pulled in by Erin's scent. Rather, he was enjoying the attention of her friend.

I inhaled. I couldn't even distinguish the friend's scent. Only Erin pervaded my senses, even though the bar was nearly full.

River was wrong. This wasn't just an enticing scent that I'd get used to.

No, this was something more. So much more.

I closed my eyes, willing my cock not to harden, my fangs not to descend.

I was successful with my fangs. Not with my cock.

In my mind I saw myself taking Erin to bed, kissing her ruby lips, her pink nipples, her glistening pussy.

And then marking her. Erasing those bite marks from her thigh by replacing them with my own.

Mine.

She was mine.

I could take her to bed, fuck her sweet body, touch every part of her with my fingers and my tongue...but that would not make her mine.

She would only be mine when I took her blood, when I marked her. Instinctively I knew this, even though someone else had fed from her.

The memory of those marks on her thigh pushed rage into me, and my gums burned.

No other man—human or vampire—would touch her.

Ever. I'd make sure of it.

I jerked.

Her smooth hand was on mine, and her touch ignited me.

"Are you all right?" she asked. "You haven't spoken for about ten minutes."

A second empty martini glass sat in front of her.

"Yeah. Fine." I gulped down the rest of my bourbon in one swallow. It was my third. At least I thought it was. I was feeling...interesting.

She *could* be mine. Maybe tonight. Why not go for it? All thoughts of keeping her safe fled as inhibition swept away from me in a current of lust.

"Do you want to dance?" I asked.

She looked toward the small dance floor. No one was dancing. "Yeah. Sure." She stood.

I took her hand—sparks flew through me—and led her to the floor.

"Hey, kids," Lucy laughed. "There's no music."

Really? I hadn't noticed. Music floated all around us—grand concertos mixed with jazzy blues. Just being in Erin's presence created melodies I'd never imagined.

Erin was wearing a tight black dress that illuminated her fair skin even more than usual and made her peridot eyes sparkle with fire. Her dark hair hung in subtle waves halfway down her back.

She was the most beautiful woman I'd ever seen. I'd seen some amazing women that fateful night, had been turned on beyond my wildest dreams...

Now, all that seemed like adolescent fantasy.

This was real.

I took her in my arms and held her close, resisting the urge to bury my nose in her hair and inhale. I closed my eyes, trying to ignore the tightening in my groin, the tingling in my gums. If I could just hold her, feel her close to me...

But as inhibition eluded me, so did control. My fangs descended, and I lowered my head toward her milky neck. The pulse from her carotid artery thrummed softly against my lips.

Next to it, the blood flowing through her jugular to her heart whisked gently to my ears.

Arteries were easier to feed from, but veins made less of a mess.

The jugular it would be, then.

Just a taste. One taste.

I let my tongue touch her skin, so soft and silky, so warm with the flow of her blood just millimeters away. Her beautiful pulse thumped gently against my flesh. My eye teeth lengthened, their itching intense.

Yes...just one taste...

No inhibition. I nicked her warm skin with my left cuspid.

SIX

Erin

"**O**uch!"

I pulled away from Dante, touching my neck. When I looked at my fingers, they were smeared with blood.

"I'm sorry." He walked briskly back to the bar, grabbed River, and the two of them left.

Just like that.

Again. He freaking left me *again*.

I rejoined Lucy at the bar.

"What was that about?" Lucy demanded. "Detective Hottie and I were headed for the sack."

"He...*bit* me." I rubbed at my neck. "I think."

"So?"

Did Lucy truly think biting was normal behavior on the dance floor? "So? We were dancing—"

"With no music, by the way."

"Quit interrupting me. And there *was* music."

"Uh...no, there wasn't. Ask anyone in here."

"It was a soft jazzy kind of instrumental thing. It was perfect, actually."

"You've had one too many martinis, hon." She turned toward the bartender. "Hey, barkeep. Why isn't there any music in here tonight?"

"Our sound system is down," he replied. "Sorry about that. It should be up tomorrow."

"See?" Lucy said to me.

I listened. Sure enough, no music. But the tune *had* been playing while Dante and I were dancing. I was sure of it.

Damn. Maybe it *was* the alcohol. It must have been. Two martinis on a pretty empty stomach, and I'd had a glass of wine at the dance club. Still, alcohol didn't usually make me hear things. Not that I remembered, anyway.

"Quit changing the subject. Dante bit my neck."

"Let me look," Lucy said, examining me. "It looks like a bug bite. Certainly not a human bite. He probably just scraped it and made it bleed."

"But I felt something pierce my skin."

"You felt him scrape thin skin that was healing. Go to the bathroom and look at it in the mirror. You'll see. Listen to me. I'm a nurse, you know." She chuckled.

"Ha-ha. So am I." I opened my purse and removed a small compact. I had to agree with Lucy. It looked like a bug bite. She was no doubt right. In fact...

I'd seen a similar bug bite on my brother when we had breakfast a few days earlier. Mosquitoes, maybe? I didn't recall being bitten, but that wasn't abnormal.

"You want another drink?" Lucy asked.

"No, I've had enough."

"Yeah, I think you have," Lucy said, "since you've been

hearing things. But I'm starved, and you cost me my night with Detective Hottie, so you're buying me a late dinner."

I laughed. "All right. I'm hungry too. I need to get something in my stomach."

We walked a few blocks down to a little restaurant and edged in for their last seating.

I ordered some gumbo and then turned to Lucy. "Did you think Dr. Bonneville was acting weird during our last shift?"

"What do you mean?"

"After we lost that heart attack, she asked me to have coffee with her. She's never done that before."

"Really? What did you talk about?"

I took a sip of water, thinking. My mind was fuzzy from the martinis, and for some reason, I couldn't remember much about my time with Dr. Bonneville. "Just about how she hated losing patients. That she died a little inside each time."

"I think that happens to all of us."

"It does, of course. But she takes it really hard. I don't get it. She's such a bitch most of the time, but when she loses a patient, she becomes... I don't know. Human?"

"She may be a bitch, but she's a top-notch physician," Lucy said.

"I know that. She's just such a riddle, you know?"

"I wouldn't waste your time overthinking it. She'll be back to her old self the next time we share a shift. Just be happy she showed you a little kindness."

"Oh, I am. And trust me. I don't expect her to repeat it."

"Good thinking."

The waiter delivered our food, and after a few bites, Lucy spoke again.

"So what was up with River's cousin?"

"I'm not sure. I'm pretty certain he was drunk, though."

"He seems to have a thing for you."

"I'm not so sure he does." I hadn't told Lucy about my previous run-ins with Dante. I wasn't real excited about telling my best friend that a guy had run out of my house after seeing my goods.

"Are you kidding? He couldn't take his eyes off you. I asked River what was going on with him, but all he said was that Dante had had too much to drink."

"See? That's what I told you."

"I know. But he had a look about him, Erin. A look of... The only word that comes to my mind is *hunger*."

"Like you said. He was drunk."

"Alcohol didn't cause the look I'm talking about."

"His own cousin attributed it to the drinking."

"Yeah. But I think River was lying."

"Why would you think that?"

"Just a tell he has. He looked away from me when he said it."

That *was* a classic tell. Lucy was very intuitive, but she didn't know River well at all. Yet. I had no doubt they'd hook up eventually. When Lucy wanted a guy, she almost always got him.

"You know I'm good at reading people," Lucy continued. "And I'm telling you. River was lying, and Dante was hungry."

"Well, he's had more than one chance to satisfy his hunger with me," I said, "and he hasn't stuck around for any of them. So he's clearly not *that* hungry. At least not for me."

"Okay... We're definitely going to revisit that subject. I see you've been keeping things from me. But I'm not talking about a hunger for sex. Or even a hunger for sex with you."

"Then what are you talking about?"

"I'm not sure, honestly." She took a bite of gumbo. "But it's there. Believe me."

Something in her voice convinced me. I believed her. I just wasn't sure what I was believing.

I rubbed the raw spot on my neck.

And tingles shot through me.

SEVEN

DANTE

"You've had too much to drink," River said when we returned to Bill's place. "That's all it was."

"That's not true. I couldn't resist her. You saw me. You're telling me there was no music in that bar, but damn it, I heard music."

"It's the alcohol, Dante. You're not used to it. I shouldn't have let you drink so much."

"For God's sake, Riv, I'm twenty-eight years old. I don't need my *younger* cousin to monitor my drinking."

"Look, I may be younger by a few months, but I've got ten years on you in life experience."

Defensiveness rose within me. "That's not my fault."

"Damn it, Dante, no one said it was your fault. But there are things you're not used to. Like the urge that comes when you scent a dark-haired female with vampire blood. And the effects of alcohol on your system."

"Has alcohol ever made you *hear* things?"

He shook his head. "But it affects everyone differently.

Auditory hallucinations *can* happen."

"How do you know that?"

"I searched it while you were dancing to no music. You freaked me out, Dante."

"Right. You searched it. While you were sitting at a bar." I rolled my eyes.

"Yes. I did. On my phone."

"Oh." I kept forgetting that cell phones were now minicomputers.

Bill shuffled in wearing lounge pants and no shirt. For one hundred and two, he looked great. Still had the musculature of a forty-year-old. "How was your night out?"

"Great. Dante drank a little too much."

"For Christ's sake, Riv." I didn't need a lecture from Bill.

"What? You did. You were hearing things."

"Hearing things?" Bill asked.

Thanks a lot, Riv. "I'm fine, Bill."

"What did you hear, Dante?"

"I really don't want to talk about this."

"Music," River said. "He was dancing with a woman to music that wasn't playing."

"Really?" Bill inhaled, his forehead creasing. "Interesting."

"It was the alcohol," River said.

"Yes, probably," Bill agreed.

But I wasn't fooled. Bill *didn't* think it was the alcohol. Something else was going on. Something he'd no doubt refuse to tell me. After all, I wasn't *ready*.

When *would* I be ready? When I told Bill what I had been through? I wasn't even sure how much of it was real. Much of it was, unfortunately, but I'd had so many nightmares as well.

I turned to Bill. "Do we have a queen?"

"What? You mean like the Queen of England? Of course not," he said.

"That's not what I mean. Do we—*vampires*—have a queen?"

"No," Bill said. "We are citizens of whatever country we live in. We recognize the government of our country. We have a council of elders who make decisions regarding the *Texts*, but it's not a governing body. You know all of this, Dante."

"I'm asking historically, Bill. Was there ever a time when our ancestors recognized any kind of royalty?"

Bill narrowed his eyes. "I suppose there is history from long ago that was never recorded. Maybe there was some kind of royal hierarchy at one time. But certainly not now."

She was no queen. But what *was* she then? She had power from some source, money to hire goons, a hidden dungeon to keep me in. *She* was *something*.

"Why would you ask that?" Bill's eyes were still narrowed, his forehead still creased.

My grandfather's question was valid, but I couldn't answer. Not yet.

There had been times when she'd made me say it, had tortured me so badly that not only would I say she was my queen...I actually believed it.

I almost believed that black was white after I'd been beaten, shocked, tortured into submission.

And then she drank from me. Made me drink from her.

I hated it.

And Bill wanted me to tell him what had happened.

How could I tell him—or anyone—what I'd let *her* do to me?

"Dante?" Bill's voice.

I jerked out of my thoughts. "What?"

"Why are you asking, if you know we have no queen?" Bill said again.

"No reason."

"I think there *is* a reason. I think it has something to do with where you were for the last ten years. You need to come clean."

"Come clean? You make it sound like I was gone because I *wanted* to be gone. Trust me. That's not the case."

"I chose the wrong words. I'm sorry." Bill put his hand on my shoulder. "I can help you if you let me."

"Help me? I've *asked* for your help, and you've refused me every time. I have things going on inside me that I can't explain. River says it's because I'm not used to all the scents around me. Or he blames it on alcohol. That I'm not used to it. I don't discount either of those explanations. They are probably partially to blame. But I'm telling you. There's something more."

"He's drawn to the scent of a certain female," River volunteered. "One that's descended from vamps at some point in her ancestry. I'm familiar with the scent, because her brother is my partner. It's a difficult scent to resist, and he's not used to using self-control."

"Thanks for that," I said with an eye roll.

"Hey, you wanted his help. Have you told him any of this?"

"Let me ask you this, Dante," Bill said. "Have you met River's partner? The brother?"

"Briefly."

"And how does *he* smell to you?"

"Good the first time I met him." That night, with the homeless man. "But now...I don't know."

"What do you mean you don't know?"

"I mean exactly what I said. I don't know. That's my point. When Erin is around, I can't smell anything else. It's like she's the only blood on the planet. In fact..." My thoughts churned. Had I even scented another being since I'd met Erin?

No. I hadn't. I'd smelled the testosterone and adrenaline in the man from her bedroom, but I hadn't smelled *him*. His own unique scent.

"I already told him that vamps don't have fated mates," River said.

"No, we don't," Bill agreed.

"Then what's going on with me?"

"Truthfully?" Bill rubbed his chin. "I don't know. But if you want to figure this out, you need to tell me what happened to you, Dante. You need to tell me everything."

Crazy. I'd escaped. The smells had overwhelmed me—every human and animal that had crossed my path, the homeless man from whom I'd stolen money and clothes.

Erin's brother—the detective who'd stopped me that night. I'd smelled him then. He smelled similar to Erin...yet different. So much different.

Then I'd picked up the various scents at the hospital, and I'd run.

And then...*Erin*.

Her scent.

She was inside me. So much a part of me that my olfactory sense hadn't picked up another since I'd found her.

"I don't think I've smelled anyone since I met Erin."

"Really?" Bill arched his eyebrows, looking pensive. "Why didn't you tell me that?"

"I didn't realize it until just now. And before, when I was

trying to make you understand, you kicked me out of your office. And when I tried to talk to *you*"—I turned to River—"you couldn't hear what I was saying. When you, your partner, and Erin were all in the same room, all I could smell was Erin."

The wrinkles in Bill's forehead became more pronounced. He was concerned. "Are you sure?"

"Only since I met her, I mean. When I first escaped, I could smell everyone and anything around me. But since meeting her—" I raked my fingers through my hair. "It hadn't occurred to me that I can't smell anyone else's scent. But I can't." I inhaled. "Nothing. Has anyone been here recently?"

"The kid down the street came by selling something for school," Bill said. "His scent is still in the air. It's young blood, tinny and full of testosterone."

I inhaled again. Nothing. I shook my head.

"Maybe your sense of smell just hasn't evolved," River said. "Because you've been gone and all."

"I just told you I smelled everything when I escaped. You're not listening again, River."

"If you're correct, Dante, and you can't smell anything—"

"Of course I'm correct!" I interrupted my grandfather. "I know if my nose is working or not!"

"All right," Bill said. "Then this is serious. In the past, a vampire needed his sense of smell to protect himself and others. While it's not as necessary today, we still depend on it."

"She did something to me…" I murmured.

"Who did? Erin?" Bill began pacing across the floor.

"No. No. Not Erin."

"The person who took you," Bill said. "She was a female, wasn't she?"

I pulled at my hair. "I can't. Can't go there."

"Dante," Bill said seriously. "You *have* to."

River nodded, touching my forearm. "Please, Dante. You were taken against your will. If you can't talk to Bill, please talk to me. I'm a detective. I *will* find whoever did this to you. I promise you. But trails grow cold quickly. Please. Tell us all you know, and I will put whoever did this to you behind bars."

EIGHT

Erin

Whatever this "hunger" was that Lucy thought she saw in Dante, I couldn't get her to elaborate on it. Instead, she changed the subject, and we spent the remainder of dinner sobering me up. Good plan.

The next night in the ER, Steve ran up to me as soon as I arrived. "You'll never guess what happened. Remember that patient, Cynthia North, who went missing from the ER last week?"

"Yeah, of course."

"She's back. She appeared on the ninth floor an hour ago, around ten."

My heart thumped. "Is she okay?"

"Yeah. She's stable, in a drug-induced coma. No one knows where she's been or how she got back."

"Stable? She was a bleeder..." My thoughts raced back to the night she came in. Dr. Thomas had been on duty. *She's a bleeder.* Had we gotten her stabilized before she'd disappeared?

Why was my memory so fuzzy?

"Yeah, I know. It's all pretty freaky. Dr. Thomas and your nerd, Dr. Crown, are with her now, running some tests."

"Who's running things down here then?"

"They called in the hag. So watch your step."

Just what I didn't need. Though Dr. Bonneville had been nice to me the last time we'd worked together, after we lost the heart attack.

The heart attack. I'd grown used to identifying patients by their condition in the ER. But that man wasn't a heart attack. Even though we hadn't known his name, he was a person.

I needed to remember that.

I didn't yet know if his family had been found, or even if they existed. Poor man.

"Is Lucy in yet?" I asked.

"I haven't seen her." Steve checked his pager. "Gotta run. The hag needs me."

I wanted to run up to nine to see the patient who had reappeared, but she was in good hands. She was stable. And alive.

More than I could say for the heart attack from two nights ago.

I went into the office, clicked on my computer, and did a quick search. Howard Dern. That was his name. Now he was no longer the heart attack in my mind.

Unfortunately, I didn't feel any better knowing his name. He was still dead.

My side trip to the computer was the only relaxation I got that night. I did a lot of boo-boo mending. No real emergencies, which was always good.

But I did see an old friend—Mr. Lincoln, the homeless man whose drug panel had come back clean. He came in with a superficial stab wound. I cleaned him up and got him comfortable.

"You look familiar," he said.

"I took care of you a week or so ago," I said. "When you came in unconscious. Remember? My name is Erin."

"That's a pretty name." He smiled. "Yes, I do remember. You thought I was on drugs."

I said nothing. I still hadn't ruled out the possibility. Labs weren't foolproof.

"I don't do drugs," he said.

"I'm sure you don't."

"You don't believe me. Just like you didn't believe me about the vampire."

"The vampire?"

"Yeah. I told you about the vampire I saw that night. Asked you if you'd seen him."

It sounded vaguely familiar. "Uh-huh," I said absently.

"I saw a ghost that night too."

I stopped myself from rolling my eyes. "I'm sure you did. Are you feeling any pain relief yet?"

"Not yet." He winced. "Don't you want to hear about the ghost?"

"Sure," I said, listening with one ear. Since I'd moved to New Orleans, I'd heard every ghost story in the book, but I hadn't yet seen any evidence of phantom activity. Though I did get goose bumps walking around certain parts of the city.

Come to think of it, I'd had goose bumps while I was at

Dante's grandfather's house, a known haunted location. I'd just chalked it up to being close to Dante.

Until he'd kicked me out, that was.

"It was a different kind of ghost," Mr. Lincoln said.

"What do you mean?"

"It was a *vampire* ghost."

Chills erupted on the back of my neck. "Oh?"

"Yeah. He was helping the vampire I saw. He protected the vampire from the cop."

"I see." If the man wasn't on drugs, he was a few bricks shy.

"The vampire stole my clothes and what little money I had. That's why I came in that night without clothes. Remember?"

"I do." That was a visual I couldn't unsee. Mr. Lincoln was a nice man, but homelessness had taken its toll on his body. A young man of twenty-five or so should have been robust and healthy. Instead, Mr. Lincoln was too thin, and red patches marred much of his skin.

"He hypnotized me."

"What?"

"The vampire. That's how they feed on humans. They hypnotize you so you don't remember."

He truly was off his rocker. "I see."

"Do you?"

What was I supposed to say to that? I had nothing, so I asked a question instead. "If you were hypnotized, how did you know a ghost was there?"

"I could still see. I just couldn't talk or move. I remember everything. Maybe that's because I don't usually get hypnotized. I just let them bite me. They don't take much, and they always buy me a hot meal afterward. It's a good deal." He touched his neck. "See? These marks. That's where they bite me."

I looked him over, palpating the marks. Mosquito bites, most likely, just like the one I had on my own neck.

"Just how many vampires live here in New Orleans, Mr. Lincoln?" Might as well humor him. It would help him take his mind off the minor stabbing.

"We're friends, aren't we, Erin? You should call me Abe."

"No kidding? Your name is Abe Lincoln?" Definitely not ruling out drugs.

"It is."

"Do you have any ID?"

"Nope. But that's the name my *maman* gave me."

"Your mother was French?"

"Yes. Cecile Lincoln. Born Gervais. And about two hundred or so."

"Two hundred or so what?"

"Vampires. You asked me how many vampires live here in New Orleans."

Right. I had. "That's a lot of vampires."

"Not really, when you consider the population of the city is almost four hundred thousand."

He had me there. "Did a vampire stab you?"

"No. Most vampires are decent people. It was some stupid kid looking for drugs. I didn't have any, but he stabbed me anyway."

"I'm very sorry this happened to you." And I was. The man might be delusional, but he didn't deserve this shitty luck. No one did.

"It's part of life on the streets."

"Don't you have any family who could help you out?"

"Nope."

"Have you tried the missions? I can get a social worker in

here to talk to you. I'm sure there's help available."

"I'm fine. I'm comfortable unless it gets below forty degrees, which it doesn't often, luckily."

"Even at night?"

"That's when the vampires help me. They come out at night."

"Because they'd burn in the sun, right?"

He shook his head. "That's a myth. They just have really sensitive skin and need to wear a lot of sunblock."

"I see. So do I, actually."

"Yeah, you're pretty pale."

"Thanks. I think."

"I didn't mean it as an insult, Erin. You're very pretty."

This conversation was rapidly going way out of my comfort zone. "The pain meds will kick in soon, Mr. Lincoln." No way was I calling him Abe. "I need to see to some other patients."

"Wait!"

"Yes?"

"You need to believe me."

"Why? You asked me that first night if I'd seen the vampire. But you allegedly saw the vampire before you came to the hospital. I wasn't with you then, so how in the world could I have seen him?"

"Because he was here. In the emergency room."

Again, my neck went cold. "I need to see other patients," I said again. I walked out of the room and hightailed it to my computer to make a note for a social worker to visit with Mr. Lincoln. The man needed some serious help.

I jerked when a hand clamped down on my shoulder.

"I need you for a few minutes, Erin."

NINE

DANTE

"*T*he queen says you've been obstinate and you need to be punished."

My heart sped up like a freight train. "I've done nothing."

"You haven't been eating."

"I'm not hungry."

"You need to eat your protein. Red meat. We feed you excellent meals."

"What good are excellent meals when I'm tied down? I can't even take a shit without you unbinding me."

"The queen's orders."

"Fuck the queen!"

"You won't say that again, you piece of shit."

"Fuck her, fuck her, fuck her!" I spat.

The masked man inched toward me. "I've been warned not to spill a drop of your precious blood. Luckily, I'm skilled at many levels of torture, and your blood will be spared."

"What are you going to do to me?" I said through clenched teeth.

"I'll leave that to your imagination," he said, his voice low. "Anticipation and all that."

I was already naked. They'd taken my clothes away.

He unclamped my bindings. "Stand up," he ordered.

"Why doesn't the queen dole out her own punishment?"

"You'd have to ask her that," he said. "But it works out well for me. I enjoy it."

Fucking sadist. I lunged toward him, but he poked me with a cattle prod.

"Aaauugh!" The jolt shot knives of pain through my body, making me tremble.

"You're a pretty young man, Dante. A young vampire on the cusp of true maturity. Too bad I can't really fuck you up. It's almost a shame to hurt you."

"Then don't." My voice cracked, sparks still snapping inside me.

"I have my orders, and as I said, I enjoy it." He eyed his tool, a sick smile curving his lips. "Funny thing about electricity. As long as I gauge the current, I can cause you unbearable pain without harming your body at all."

I shot up in bed. Bill was in his study, and River had gone to work.

I hadn't told them anything, even though Bill had pressured me. River wanted the truth for a different reason—to investigate. To find who'd done this to me. He was still skeptical that something different was going on with my scenting of Erin, but Bill believed me. I could tell by how he'd looked at me.

But he was a little freaked out. He didn't know *why* it was happening. That bothered him. Bill didn't like not knowing.

I rose, drank some blood and made some breakfast, and then decided to search the *Vampyre Texts*. Bill had two copies— one he kept in his office, and another more ornate version that he kept in the living room. As kids, we'd been warned not to touch it. I was no longer a kid. I picked up the heavy tome, sat down on the couch, and opened it.

To no avail. The words were written in ancient French, and I couldn't decipher them. Could anyone in this day and age? I'd need to find a linguist. A linguist I could trust.

Yeah, right. Linguists were a dime a dozen. Not.

Bill was one hundred and two years old. Still, ancient French hadn't been spoken since the fourteenth century. I wasn't sure how I knew that. Must have learned it in history class a long time ago.

My grandfather was the only person I knew who might be able to make some sense of the *Texts*. I put the book away and walked to his office.

"Come in, Dante," he said before I could knock.

I entered, trying to figure out what I wanted to ask.

"The *Vampyre Texts*," he said. "You learn the important content at the age of eighteen, after you complete your high school studies."

This was the third time since I'd returned that he'd read my mind. I wasn't at all comfortable with it. He'd always been intuitive, but this was getting beyond strange.

"I'm well past eighteen. Can you teach me?"

"It's not that simple. The content of the *Texts* is taught through symbolry and example."

"So? You taught River and Em, didn't you?"

"I did. But they were ready."

I am *ready.*

"You're not," he said.

"Why do you constantly say that?" I demanded. "You have no idea what happened to me." Then it dawned on me again. I hadn't said those words aloud. "Stop it! Stop getting into my head!"

"I'm not."

"Bullshit. You've been reading my mind since I got home."

He looked up, his eyes wide, and removed his glasses. "You're mistaken. I don't have that ability." He cleared his throat.

His tone was familiar—the same one I remembered from my childhood. *We're done discussing this. Drop it.*

But I was no longer a child. Bill was hiding something. Either he'd been reading my mind, or he knew things he should have no way of knowing. Which meant he *had* a way of knowing. I just didn't know what it was.

All of that was the least of my concerns at the moment, though. I needed to learn the content of the texts, and I'd find a way to do it, with or without my grandfather's help. I had no other choice. I had to figure out what was going on with Erin. The answer must be within those pages somewhere. It had to be.

I turned to leave Bill's office—

A knife of ice speared into the back of my neck, and I gasped.

"Dante..."

But I ignored my grandfather's voice.

Erin.

Erin was in danger.

✤

I screeched into the hospital parking lot. I was a good driver, but my license had long since expired—something else I'd have to take care of.

Erin's scent...

She was in the hospital.

Someone was with her. Someone who meant her harm.

I wasn't sure how I knew, but I did. I smelled only Erin, but she was not alone.

My gums prickled as my fangs descended. I needed to keep my mouth closed. No way did I have enough control to make them retract. Not right now. Not when my blood was boiling beneath my skin.

And then—

The other individual was gone.

The prickling on my neck ceased. My teeth began to shorten. Erin was fine. No longer in danger.

I stopped in the middle of the driveway to the ER and stood, immobile.

Erin was inside.

Erin...who I wanted more than my next breath of air, my next drop of blood.

I continued standing as an ambulance blared up to the door, stopping just before hitting me.

"Hey!" An EMT rushed over to me. "Get out of the way! You could have been killed!"

Still I stood, my gaze riveted to the door of the ER, until something buzzed against my skin.

My new phone. It was River.

"Hello?" I said.

"Dante, you need to come over to the ER. It's Emilia."

My heart raced. "I'm *at* the ER. Is she all right?"

"We're at Tulane. Where are you?"

"At University. I'm on my way."

My sister lay in a hospital bed in one of the ER exam rooms. I felt helpless. Helpless in a different way than I'd felt when I'd perceived Erin in danger.

How had I made such a mistake? Erin was fine. Could I no longer trust my instinct? Erin had wreaked havoc on my senses, and not necessarily in a good way.

I'd been sure another person had been with her, hurting her.

My mind was unstable. That was the only explanation. Being held in captivity, tortured, violated—it had taken its toll.

Of course it had.

I needed help.

I didn't know any vampire therapists, and how could I explain to a human therapist what I'd been through?

River and Bill sat in chairs next to the bed where Emilia lay. I took her hand. "Doing okay, little sis?"

"I'm fine. I guess I fainted at work."

"You've been working too hard, Em," River said.

"I haven't been doing anything more than I always do. I'm not sure what's going on."

"I can answer that." A man in a white coat walked into the room. "Could you all excuse me for a few minutes? I need to talk to the patient alone."

"They're family," Emilia said. "I want them here."

"Are you sure?"

"Of course I'm sure. What could you possibly have to say that I wouldn't want them to hear? Please. Go ahead."

"You're pregnant."

TEN

Erin

Dr. Bonneville had wanted me to stop at the Tulane ER on my way home and make arrangements to replenish our B positive blood from their stash. I'd asked why we couldn't just email them, but she'd been clear that the blood would arrive faster if a staff member made the request in person. Since it meant I got off an hour early, I didn't complain.

As soon as I got out of my car at the Tulane parking lot, something gripped me.

A pull. A tug. And then pinpricks erupted on my flesh.

I must have been more freaked out from Abe Lincoln's vampire tales than I realized. I took a few deep breaths and walked toward the entrance.

"May I help you?" the receptionist asked.

"I'm Erin Hamilton, a nurse from University ER. Dr. Zabrina Bonneville asked that I come over and make arrangements to get some B positive blood transferred to our blood bank. We got shorted on our last delivery, according to her, and apparently you have more than enough here to help us out in the meantime."

"You'll need to speak to our admin about that, and she's not in yet."

I looked at my watch. Seven a.m. "When does she get in?"

"Eight o'clock."

I didn't feel like waiting around for nearly an hour, but I didn't have much of a choice. "I guess I'll wait. Can you point me toward the cafeteria? I'm starving."

"Sure. Follow the hallway to the main hospital. You can't miss it."

"Thanks."

I turned, and—

A gasp left my throat.

Walking toward me, as if in slow motion, was Dante Gabriel.

I perked my ears. No music this time. Just Dante in all his male glory. Dante, who I'd last seen when he left the dance floor—and then the bar—abruptly.

He had a habit of leaving me in limbo.

He walked toward me quickly. "I knew you were here."

"You did?"

"What are you doing here?"

"An errand for one of the doctors. Looks like I'm stuck here for an hour. Why are *you* here? Are you okay?"

"My sister."

"Is *she* okay?"

"Sort of. I mean, yes. She's...pregnant."

"Oh! Well, congratulations, then. I didn't know she was married."

"She's not."

"Oh." Warmth crept up my cheeks. "Congratulations anyway. That's wonderful news. Isn't it?"

"She's always wanted to be a mother."

"Good. I'm sure she'll be a great one."

"I hope so. I mean, I hope she has the chance."

"What do you—"

He grabbed my arm and led me out of the ER and down a secluded hallway. He pushed me against the wall.

"I've tried to stay away from you, Erin. God, I've tried, for your own good. But I can't stop thinking about you."

My skin tingled all over, and my blood flowed like tiny rivers of warm honey in my veins. "I can't stop thinking about you either, but why—"

His lips clamped onto mine. I didn't even think about letting him in. I parted my lips on instinct, letting him sweep his warm tongue into my mouth. Never mind that he'd run from me twice now. Never mind that I still knew next to nothing about him. Never mind that my first contact with him had been catching him in a criminal act.

I wanted him. Wanted his mouth on mine, his hands on my body.

I cupped his cheeks and pulled his face as close to mine as I could until our lips were smashed together, our tongues tangling. We kissed ferociously, until I had to push him away to take a much-needed breath.

"My God," he groaned.

"My God is right," I replied.

"I want you so fucking much."

"You have a funny way of showing it."

"That kiss. Can't you tell how much I want you?" He nudged his bulge into my belly.

"Yes. But you always—"

He took my lips again.

Would we ever talk? Ever discuss why he was acting so weird?

Right now, I didn't care. All I wanted for the rest of my life was to keep kissing Dante, keep caressing his broad shoulders, his cheeks, his neck. I threaded my fingers through his silky hair, relishing its softness. I slid my other hand over his shoulder and down his muscular arm, entwining his fingers with my own.

He pushed his erection into me farther. Without thinking, I whisked my hand out of his and cupped the denim-clad bulge.

"Oh, God," he groaned again against my mouth. "I want you so much."

"I want you too." No truer words. I was ready to fuck him right in a hospital hallway.

He deepened the kiss, cupping one of my breasts. My nipple was already hard, but the feeling intensified as he inched his fingers toward it. When he pinched it, I nearly climaxed.

I boiled over, my pussy pulsing along with my heart. He dragged his hand away from my breast and down to my crotch. When he began rubbing me there, I let out a long, low groan.

"Good, baby?"

God, yes. So good. But I couldn't form the words.

"Do you want me as much as I want you?"

Still no words, but I nodded against him.

He pushed me harder against the wall. "I want to make you...come."

I held onto him, fearing my legs wouldn't hold me up. "Not here. Not in..." The last words came out only as a sigh.

"Please, Erin. I know I've left you hanging. I know you don't understand why. I want you so much. Want you to feel good—"

Then footsteps.

He broke away.

"Dante." His cousin River walked toward us. "There you are. I need to talk to you. Pronto."

ELEVEN

DANTE

Erin looked up at me, her green eyes glowing, her lips swollen and red from our kisses. River would know what we'd been doing.

I didn't fucking care. The jolt from his interruption had taken care of my teeth but not my cock. It was still hard in my jeans.

I let go of Erin, only to grab her again as she started falling. "You okay?"

She nodded but gripped my forearm, the heat from her grasp transfusing into my skin. Her blood. It was close to the surface of her palm and fingertips. I drew in a deep, calming breath.

"Riv, you remember Erin."

"Yeah. Nice to see you again." He turned back to me. "I'm really sorry to interrupt. I mean *really* sorry. But this is important."

Erin cleared her throat, her cheeks red with embarrassment. "I have to get back to the ER anyway. The administrator I came to see should be in soon." She let go of my arm and walked away, her gait slightly unsteady.

"What was she doing here?" River asked. "Is that why you ran out of Em's room?"

"Shit."

I'd made like a jackrabbit as soon as the doctor said Em was pregnant. I'd smelled Erin, felt her presence, needed to see her. What must my sister be thinking?

"How long have I been gone?"

"About twenty-five minutes."

I'd been making out with Erin for twenty-five minutes? Time was truly suspended when I was with her.

I inhaled. Her scent still clung to the air. My mind was muddled.

"What did you want again?"

"I know who the father is."

"Huh?"

"Emilia wouldn't tell us, but I *know*, Dante."

I shook my head to clear it. Erin's fragrance still hung inside my nose, nearly debilitating me.

"She wouldn't tell you?"

"Said it was none of my fucking business, and that she was having the baby, damn it."

"Okay. Okay." I rubbed at my forehead. That sounded like the Em I remembered from when we were teens. "Now what?"

"She refuses to terminate the pregnancy."

Now I understood. Our mother had died giving birth to Emilia, and full vampire women were rare. "Wait. Begin again."

"She wouldn't tell me who the father was, but I know who it is. Em has had a strangely familiar smell to me for a few weeks now, but I chalked it up to her hormones or whatever.

Plus, she hadn't been feeling well. But when the doctor said she was pregnant, I knew right away who the father is."

"Don't keep me in suspense."

"My partner. Jay Hamilton. Erin's brother."

Whoa. My head spun with haze. "What?"

"What the hell is the matter with you, Dante?"

I was awash in Erin, unable to form a clear thought. But I had to. I willed myself back into my right mind. "I'm fine. So tell me again."

"Jay Hamilton is the father of Em's baby."

"How could that be?"

"Either she had herself artificially inseminated with his sperm," River said, "or more likely, they slept together."

"She's so young!"

"She's twenty-five, Dante. Not fifteen, like she was when you left."

My ire awakened. "Stop saying that."

"Saying what?"

"That I *left*. You make it sound like I had a fucking choice in the matter. If I'd had it my way, I never would have gone. I'd have been here, learning all the shit that you already know. That Em already knows. I'm severely handicapped solely because I was taken against my will."

"Look, I know you've been through a lot."

"You don't have half a fucking clue what I've been through. I've been through things you can't even imagine in your tiny little mind."

"Tiny little mind?" River advanced toward me. "Who do you think you're talking to?"

My guard went up. Quick as a flash, I grabbed River by his collar and flattened him against the wall, fangs elongating.

"Who the hell do *you* think you're talking to? I've had things done to me that I wouldn't wish on my worst enemy, and you say you *know* I've been through a lot? You don't know shit! I ought to take your fucking head off."

"Hey, calm down. Calm down." He slowly moved his arm upward until his hand was over mine. "Let go of me."

I unclenched my fist and moved away from him. Self-control.

I didn't have it.

Not even slightly.

If I couldn't control myself around River, how would I ever control myself with Erin?

"I'm sorry," I said grimly, though my fangs didn't withdraw.

"You're right," River said. "I can't imagine what you've been through. I'm sorry. Trick of the trade. As a cop, I have to turn off my emotions in the line of duty a lot. If I didn't, I couldn't live with what I see sometimes. It's fallen onto you, cuz, and I'm really, really sorry."

I opened my mouth, but he held up his hand.

"Let me be sorry, Dante. I've been a douche. I get that you're not ready to talk yet. Maybe you'll never be ready, and that's okay, even though I'd love to lock up whatever fucker did this to you. But this is about Em. And my partner. Em is determined to have this baby."

I closed my eyes and inhaled, giving myself a few seconds. Then, "She'll be okay. Emilia is strong. She has to be. I can't lose her now that I just got her back."

"We'll get her the best care," River said. "She won't even talk about terminating. It'd be one thing if she were married and had been trying to get pregnant. But that's not the case. This is just an unfortunate accident."

"It wasn't an accident if she had herself inseminated."

River didn't respond.

"What about your partner? Does *he* want the baby?"

"My partner has never mentioned Em to me. Either he donated anonymously to a sperm bank, or he fucked your sister. Which do you think is more likely?"

My hackles rose. Now that I was in my right mind again, reality had hit me over the head with a mallet. Those teeth were never going to retract now. "Call your partner. Tell him to meet us here so I can kill the motherfucker."

"I think you mean sisterfucker."

"Not funny." I clenched my hands into fists. "Why does she want to have the baby?"

"I don't know," River said. "But Emilia is strong-willed. Maybe you can talk to her. Convince her that the timing isn't right. I hate the idea as much as you do, but I'm scared of losing her, man."

"I can't do that." Absolutely not. I'd had my own will stolen for ten years. I would not try to make a decision for my sister, especially a decision I wasn't sure was the right one, even if it would guarantee she'd live. "I *won't* do that. She's strong. She'll make it."

"Your mother was strong too. So was mine."

An image of my mother popped into my mind. She was dark with blue eyes. Em looked a lot like her, while I favored my father. She was beautiful, but I had no real memories of her. I'd been three when she passed. My father had cared for us then, and Em, being a newborn, had taken most of his attention away from me. That was when I had begun to rely more on Bill.

"Yes, they were. Bill has money. We'll get Em the best care out there."

"Yeah, okay." River sighed. "You're right. I'm just scared shitless."

"Me too." I inhaled. Erin's scent still hung in the air, though it was dissipating.

Emilia was fine for now. River was fine.

I was *not* fine. I'd promised Erin an orgasm, and I hadn't delivered. I still didn't trust myself with her, but I had to be near her. Had to feel her.

"Hey, I've got to go."

"Where are you—"

I walked away from River.

And toward my heart's desire.

TWELVE

Erin

I'd been light-headed all through my meeting with the Tulane ER administrator, but fortunately, I was able to get the job done. I headed straight home for a quick breakfast and some shut-eye.

Dante never left my mind.

His kisses were unlike any kisses I'd ever experienced. They both excited me and subdued me. Gave to me and took from me. Fueled me with passion and desire, as well as agony... in a good way.

What I'd have given to have that orgasm he promised me. If only River hadn't interrupted us. I'd never be able to look my brother's partner in the eye again.

Once I'd eaten an English muffin and some granola, I yawned and headed upstairs for a hot bath. Yup, a nice fizzy bath bomb scented with lavender sounded heavenly.

I started running water in my tub, got out of my clothes, and threw them in the hamper. Then I tossed in the fragrant bath bomb and inhaled. Mmm, if that couldn't make me relax, nothing could.

I stepped into the hot water and immersed myself.

Closing my eyes, I inhaled again, letting the tranquilizing fragrance soothe all of my senses.

"I've never seen anything more beautiful."

My eyes shot open.

I knew that voice. The voice from my dreams.

Dante stood next to my tub, his dark eyes full of fire.

I rushed to cover myself with bubbles...until I realized I hadn't used bubble bath.

Oh, well. He was going to see me naked eventually. At least I'd hoped so.

Emotion coursed through me. Not fear, though that would have made more sense. He'd never harmed me, and I had no reason to believe he would now. No, this was a deeper emotion—lust, desire, passion. Pure, raw need.

"How did you get in here?"

"You left your door unlocked again."

"No. I didn't." I couldn't have. I remembered locking it. Didn't I? I'd been so light-headed after my necking session with Dante. Had I forgotten?

I had to stop doing that. My neighborhood was pretty safe, but still. Not smart. Especially if, as Abe Lincoln swore, ghosts and vampires walked the streets of New Orleans. The thought made me smile. He was a nice enough young man, but so delusional. Abe Lincoln couldn't possibly be his real name.

"What do you want?"

"You."

"I'm kind of in the middle of something here. Then I need to get some sleep. I work again tonight."

"I won't touch you."

"You just said you wanted me."

"I do. But I won't touch you. I can't."

"Why not?"

"Because I can't. Can we leave it at that?"

"No, we *can't* leave it at that. It doesn't make any sense. First you're all over me, and then you take off. How many times has that happened now, Dante? How many times am I supposed to put up with it?"

No response.

"Aren't you going to answer me?"

"I can't. You're naked. In a tub. You're wet and naked. How am I supposed to concentrate on anything but that?"

"For God's sake." I stood and stepped out of the tub, brushing past Dante, and wrapped myself in a large brown towel. "Get out."

"No."

Tell him again. Tell him to leave. To get out. But the words wouldn't form on my vocal cords.

Instead, other words crystallized. *Stay. Please stay. Make love to me. Take what you need from me. Anything you need.* I had to choke them back to keep them from spewing out of me.

"That towel makes your eyes so green," he said.

I opened my mouth but shut it quickly. God, the man was beautiful. His wavy dark hair sat on his shoulders, and his big espresso eyes were heavily lashed and full of fire.

His dick was hard. The bulge in his jeans was apparent.

He looked so different from the first time I'd laid eyes on him only a short time ago. He'd been beautiful then, but now...

Please. Tie me up. Blindfold me. Whip me.

Where had those words come from? Luckily I kept from

voicing them. But though I stopped my words, I couldn't stop my body. I walked toward him and dropped my towel.

"What do you want from me?" I asked.

"I want you to touch me, Erin. Please."

I reached upward and cupped one of his cheeks, his stubble growth prickly against my palm.

He closed his eyes. "Your touch ignites something in me. Something I've never known. I can feel the blood beneath your fingertips, the warmth."

His words were oddly arousing. I caressed his cheek, marveling at his beauty.

"And your scent," he continued. "I can't get enough of it."

"It's just a lavender bath bomb." I inhaled.

Then I smashed my naked body against him, as if he were a magnet and I were a giant paper clip.

His arms did not go around me.

He was holding to his promise not to touch me. But I didn't know why.

"Touch me, please, Dante. I need your touch. I yearn for it."

"I can't, love, no matter how much I want to."

I moved slightly away from him, far enough that I could look into his gorgeous eyes. "Why not?"

"Someday I hope I can tell you. I hope I can share all that I am with you. But I can't right now. Not today."

"Please. You can trust me."

"Yes, I think I can." He smiled. "I feel that I can."

"Then why not now?"

THIRTEEN

DANTE

How I wanted to respond. Wanted to divulge to her every secret I held.

But I couldn't risk it. Not when even *I* didn't understand so much of it.

I'd vowed to protect her from me. Being here was in itself a violation of that promise, but I had to have what I could of her, I had to let her touch me.

I needed that much, at least.

If I didn't touch her consciously, I could keep the blood lust at bay.

At least that's what I told myself. It was something I recalled hearing long ago, before I'd been taken. I couldn't recall the source, but it had to be true. Didn't it?

"Just touch me. Please, Erin. Run your fingers over every inch of my body. Let me feel your touch. Your caress."

"I don't understand."

"I know. And I'm sorry."

She pulled back, releasing me. "That's not what I mean. I

mean I don't understand why moving away from you is so...so... difficult. It's like I'm meant to be near you."

So she felt it too.

"Yet you tell me you won't touch me. You've left me so many times after touching me. It's as if something about me... *repulses* you."

I closed my eyes, envisioning the bite marks on Erin's supple inner thigh. Had I actually been repulsed? My heart sped. Not repulsed by Erin, but yes, the bite marks—someone else's bite marks—on her beautiful body had repulsed me. Angered me.

Made me go mad with a lust to eliminate whoever had marred her, whoever had taken blood that was mine.

I hadn't been able to protect her from whoever was feeding on her. Hadn't been able to protect what was mine.

I opened my eyes and gazed into hers.

I had no business being here.

Not when I couldn't protect her from the world.

I could at least protect her from me.

"I need to leave." I pushed her away.

She shook her head, letting out a huff. "You're really going to do this again, aren't you? You're going to get me all hot and bothered and then leave me. Fine. Two can play this game. If you leave me now, don't come near me again, Dante. I mean it."

Her words fueled something in me, a compulsion I couldn't control.

She stood against the closed door of her bathroom, her hands splayed against the wood, as if she were trying to keep herself from flying back into my arms.

Yes, she felt something. She felt the same pull I did. She *said* the words—told me to leave—but she didn't mean them.

"Tell me what you want, Erin. Tell me what you want me to do to you."

She closed her eyes. "Get out. Now. Don't ever come near me again."

"That's not what you really want."

"It is. It truly is."

I advanced toward her and cupped both her cheeks, reneging on my vow not to touch her. The bursting of her capillaries awoke the hunger in me even more. I consciously tamped it down. "Open your eyes. Look at me."

To my surprise, she obeyed, her light-green eyes glazed with desire.

"I wish I could make you understand. I wish I understood myself what I'm feeling. I wish—" My lust took over, and I crushed my mouth to hers. We kissed for a few precious moments, until she broke the kiss with a loud smack.

"You asked me what I want. I want you to take me to my bed. I want you to use that gorgeous body of yours to give me pleasure. Every single dirty pleasure you can think of. I want your tongue in my mouth, on my nipples, in my pussy. I want you to bring me to orgasm like you promised to earlier. And then I want to bring *you* to orgasm. I want to feel your body shiver as you climax into me. I want *you*, Dante. I want you to make love to me."

My loins ignited.

I was already hard, but now the zing in my gums began.

I squeezed my eyes shut, willing my fangs not to elongate.

Please. Please. Let me be with her just this once. Let me know what she feels like against my body. I won't take her blood. I will control myself. Please.

But my teeth had a mind of their own. They grew, and my

need for her blood ached within me.

I'd known coming here was a mistake, but I hadn't been able to stop myself. The drive inside me, the pull, had overtaken me.

I turned away from her so she wouldn't see my teeth. "I need to go."

But she launched herself at me, both of us landing on the hard tile floor of her bathroom, she on top of me.

My lust was so overpowering I felt no pain from the fall.

"No," she said, her voice lower than usual. "You're not leaving. Not until you give me what I want. What *you* came here for."

She ripped open my shirt, and buttons went pinging against the glass doors of her shower. She gazed at my chest, sliding her fingers over my shoulders, my pectorals, my nipples, which were already hardened.

"You're amazing," she said, her voice a husky rasp. "I've never seen a man so magnificent."

I kept my lips shut. My fangs were still elongated, and I couldn't risk her seeing them.

"You're going to shut up," she said. "You're not going to say a fucking word. No more crap about leaving. No more crap about how I won't understand. You're going to keep mum while I get rid of your clothes and give you the fuck of your life, Dante. Got it?"

I nodded. Keeping my mouth closed was a necessity, though she had no way of knowing that. I'd keep my will strong, hold myself in check, let her take what she wanted from me. I owed her that much.

She lowered her head and brushed a soft kiss against my chest.

Shivers ran through my body. God, the heat of her lips, the blood flowing to them. The need to consume her clawed at me…but still I kept my mouth shut. Couldn't let her see what the blood lust had brought me to.

"Your skin is so soft, Dante. So soft and fair, yet your muscles are hard underneath. You're amazing." She trailed her lips over the indentation of my clavicle, tracing tiny circles with her tongue.

My erection was granite inside my jeans, and every part of me itched to take control, to stand and throw her down on the tile floor, unzip my pants, free my aching cock, and drive it into her.

And then…that beautiful jugular at her neck, pulsing with the life force within her…

I'd drink from her, draw strength from her, become one with her…

My lips began to part, but I pressed them together. *Must be strong. Must be strong.*

She slid her tongue over one nipple.

I shuddered. How could that feel so good? I'd been tortured there. Made to—

God, can't go there right now.

I had no right to be here. No right—

"Oh, God." The words tumbled from my mouth despite my vow to keep my lips closed.

She fiddled with the snap to my jeans and then unzipped them, grasping my erection.

"Erin, please…"

"Shh. You're not allowed to speak, remember?"

Yes. I didn't like taking orders, but for now it was just as well. If she looked closely, she'd see part of my guarded secret.

Couldn't let that happen, couldn't—

I sucked in a sharp breath when she edged my jeans and underwear over my hips and released my swollen cock.

I expected her to tease it. Maybe suck on it. Something I'd never experienced. Something nothing could have prepared me for.

Instead, she held a condom—where had that come from?—and ripped open the foil wrapper. She slid it over my cock with her lips.

Being covered felt...odd—smothering, almost—but the slow and erotic movement of her full lips pushing the rubber onto me... I closed my eyes and sucked in a breath.

I'd come at any moment now. I'd disappoint her. I balled my hands into fists, gritted my teeth—anything to hold on to my waning control.

I didn't want the condom, didn't want any barriers between us, but I understood her need for assurance. In truth, we barely knew each other. She was being sensible, and I was committed to keeping her safe. I could never harm her. The need to shield her from any potential threat rose within me with savage ferocity.

But nothing could override my urge, my drive, my lust to be part of her. I wanted her to slide onto me so badly. To take me—take me to a place where I could forget everything I'd been through, everything I'd let happen.

Then she grasped my cock, her naked body hovering over me.

"Now I'm going to take what I want."

"Now I'm going to take what I want."

But it wasn't Erin's voice. I looked up, and it was her masked face above me, her fangs protruding as she ground against me, forcing my untried body into an unwanted state of arousal.

My body tensed, my fangs shrank. But only for a moment.

I squeezed my eyes shut, balling my hands into fists and straining against my bindings.

"No!"

"I love it when you struggle," she said, her voice laced with venom. "It's all the better for me. Makes your blood taste even sweeter." She lowered her lips to my neck.

"No! You can't! I won't let you!"

FOURTEEN

Erin

"No!"

Dante pushed me away, and I tumbled onto the floor, nearly hitting my head on the corner of the countertop.

"No!" he yelled again, pulling off the condom and replacing his jeans around his hips. "You can't! I won't let you!"

His shirt hanging open, he stumbled out of my bathroom.

Shocked and dazed, I stood to go after him. What had gone wrong this time?

He couldn't leave. I couldn't allow it. I needed him. Needed him inside me. Not just in my body but in my very soul.

I walked, light-headed, out of the bathroom and into my bedroom.

He was gone.

Still naked, I headed down the stairs. "Dante!"

Nothing.

He was gone. Just like that, quick as a bolt of lightning, he was gone.

My body throbbed with unsated desire, and my legs itched, aching to go after him.

No.

That was the last time. The last time I'd allow this to happen. Never again would he run from me.

I walked slowly to the door, my heart stampeding in my chest, and locked it.

Yes, I *locked* it. This time I committed the turning of the deadbolt to my memory. I locked the damned door.

I walked to the kitchen, poured myself a large glass of ice water, and downed it, attempting to cool myself off.

Didn't work.

Didn't matter. I had to get to bed. I had work tonight.

When I reached the ER at eleven p.m., I was pleased to see that Dr. Thomas was on duty. I couldn't deal with Dr. Bonneville tonight. I'd slept fitfully, visions of Dante invading my dreams.

My brother met me at the entrance.

"What are you doing here?" I asked.

"River's inside talking to Cynthia North. She's conscious."

"Oh, that's great! What do you know so far?"

"She has no memory of anything after being shot. She was agitated, and she seemed to be responding better to River, so I let him take the lead. I figured I'd just wait out here. It's a nice night."

"Yeah. Unfortunately, I can't enjoy it. I'm due on my shift."

"I know. I won't keep you."

"Why don't you come inside? Steve can make you one of his famous lattes."

"Steve's not on tonight."

"Oh. Suit yourself, then." I walked into the ER.

"Erin, there you are." Dr. Thomas motioned to me. "Lucy's not in yet, and Dale and Renee both called in sick. I need you to take some blood for labs for the patient in exam room four. She's got symptoms of the flu."

"Yes, Doctor." I placed a surgical mask over my face. I'd had a flu shot, of course, but I wasn't too excited about exposing myself to the nasty virus. Flu shots were no guarantee against infection. But this was what they paid me for.

I grabbed the chart off the door and entered the examination room. "Hi there"—I scanned the chart—"Ms. Moore. So you're not feeling too great, huh?"

The older woman shook her head. "It's Mrs. Moore, dear. And no, I'm afraid I'm not."

Unfortunately, the flu flocked to the elderly due to their decreased immune systems. "You're ninety years old?"

"Yes. Been around the block a few times."

"Congratulations on living such a long life." I smiled.

"It's not all it's cracked up to be. I've buried a husband and a son. But I get along."

"I'm sorry for your loss, ma'am. I'm afraid I'm going to have to take some blood. I'll try not to hurt you too much."

"Poke away. It won't be the first time, and God willing, it won't be the last."

"I'm sure it won't be," I said, hoping I wasn't telling a huge lie. The flu could ravage a ninety-year-old woman, though Mrs. Moore appeared to be in decent shape for her age. I tied the rubber banding above her elbow. "Can you make a fist for me?"

She needn't have bothered. The veins in her arm stuck out like tiny blue streams, and her skin was so fragile it was translucent. I hated to stick a needle into someone so old. I did it as quickly as possible. She didn't even flinch.

"I had the best physician when I was younger," she was saying as she watched the blood fill up the crystal tube. "I believe her daughter must work here."

"Oh?"

"Yes. When I was being wheeled back here to the exam room, I passed the photos of the doctors on the wall. There was a photo of a woman who could be my doctor's twin, except she had blond hair. My doctor was a brunette."

"Really?" I removed the first tube and inserted the second.

"Yes. She had the most interesting name, too. Like Sarah, but she spelled it with a Z. Such a gifted doctor. I've always wondered what happened to her."

I stiffened a bit, forcing my eyes not to widen. Sarah with a Z. Like Sabrina with a Z. "Was her last name Bonneville?"

"No. But her last name was also French. I think it began with an L. Le Grand or La Grande. I can't remember. Maybe Lagrandaise. It was so long ago, and my memory isn't what it used to be."

"We have a Zabrina Bonneville here. Like Sabrina with a Z. She has blond hair."

"Maybe that's whose photo I saw. I don't know. It couldn't have been my doctor. She's be in her seventies by now."

"What did you see her for?" I asked.

"She was my general practitioner. She saw our whole family for a while, but she was really good with my second son, Carlos. He had a blood disorder. We never did find out exactly what was wrong with him, but Dr. Zarah—that's what we called her—found a treatment that kept him in remission when no other physician could. Unfortunately, Carlos died in a car accident when he was only twenty-four. But I have no doubt that he would have lived a long and healthy life thanks to her."

"I'm so sorry for your loss." The words came out mechanically, though I didn't mean for them too. I'd said them so many times as part of my work that I felt they no longer had meaning, but I always meant them in my heart. Words were so useless sometimes.

"Carlos is in a better place," Mrs. Moore said, and then launched in to a coughing fit, sputtering and wheezing.

"Let me see if the doctor will let me give you a breathing treatment, ma'am," I said. "Please excuse me for a minute."

I got the necessary permission from Dr. Thomas and prepared a nebulizer. Then I headed back into room two.

Mrs. Moore had fallen asleep. Poor thing. I prepared the treatment and placed the mask over her face and started the treatment.

Then—

Oh, God. Her lips were tinged with blue.

My nerves jumped. Lack of oxygen. I felt her neck for a pulse. It was weak, but it was there. "Code blue!" I yelled.

Dr. Thomas came running, along with Dr. Crown.

"Status?" Logan said.

"Patient is ninety years old. I went to get permission for a neb treatment, came back, and now her pulse is faint. Lips and nail beds show signs of cyanosis."

"She's still breathing. Get some oxygen ready," Dr. Thomas said. "Stat. Then hook her up to the EKG."

I prepared the tank and got the tubes hooked up to Mrs. Moore's nose. Logan cut her blouse down the middle, and I hooked up the EKG.

"Pulse rate is below forty," Logan said. "Bradycardia."

Then the dreaded shrill buzz.

"Flatlining!" Logan yelled. "Prepare the paddles, Erin."

Logan and Dr. Thomas tried for several minutes to jumpstart Mrs. Moore's heart while I watched, white noise permeating my ears.

"Time of death, twelve twenty-four a.m.," Dr. Thomas said.

I bit my lower lip.

Mrs. Moore was ninety years old. She'd lived long, had lost a son, a husband. The flu would have ravaged her body and might have killed her in the end. Perhaps this was a blessing.

How I wished I believed all of that bullshit.

It never got any easier.

I arched my eyebrows at Dr. Thomas, and she nodded, so I left the exam room.

I didn't cry over patients. Not anymore. But I always needed a moment after losing one. Dr. Thomas understood that. Even Dr. Bonneville understood that.

I slumped against the wall in the hallway and let out a heavy sigh.

Logan walked up to me. "Hey. You okay?"

Logan and I hadn't talked about what had happened—or rather, what *hadn't* happened—between us, why a maniac had chased him out of my home after I'd thrown myself at him. But that didn't matter at the moment. As healthcare providers, we understood each other in this situation.

"We were in the middle of a conversation. She was alert, lucid. Then she started coughing, and I only left the room for a moment to prepare a neb."

"She was ninety, Erin."

"I know. It's just that—"

"Hey. It's okay."

Then the tears came. I buried my head in Logan's smock and cried.

Why? I never cried over patients.

But this one had been special. I didn't know how or why, but in the marrow of my bones, I felt it. Mrs. Moore had something to tell me.

Something I'd never know now.

FIFTEEN

DANTE

Bill was in his office, as usual. I knocked.

"Come in, Dante."

I entered, images swirling in my mind. I opened my mouth, but words did not come.

"Are you ready?" he asked.

I sat down in a leather chair across from his desk. "Yes."

"Good," he said. "I'm working on having some portions of the texts translated, and when you're—"

"No." I held up my hand. "I mean yes. I'm ready to learn the texts. But I'm also ready to..."

"Yes?"

I inhaled deeply. I had to talk. Had to tell someone what had happened to me, at least the parts I could remember. Bill was the logical choice. I scanned his office. On his wall hung a photo of him when he was a young father. Next to him was Marcheline, my grandmother, who had died before I was born. They each held one of their twin sons. Uncle Braedon sat on Bill's lap, while my grandmother held my father, Julian.

Next to that photo hung an older photo of Bill as a child with my great-grandfather. His mother had died in childbirth. I shuddered inwardly, trying not to think of Emilia suffering the same fate.

Photos of River, Em, and me as kids were scattered here and there. River and I could have passed for twins when we were toddlers. We'd gone everywhere together, had been inseparable. Up until that night ten years ago...

I cleared my throat.

"I don't remember what happened. Riv and I sneaked out to the French Quarter."

"Yes, I know. He came back. You didn't. His memories begin when he got back here, and he was badly burned. He said the two of you drank a lot."

"Yeah. We gave money to a homeless guy to buy us liquor. We let him keep the change."

"Yes. That's what River says."

"We drank this bottle of rotgut really fast, and things get pretty fuzzy after that."

"What's the next thing you remember?"

"Waking up in a dark room. I was lying down, and I couldn't move. I didn't realize it at first, but my ankles and wrists were bound."

"Was anyone else there?"

I closed my eyes. "No. Not at first. I don't think so."

Darkness. Were my eyes open? Throb. Throb. *My head pulsed in time with my heart, each beat like a jackhammer inside my skull. Even my teeth hurt.*

I willfully forced my eyes open.

Still, darkness.

I was dying. That had to be it. My head would explode any minute now.

Throb. Throb. Throb.

I held up my hand in front of my face.

Couldn't see it.

Wait. Was it there? Had it moved?

I pulled against resistance.

My hand. Couldn't move my hand.

My skin went cold as my heart sped up. What was happening?

"Help! Someone help me! Please!"

My nerves skittered beneath my skin as raw fear pulsed through me.

My hands, my legs. Couldn't move.

"I'm dying! Please! Someone help me! Help! Help! Dad! Help me!" My voice was hoarse, raspy, and it hurt to yell.

Couldn't see. So dark... Even my acute vampire vision couldn't decipher anything.

Then a sliver of light. A door opened.

"Who are you?" I yelled. "Why am I here?"

"I couldn't see. I didn't know why at the time. I always thought vampires could see in the dark."

"We can. Unless there's nothing to see."

"Yes. Yes." Memories rolled back into me. Memories I'd wished to forget. "It was a dark, empty room, and I was on my back. Couldn't move. Nothing to see but the ceiling, and I couldn't even see that."

"What do you remember next?"

"My head hurt. Worse than ever. I swear I thought I'd die from the sharp pounding."

"You were hungover."

"Maybe. I was sure it was something else. I couldn't move. Couldn't see. Everything hurt. My head. My arms. My neck. My legs. My teeth. My fucking teeth hurt, Bill."

"You could have been drugged. Rohypnol, most likely."

"Rohypnol?"

"Commonly referred to as the date-rape drug. Someone might have dropped it in your drink. Because River doesn't have any memory of getting home, we think he was roofied too."

"Roofied?"

"That's what they call it on the street. Think hard, Dante. Do you remember seeing anyone unusual that night? Before you woke up?"

"It was Mardi Gras. Everyone was masked."

"Yeah. That's what River said."

"It's been ten years. Why would I know anything more than what River has already told you?"

"I'm just trying to help you, Dante."

"I know. I'm sorry. But I don't remember anyone unusual. I mean, *everyone* was unusual."

Women had been flashing their tits to get beads. Riv and I hadn't been able to stop ogling them. I'd been erect the whole damned time.

I'd thought I was in heaven.

God, how stupid.

Heaven didn't exist. But hell sure did. I'd experienced it firsthand.

"What's the last thing you remember before you woke up?" Bill asked.

I squeezed my eyes shut again.

Tits. Tits everywhere. Someone handed me a drink. Someone with tits.

And a mask.

And very fair skin.

"A woman," I said. "I remember now. She was topless. She gave me a drink."

"All right."

"She had very fair skin and searing blue eyes." My insides turned to ice. "Oh my God. She was a vampire, Bill."

SIXTEEN

Erin

"What?" I sat across from Lucy at breakfast after work, hoping I hadn't heard her right.

"I'm going out with Detective Hottie tonight," she said again.

I scoffed. "Good luck."

"Thanks. I think."

"If he's anything like his cousin, don't expect to get very far."

"What happened now?"

I didn't feel like rehashing the previous morning. It was too humiliating. "Suffice it to say, I'm done with him."

Words were words and nothing else. Even after saying them, I knew, if I saw Dante again, I'd feel that same uncontrollable pull.

The answer? Never see him again. Which would be difficult if my best friend started dating his cousin. Not to mention his cousin being partners with my brother. All I could do was hope that Lucy fucked River and got him out of her system, and that Jay got reassigned.

"Hey," I said, remembering Mrs. Moore, "do you know if Dr. Bonneville's mother was also a doctor?"

"I have no idea. Why?"

I filled her in on my conversation with Mrs. Moore.

"It's possible," Lucy said, and then she chuckled. "The Z names are interesting. But somehow I never really thought of her as having a mother. I just assumed she was conceived out of pure evil."

I joined her in laughter. "True. But she does take losing a patient very hard, so she must have some shred of humanity left in her."

"That just means she cares more about the dead than the living. It's her ego. She couldn't save the patient, so she takes it hard. It has nothing to do with the actual loss of a human life."

"Hmm. I never thought of it that way." I took a sip of my decaf. "She is a brilliant physician, though."

"Genius has nothing to do with kindness. Sometimes the more scientifically brilliant a person is, the more lack of regard he has for what's truly important."

I swallowed a bite of English muffin. "Maybe. But Dr. Thomas is intelligent too, and she's a great person."

"Dr. Thomas is an excellent doctor, but I wouldn't put her at Bitchville's level. That woman must have an IQ of 160 or above."

"Yeah, you're right," I said. "I just like Thomas so much better, so I'd prefer to think she's just as gifted. At least she understands bedside manner. That's nearly as important as aptitude when it comes to being a good physician. Or nurse, for that matter."

"And she treats her colleagues with respect," Lucy agreed.

"Hey, can you do me a favor?" I asked.

"Sure."

"When you go out with River, can you get the scoop on Cynthia North?"

"I can try. But why don't you just ask Jay?"

"I intend to. But Jay said she was responding better to River, so he left him alone with her last night. I'd like to get his take on the whole thing."

"I'll ask. But why are you so interested? She's back, and she's recovering. She's no worse for the wear that anyone can see."

"She was taken from our hospital," I said.

"And returned unharmed."

"True, and I'm thankful for that. But doesn't it bother you that she just disappeared for a few days?"

"Of course it bothers me, but I have enough to worry about."

So did I. But something niggled at me. Just as I felt Mrs. Moore had had important information for me, I now felt Cynthia North did too. The question was...what was it?

Work the next night was quiet, so I decided to visit the blood bank.

That was where I'd first laid eyes on Dante, and though I wanted more than anything to forget him, I couldn't.

So I'd try to figure out exactly what it was about him that called to me.

He was gorgeous, no doubt, but I'd felt the pull the first

time I'd seen him, looking like a maniac with blood on his hands and face. Not something that would normally entice me, no matter how physically attractive the person was.

I walked in, rubbing my arms against the chill. Of course the bank was immaculate. Nothing like it had looked when I'd found Dante vandalizing it.

Why would a person vandalize a blood bank?

Why would a person even seek out a blood bank and mistake it for a regular refrigerator?

I shook my head. I had no idea.

Nope, nothing to be learned here. I turned to leave, when I noticed one of the shelves was empty.

No B positive blood.

B positive was the type Dr. Bonneville had sent me to Tulane to order. It must not have arrived yet. Odd. She'd sent me personally for that very reason, to get it here quickly.

Oh, well. No worries. The B neg shelf was full, and B neg would suffice for anyone who was type B pos.

I walked back up to the ER. Dr. Anderson was on duty tonight, and he kept to himself unless he needed help. Some docs were like that. They didn't trust the nursing staff. Fine with me. I could catch up with paperwork. But first, a look at the news.

"What?" I said aloud when I saw the first headline.

Apparently, the woman who'd disappeared from the free clinic around the same time that our patient had disappeared had been returned as well, also in a drug-induced coma.

"That is that," I said aloud, standing. I checked in with Dr. Anderson and got permission to leave a few minutes before my shift ended.

Attending physicians did their rounds early in the

morning, so Cynthia North would be awake. She and I were going to have a talk.

DANTE

"*Good morning, you piece of shit.*" *The masked servant—I didn't know his name, but he was the more odious of the two—glared at me and then moved his gaze to my cock, licking his lips lasciviously. "It's torture time. I'd love to put a vise clamp on you here, but unfortunately, the queen forbids it. A shame."*

Though I hated her, I couldn't help but feel a tiny sliver of gratitude.

This sadist wouldn't touch my cock, thank God.

"She likes you to look pretty. Too bad. I really want to use my whip and watch that perfect skin crack open, watch your fucking blood drip everywhere. Can't waste the blood, though."

I closed my eyes and tried to zone out. Tried to stop hearing his evil voice.

Tried, but—

"Aaauuggh!"

My eyes shot open to see a silver clamp pinching my right nipple. Sharp pain lanced into my flesh, as if the nipple had been ripped off my body.

"Hurts. Yes, that's good. Scream for me."

I clamped my mouth shut. I would not scream again. Wouldn't give him the satisfaction.

I kept that vow.

Time and time again.

"Are you sure she was a vampire? Maybe just a human with fair skin?"

It was the eyes. *She* was the queen. *Her.* The one who'd fed from me and had me tortured, forced me to drink her blood. *She* had been there that night, had been the one to drug me and take me.

"I'm sure."

"Anything else?"

I let out a long breath. "Not that I can remember. The next thing I recall is waking up in the dark room. Not being able to move. God." I pushed my hair out of my face. "How did I survive?"

"You survived because you're strong, Dante. You're descended from a long line of strong and resilient vampires. The Gabriel line is known for both its physical and mental strength."

"There were times when I wanted to die."

"But you didn't."

"No. I didn't. Sometimes the pain was so bad I didn't think I could possibly live through it."

"But you did."

"I did." And after that last time, I hadn't given my torturer the satisfaction of ever hearing me scream again.

"How long after you got there was it before someone came to you?"

"I honestly don't know. Time didn't seem to exist in that place. I didn't see natural light the entire time I was there."

"Did they feed you?"

"Yes. Eventually. Three meals a day. Lots of water."

"Good. So whoever had you didn't take you with the intention of killing you. That's clear, since you lasted ten years there."

"Does our family have any...enemies in the vampire world?"

Bill shook his head. "There are so few of us left. Millennia ago, when we lived in clans, we were probably friends with some clans and enemies with others. But no written history has been kept of any of that."

I sighed.

"What do you recall next?"

"I was in pain. My head was pounding for what seemed like days. And my stomach. I was hungry, thirsty. Just when I thought I might die from thirst, someone entered."

"Who?"

"One of the two servants who fed me. And tortured me. I could smell them. They weren't vampires. They were human." The scent rose up in my memory. No human smelled bad to a vampire, but by the end, all I smelled when either of them entered was rotten fish.

The scent of evil.

"I see. Interesting. They were male?"

"Yes. Human males. Human sadists. I mean *real* sadists. This wasn't for sexual gratification. This was just because they enjoyed inflicting pain." I closed my eyes, humiliation rising within me. I rubbed my arms against a sudden chill.

"Dante?"

I opened them. "I'm all right. It's just...embarrassing."

"You had no control over what happened to you. There's no reason for you to feel embarrassed."

"Yeah? Tell that to my brain. I can't help it. I'm a Gabriel vampire. I should have been able to fight them off."

"You were eighteen years old."

"And I was twenty-eight by the time I escaped. I should have been able to escape way sooner than that."

"Something kept you strong, Dante. Your blood."

"You mean *her* blood," I said quietly.

"No. I mean *your* blood. Your father's blood. My blood. My father's blood. It all flows within your veins." He cocked his head. "Wait. What do you mean...*her* blood?"

EIGHTEEN

Erin

"I wish I could tell you more, but I just can't," Cynthia North said. "I've already told the police that I don't remember anything."

"Do you remember being shot at all?"

She's a bleeder. Dr. Thomas's words when Cynthia North had been wheeled in by the EMTs. The words that had sent me down to the blood bank for O neg.

The words that had sent me to Dante.

"No. Just that bitch coming at me. I panicked. And then... nothing."

Cynthia had apparently gotten over the agitation Jay had witnessed, because her demeanor with me was good. Her complexion was rosy. She'd been transfused before going to the OR for surgery—the surgery she never made it to. She looked and sounded remarkably healthy for someone who'd been near death only a little over a week ago.

Wherever she had been, she had received excellent care.

"How do you feel, Ms. North?"

"Cynthia, please. I feel...good, actually. I'd really love to get out of here."

"That's up to your doctors. Who's been working with you?"

"Dr. Leonard Brown mostly. Oh, and another has been by a few times. A woman. Dr. Bonneville."

"Dr. Zabrina Bonneville? She's an emergency room physician."

"Really? She told me she was a hematologist."

A blood doctor? Maybe. Her residency could have been in hematology. Maybe she switched to emergency medicine later. I'd have to check.

"Are you having any blood problems?"

"She just took some of my blood. Wanted to rule out a few things."

"Have you heard back on those tests?"

"Yes. I'm fine, apparently."

"That's good to hear." I patted her hand. "Thank you for your time, Ms.— Cynthia. I appreciate it."

"You're welcome. And if you could put in a good word for me with either of my doctors, I'd appreciate it. You know, to get me out of here sooner." She smiled.

"I'll do what I can." I thanked her again and left her room, leaving her door open.

❧

I got home with renewed energy. The shift had gone well, even if I hadn't gleaned much information from Cynthia North. A night that kept me busy but resulted in no fatalities or even a critical condition was a good night.

I fixed myself a quick breakfast and pulled out my laptop.

Time to do a little research on Dr. Zabrina Bonneville. She was a hematologist now?

She was really good with my second son, Carlos. He had a blood disorder.

Maybe Dr. Bonneville wasn't a blood doctor. But her apparent doppelganger, Dr. Zarah, had been.

I searched furiously for an hour. What I found astounded me. Or rather, what I *didn't* find.

Dr. Bonneville had not published *any* articles in medical journals, nor had Dr. Zarah. I checked all three surnames Mrs. Moore had given me. If Dr. Zarah had truly come up with some kind of protocol to keep Mrs. Moore's son alive, why hadn't she written about it? Documented it?

Dr. Bonneville was also known for her brilliance as a diagnostician. Lucy had talked about her ego. Wouldn't her ego demand that she publish her findings?

Where had she gone to med school? Done her residency? Any fellowships? I couldn't find any documentation. On the internet, Zabrina Bonneville didn't seem to exist.

Not possible. She'd been hired at University, so she clearly had credentials. Why they weren't documented anywhere online was more than a puzzle, though.

I'd never questioned her ability as a physician. She was top-notch. It was her personality that drove all of us in the ER crazy.

I'd attack this from a different angle. Mrs. Moore's son. She'd said his name was Carlos. Mrs. Moore had been ninety when she died, and she'd said Carlos had died in a car accident at twenty-four. She'd also said Carlos was her second son. If she'd given birth to him between twenty-five and thirty, I was looking at around forty years ago. The internet hadn't existed forty years ago. Still, I might be able to find something. Many newspapers had already moved all their old microfilms and microfiches to the internet.

It was worth a look.

Carlos Moore was a more common name than I'd thought. I found a writer and an attorney in the area with that name. But the name did not come up in any automobile accidents within the time frame I was researching.

They could very well have been living somewhere else. I was truly looking for a needle in a haystack. I was about to give up when something caught my eye at the bottom of my search screen.

"Carlos" and "Moore" showed up separately in an article about an automobile accident during the correct time frame. What the heck? I clicked.

Three people are confirmed dead after a horrific four-vehicle crash on Gayoso Street on January 9.

A station wagon driven by Mark Strahan, thirty-eight, plowed into a sedan driven by twenty-four-year-old Carlos Mendez, son of Juan and Irene Mendez, who was pronounced dead at the scene.

Strahan was rushed to Tulane Hospital and is in critical condition. His blood alcohol level indicated he was intoxicated while driving.

Two pedestrians, both minors, were killed when the vehicle driven by Mendez was pushed into them during the accident. The minors' parents asked that their names not be released.

"This is yet another accident clearly caused by drunk driving," NOPD Officer Joseph Moore stated. "Three innocent lives have been lost due to one person's inebriation. Let this be

a wake-up call to all drivers who get behind the wheel after drinking."

Strahan, if he survives, will most likely be charged with vehicular manslaughter.

Hmm. The age was correct. What was Mrs. Moore's first name? Had it been Irene? Perhaps she had remarried.

I'd check tomorrow at work.

Then a flash bolted into my brain. Why hadn't I thought of this before? Mrs. Moore had said she'd buried a husband. Maybe Mr. Moore was her second husband, and Juan Mendez had been her first. Mrs. Moore had said Carlos was her second son. Her first son was most likely still alive...and her next of kin.

He would have been notified of her death.

He could tell me everything I needed to know.

NINETEEN

DANTE

*D*espite my fuzzy mind, still I resisted her blood, my cheek burning from where her goon had hit me.

"No!"

She turned down her lips into a pout. "And after all I've done for you."

"All you've done for me? Are you kidding? You're keeping me here against my will. You're taking my blood."

"And I'm about to give you my own."

"We can't drink from each other. Everyone knows that."

"Ah...what you've been told. There are some negative side effects that can be treated. Not all effects are negative. My blood will give your body the ability to stay strong while you're my captive."

I pulled against my bindings, gritting my teeth. The wounds on my neck itched from closing up. Already they were healing.

"Open your mouth, Dante."

I squeezed my lips and eyes shut.

"Open his mouth again," she commanded the men, "and

make sure it stays open this time."

I opened my eyes, though I had no desire to watch what she was forcing me to do. One of the servants attached a metal clamp to my mouth, forcing my lips into an O, while the other held my head still. She held her wrist over my mouth, and I watched in horror as her blood poured into me.

Couldn't move. Couldn't...

No! No! No!

Her blood burned my tongue, took with it my skin. Then, as it clawed its way down my throat, it left an acidic trail.

Soon my reflexes forced me to swallow against my will.

"Yes," she said. "Now you're truly a part of me. You will learn to take my blood by puncturing my flesh as I puncture yours. You can never escape me now, Dante. Never."

⚜

"The vampire who held me captive was a female."

Bill rubbed his forehead. "I'd gathered as much from our previous conversations. Was it the same one who fed you drugs that night?"

"Yes. She was masked, but it had to be her."

"And when you were in captivity?"

"Masked. They were all masked."

"Do you remember the color of her eyes?"

"Blue."

"What about her hair?"

"In the beginning it was dark. Nearly black. Then...she began covering it up. She came to me not only masked but with a... I don't know. A turban or something on her head."

"All right. Any identifying characteristics other than her

eyes and hair?"

"It was dark a lot of the time when she came to me."

"And you drank from her?"

"She forced me to."

"Side effects?"

"My muscles stayed strong. They didn't atrophy. She said that was due to her blood."

"What about side effects for her?"

"I have no idea. I hope she had major side effects, but she told me she wouldn't, and that I wouldn't. That she had learned how to combat the side effects of feeding on vampire blood."

"Interesting..." Bill rubbed his forehead.

Interesting? I was spilling my guts here, my humiliation, and all he had to say was *interesting*? I stood. "I'm done here."

"What? You can't leave yet."

"I can. I thought you cared, Bill. But all you're interested in is answers. You don't want to help me."

"Of course I want to help you."

"Then don't make me relive all this shit!" I walked to the door and then looked over my shoulder. "I've told you a lot. What can you do to help me?"

"Based on what I know so far? I don't know." He bent over his desk.

I huffed. "That's what I figured."

"I'll need to do some research. There's a lot going on here that neither of us understands."

"Just teach me what I need to know, or get me the translation of the *Texts*." I turned and left the office.

Bill was holding something back. He wasn't himself. I'd suspected it since I'd returned.

But now I felt it in my bones.

Bill was different.

I had to find out why.

It was midmorning. I applied sunblock to my face and neck and left Bill's house. I needed to find a place of my own. Maybe I could stay with River for a while. Maybe my cousin and I could handle all this shit between the two of us. Forget learning it from Bill. I didn't want him getting any more into my head anyway. River could just tell me what he knew.

It was daytime, and River would be off duty. I headed toward his place.

But found myself at Erin's place instead, as if an invisible force had guided me.

I closed my eyes and turned her doorknob, already knowing what I would find.

Unlocked.

Again.

TWENTY

Erin

"**W**hat?"

I jerked my head up. I'd fallen asleep at my table, my cheek on the keys of my laptop.

My gaze flew to the doorknob.

It was turning.

"Shit!" Had I truly forgotten to lock my door again? What the hell was wrong with me?

I froze. Oddly, though, not fear but anticipation coursed through me.

When Dante opened the door and appeared in my entryway, my skin warmed.

My mind dueled with my soul.

Never again!

But God, I wanted him.

I inhaled and let it out slowly. "What do you want, Dante?"

"Why is your door unlocked again?"

"None of your business." I had no answer, anyway.

"You're not safe if you don't lock your door."

"Not when people like you don't bother to knock. Besides, it's broad daylight, Dante."

"It's nighttime for you, isn't it?"

"I was working. Notice my computer?"

"I also notice that your face seemed to be smashed into it."

I rubbed my cheek. Sure enough, little grooves from the keyboard. He didn't miss a beat. "So? What are you doing here? Why bother coming here at all, when you're just going to run off again?"

He didn't respond. Just stared at me with his dark and smoky eyes.

I inhaled. I could already smell my arousal. Just being near him...

This had to stop. I stood and backed toward the kitchen. "I don't know why you're here, but you're no longer welcome in my home. Please leave."

He took a step forward.

"I'm not kidding, Dante. I'll call the police. I'll have you arrested."

"You didn't have me arrested the first night we met, and you had every right to."

He had me there. I wouldn't call the police. I wouldn't have him arrested.

The urge to protect him speared me in the gut.

What was I feeling?

He was gorgeous, yes, but what I was feeling went far beyond physical attraction. I hardly knew him, yet the pull was undeniable.

Even now, I felt an invisible cord urging me forward, and I inched toward him.

"I shouldn't have come here," he said.

I forced my feet to remain still. "Then why did you?"

He shook his head. "I'd tell you if I knew."

I had no idea what he was feeling. I only knew what was in my own heart. No. My heart wasn't involved yet. I'd been in love before, and what I felt for Dante was different.

Different, yet just as strong. Maybe even stronger.

It was physical, mental, emotional, spiritual.

He hadn't stolen my heart.

He'd stolen my soul.

And I had no idea how or why.

I balled my hands into fists. "Stop doing this to me!"

"Erin..."

I held out my hand in a stopping motion. "Don't come any nearer. Just don't."

He ignored me, stalking toward me. Soon we were inches apart. His breath drifted over my forehead like a spring breeze.

"I can't help it," he said. "I ache for you."

I closed my eyes, inhaling his masculine scent. "God, I ache for you too." Then I opened my eyes. "But I can't do this anymore. You get me worked up and then you leave. For God's sake, what am I supposed to think? You ran away after spreading my legs."

He closed his eyes then. "I'm trying... God. I have to protect you, Erin."

"From what?"

"From..." He opened his eyes and stared straight into mine. "Someone is..." He raked his fingers through his hair. "Someone... Fuck I can't do this."

I grabbed his arm then, tingles shooting through my fingers at the contact. "Can't do what? Can't do what, Dante?"

"Fuck," he said again, and then he grabbed me and kissed me.

I tried to keep my lips closed. Truly, I did. But something within me overruled my brain. Not my heart but my soul ruled me when Dante was near.

And my soul wanted to kiss him.

It was hardly a tender kiss. It was raw, untamed, full of fire, passion, and something else I couldn't quite pinpoint.

Didn't matter. It was *necessary*. Necessary for both of us. For him as well as for me.

I could feel all of that in this kiss.

He broke the kiss suddenly. "I can't stop this time, Erin."

"Good," I said huskily, moving my mouth back to his.

"No. Wait." He moved backward.

God. Not again.

"I'm serious. I'm not stopping this time."

"You're stopping right now. Jesus, Dante."

"There's no going back after this, Erin."

My mind flooded with lust. I had no idea what he was talking about, and at that moment, I didn't give a damn. All I wanted was his lips on mine, his dick inside me. And damn it, I would have it.

No going back. That was fine with me.

"Do you understand me?" he said.

"Yeah. Whatever. No going back. I get it. But Dante, we haven't gone *anywhere* yet. Nowhere. We've kissed a few times. Done some petting. Danced to strange music that apparently wasn't there."

"Wait!" He grabbed my shoulders. "That night at the bar. *You* heard music?"

"Well, no. I mean, obviously it must have been coming

from outside or something. Lucy swears there was no music in the bar, and the bartender corroborated it. I'd had a lot to drink."

"What kind of music did you hear, Erin? What kind?"

"A soft jazzy kind of thing, I guess."

He rubbed his chin. "I don't believe it."

"It's okay. No one else believes me either."

"That's not what I mean. I *do* believe you heard it, Erin. I believe you, because I heard it too."

I widened my eyes. "What?"

"I heard the music. As clear as a church bell on Sunday. And River said the same thing. There was no music."

"Whatever. Who cares? Would you please kiss me again?"

He moved closer. "I want to more than anything."

"Do it. I won't stop you." I opened my mouth and leaned into him.

He brushed his lips against mine in a soft kiss and then backed away.

Oh, hell, no. "You're not leaving."

"I have to. I'm so sorry, Erin."

"I swear to God, if you leave me now, I'll never let you through my door again."

"You don't know what you're getting into. I'm not who you think I am."

"Honestly, Dante, right now I don't care. I only care about getting you into my bed." I laughed. "Do you think this is something I do lightly? That I sleep around? I don't. I've had one serious relationship in my life, and then you can count on one hand the men I've slept with."

"Then who has been—" He shook his head. "Never mind."

"What? Who has been what?"

DANTE

*F*eeding on you.

I cursed inwardly. Why couldn't vampires smell other vampires? Not that I could smell anyone but Erin anyway. What had happened to me?

The marks on her inner thigh had been unmistakable.

Someone had fed on her.

My cock was hard.

Harder than it had ever been.

In my limited experience, I knew I should assume this was just the adolescent me who'd never had a chance to experiment, to learn how to be with a woman.

But it was more.

In my soul, I knew it was more.

Erin Hamilton had awoken something in me. Something no one could have prepared me for, even if I'd been around for the last ten years. I wanted to possess her. I ached for completion with Erin.

Now.

I crushed my lips onto hers and drank from her. My gums tingled, and my fangs ached to descend.

I didn't care.

I was so consumed by lust that I didn't fight my physiology. Didn't worry about nicking her tongue or the inside of her mouth.

Nothing mattered.

Nothing except kissing Erin, devouring Erin. Making Erin mine.

The act would nearly complete what was already real. She was mine. Had always been mine. Had been born for me.

River said fated mates didn't exist for vampires.

He'd been wrong.

We swirled our tongues together, kissed with passion and desire. I let my tongue flow over every millimeter of her mouth, tasting every crevice of her. Passion fruit and mint, musky cinnamon and clove.

And the flavor that was uniquely Erin.

The flavor that would be magnified one hundredfold when I finally tasted her blood.

I would do so.

Soon.

I broke the kiss and inhaled deeply, as if I'd been underwater for too long. I scooped her into my arms and carried her upstairs to her bedroom.

No stopping. No going back.

This time, no matter how many bite marks I found, no matter how much my fangs ached to descend and sink into her flesh, no matter how much I longed to protect her...

None of that would stop me today.

I set her down so we were both standing next to her

bed, and I grabbed her dark ponytail, pulling it downward to expose her neck. I inhaled. Sweet, succulent Erin. Then I eyed her closely. Only one small mark, and it had come from me that night on the dance floor. That night when she and I had heard a concert inaudible to the rest of the universe.

The jazzy blues played faintly now, as I regarded the woman who was mine. "Do you hear it, Erin?"

"Mmm...hear what?" she mumbled, her eyes glassy.

"The music."

She looked at me, her eyes glazed over. "I think I do. Where is it coming from, Dante?"

I smiled. "I honestly don't know. But I know I hear it, as sure as I know the sun will rise tomorrow." I brushed my lips gently over hers. "I want to make love to you, Erin. I *need* to make love to you."

"For us to make love, Dante, you have to actually stay until the act is complete." She giggled.

"I'll stay this time. I promise." I meant those words from the depths of my soul. I had to be with her, to join with her. I lowered my head and kissed her lips, parting them with my tongue.

When something buzzed against my leg.

Erin pulled away. "I think you just got a text or something."

The buzz was a text message? I was still getting used to the constant phone stuff. "I don't care."

"You have to check."

"No, I don't."

"I'm an ER nurse, Dante. You always check. What if it's an emergency? You said your sister's pregnant."

I sighed. She was right, of course.

I pulled my phone out of my pocket. The text was from

River.

Come to Bill's right away. Important.

God, Erin was right. It had to be Em.

"I'm so sorry," I said. "I have to leave."

She laughed aloud.

Erin

Left alone again with my pussy throbbing and my nipples hard. I had only myself to blame this time. I was the one who'd insisted he look at his phone. In my line of work, you didn't ignore your phone. Ever.

I undressed and opened my dresser to get out some clean underwear, when my hand hit something hard at the back of the drawer. I pushed away the clothes—

"Oh my God."

A vibrator. I'd forgotten all about it. Lucy had given it to me as a gag on my last birthday. I'd never used it, though I hadn't eliminated the possibility. I'd taken it out of its original box and buried it in my underwear drawer, thinking I might need it someday.

Maybe today was the day.

The thing was huge. Lucy would never purchase anything average-sized.

Dante was huge, as far as I could tell from what I'd felt

under his jeans. This tool would most likely be an excellent substitute.

I shed my clothes and lay down on my cool cotton comforter. This was all new to me, but I was so ripe. I smoothed my fingers over my labia. God, yes. I was wet. So damned wet.

Wet enough to take the phallic wonder right then, but I didn't. Not yet.

First I played with my nipples a little, pinching and twisting them, imagining Dante's firm lips tugging on them. Imagining his soft hair tickling them as he tortured me in the best way.

Then I trailed one hand over my abdomen to my clit. It was swollen and hard, and after a few strokes, I was ready for Dante's big cock.

With one hand still playing with a nipple, I plunged the vibrator into my pussy.

Erin. God, Erin!

I closed my eyes as Dante hovered above me, thrusting in and out of me, the sweat from his brow dripping onto my face.

Thrust. Thrust. Thrust.

"Dante!" I screamed. "Oh my God. Dante!"

The orgasm ripped through me with the force of a hurricane, and still he thrust into me, harder and harder.

Taking me. Branding me. Making me his.

Until the contractions slowed, and I opened my eyes. And I stopped the in-and-out motion—the motion of my own hand.

It had been good. No denying that.

But even with my vivid imagination, it hadn't equaled Dante. Not Dante's lips. Not Dante's cock.

It hadn't given me the pure release I craved.

And I hadn't heard music.

TWENTY-THREE

DANTE

I rushed into Bill's house. "Where are you? What's wrong? Is Em okay?"

River came out from the kitchen, carrying two glasses of blood. He handed me one. "Em's fine."

"Then what's the big emergency?"

"No emergency. I just said it was important."

I drained the glass of blood. It sated my immediate thirst, but not the lust for Erin's blood. "I was in the *middle* of something important, Riv."

"Oh. Sorry. But this really *is* important."

My muddled mind couldn't imagine what might be more important than finally making love with Erin. "Fine. What is it?"

"First, I want you to know that I'm here for you. I'll help you in any way I can."

"Yeah. Great. Thanks. That couldn't have waited?"

"That's not why we need you here. Bill found something that might explain what's going on with you. Why your sense of smell isn't working correctly."

"Can we do anything about that?"

"I don't know. He didn't tell me much yet. Said he was waiting for you."

"I'm willing to try anything. I need my nose, Riv." More than ever, now that I had to protect Erin.

"I know you do." He looked at his watch. "It's getting close to dinnertime, and I have a date tonight, so—"

"A date? With whom?"

"That nurse from the bar. Lucy Cyrus. Man, is she hot."

"Erin's friend," I said more to myself than to Dante.

"Yeah." He sniffed. "You've been with Erin, haven't you?"

I nodded, stiffening. That River could scent Erin still bothered me more than a little. I suppressed the urge to punch him in the nose.

"No wonder you didn't want to be dragged away. Let's go see Bill. He'll explain this better than I can."

We wandered into Bill's office. He sat behind his desk, as usual.

"Dante, good. Thanks for coming so quickly."

I sat down. "I thought something might be wrong with Em."

"No, no. Emilia's at home, as far as I know. She's doing fine. She'll have the best medical care available. There's a vampire doctor on the outskirts of town, an old family friend. He's gotten many women through pregnancy and childbirth."

"That's good," I said. "What did you find?"

"It's complicated. Something that hasn't been documented in over a thousand years, and even then it was extremely rare. Most scholars assumed the trait had died out, and it hasn't been part of our teaching in centuries. I had to really dig for it."

"Wait. What? What trait?"

"I'll get to that. As you both know, in the beginning, as far as we know, humans and vampires lived in peace together, the latter feeding on the former. No one knew exactly how or why the feeding took place, but I found a theory."

"What's this got to do with me?"

"Hear me out." He cleared his throat. "As I understand it, millennia ago, humans developed a physiological need, one that isn't completely understood. Human males were drawn to female vampires, and human females to male vampires. These vampires fed from their human counterparts, getting their required sustenance, but that's not what originated the bond."

"What do you mean?" River asked.

"The human *needed* to let him feed. Needed to nourish this particular vampire."

"That doesn't make sense," I said. "Humans have no need for us."

"No, they don't. Not anymore. But at one time, they did." Bill closed his eyes.

"So each vamp had a particular human that fed him?" River said.

"Yes. The human developed a physical need to feed a certain vampire, and you can see where this led."

"No, I'm afraid I don't see," I said, rubbing my temples against an impending headache.

"The need forced vampires to procreate with humans. The humans needed the vampires to feed from them, and the vampires in response needed that particular human's blood. A bond was created. A bond that overcame all other bonds. It created a destiny for the vampire and the human."

"So that's how the interbreeding started?"

"Apparently. It was a necessity on the human's part, and it led to our demise because we stopped breeding with our own."

"I thought it was our lack of fertility that led to that."

"That didn't help our cause. But if the humans hadn't created the bond, hadn't developed the need to feed us, we would most likely have continued to breed within our own species, and more of us would have survived. It's very unlikely for one species to breed with a different species in the wild. It almost never happens. We would have never been as plentiful as humans, since they're so much more fertile, but we would have continued to thrive."

"So you're saying..."

"I'm saying that this bond on the part of humanity, that caused vampires during that time to lose their smell and thus their ability to protect themselves, and kept them from breeding with their own, contributed to our decreasing numbers."

"Humans have helped destroy us." River took a seat next to me.

Bill nodded. "Through no fault of their own, of course, at least not that we know of. They didn't ask for this bond. It evolved well before humans and vampires became self-aware."

"Then Erin..." My mind raced. Could this be possible? After all these years? It was happening now? "Did this happen to every vamp—"

"It's not something that happens to *us*," Bill said. "If I'm understanding correctly, the bond begins with the human."

"How?"

"No one knows, but the theory is that it originated as a defense mechanism. Vampires are physically stronger than humans, and their senses are much more acute. Humans needed a way to survive, to ensure that vampires wouldn't eventually conquer them. What better way than to take away their sense of smell, force a need for human blood onto them, and then interbreed until vampires eventually died out?"

"But what causes..." I sat down, my head going fuzzy.

"It hasn't worked," River said. "We're still here."

"Yes, we are. But there are precious few of us." Bill rubbed his head.

"Then it's probably not happening with me," I said.

"I'm not so sure," Bill said. "You said you and Erin heard music that wasn't there, right?"

I nodded.

"That's the mark of a blood bond."

"Music?" River said. "Music didn't even exist when all of this was allegedly happening. If we weren't self-aware, we certainly didn't recognize music, other than beating bones against skins or whatever." He rolled his eyes.

"Enhanced auditory stimulation between the bonded is how the theory puts it," Bill said. "If what I suspect is true, Erin has formed a blood bond with you. The pull you feel isn't coming from you. It's coming from *her*."

I grasped the arm of my chair, trying to wrap my mind around what Bill was telling me. "No. *I* feel the pull. I...need her. I want her. I can't stay away from her. I leave this house with the intention of going somewhere else, and I end up going to her."

"You feel *her* pulling *you*. She's developed a physiological need to feed you. And once you feed from her, that need will transfer to you. You will require her blood for survival." Bill paused.

After a few moments of silence, River spoke. "We were always taught that fated mates didn't exist among vampires or humans."

"This isn't a case of fated mates," Bill said. "Fated mates in the were kingdoms are bound by intense physical attraction and drive that evolves into more, but they can live without each other. Many never meet their intended mate. What I'm talking about goes beyond that. It's a bond of the blood, which evolves into a physical need and desire to fornicate and..."

Our bond will never be severed.

No, can't go there. Get out of my head!

"What?" I swallowed the lump that had lodged in my throat and willed away the unwanted thoughts.

"You've been through so much, Dante, and now..."

"I'll just stay away from her." Even as the words left my mouth, I knew I couldn't. The magnetic pull was too great. "If I leave her alone—"

"You can't," Bill said, sighing. "Not unless you're willing to truly let her go. Now that Erin has initiated a bond with you, she needs to feed you. If you don't complete the bond and let her give you her blood...she will die."

THE QUEEN

I do miss you, Dante, but I am keeping good company. I have a new source of nourishment, one that is feeding me well until I bring you back. Though he is satisfying, his blood is not quite as potent as what I've become used to.

My blood cries for your blood. It always will.

I have much work to do, work to assure a place for us in the future, dear Dante. I dream of the day we are reunited, the day I can once again sink my fangs into your flesh and become one with you, body and blood.

You are, and always will be, mine.

Our bond will never be severed.

BLOOD BOND SAGA

PART 3

DANTE

"I'm saying that this bond on the part of humanity, that caused vampires during that time to lose their smell and thus their ability to protect themselves, and kept them from breeding with their own, contributed to our decreasing numbers."

"Humans have helped destroy us." River took a seat next to me.

Bill nodded. "Through no fault of their own, of course, at least not that we know of. They didn't ask for this bond. It evolved well before humans and vampires became self-aware."

"Then Erin..." My mind raced. Could this be possible? After all these years? It was happening now? "Did this happen to every vamp—"

"It's not something that happens to *us*," Bill said. "If I'm understanding correctly, the bond begins with the human."

"How?"

"No one knows, but the theory is that it originated as a defense mechanism. Vampires are physically stronger than humans, and their senses are much more acute. Humans needed a way to survive, to ensure that vampires wouldn't eventually conquer them. What better way than to take away their sense of smell, force a need for human blood onto them, and then interbreed until vampires eventually died out?"

"But what causes..." I sat down, my head going fuzzy.

"It hasn't worked," River said. "We're still here."

"Yes, we are. But there are precious few of us." Bill rubbed his head.

"Then it's probably not happening with me," I said.

"I'm not so sure," Bill said. "You said you and Erin heard music that wasn't there, right?"

I nodded.

"That's the mark of a blood bond."

"Music?" River said. "Music didn't even exist when all of this was allegedly happening. If we weren't self-aware, we certainly didn't recognize music, other than beating bones against skins or whatever." He rolled his eyes.

"Enhanced auditory stimulation between the bonded is how the theory puts it," Bill said. "If what I suspect is true, Erin has formed a blood bond with you. The pull you feel isn't coming from you. It's coming from *her*."

I grasped the arm of my chair, trying to wrap my mind around what Bill was telling me. "No. *I* feel the pull. I...need her. I want her. I can't stay away from her. I leave this house with the intention of going somewhere else, and I end up going to her."

"You feel *her* pulling *you*. She's developed a physiological need to feed you. And once you feed from her, that need will transfer to you. You will require her blood for survival." Bill paused.

After a few moments of silence, River spoke. "We were

always taught that fated mates didn't exist among vampires or humans."

"This isn't a case of fated mates," Bill said. "Fated mates in the were kingdoms are bound by intense physical attraction and drive that evolves into more, but they can live without each other. Many never meet their intended mate. What I'm talking about goes beyond that. It's a bond of the blood, which evolves into a physical need and desire to fornicate and..."

Our bond will never be severed.

No, can't go there. Get out of my head!

"What?" I swallowed the lump that had lodged in my throat and willed away the unwanted thoughts.

"You've been through so much, Dante, and now..."

"I'll just stay away from her." Even as the words left my mouth, I knew I couldn't. The magnetic pull was too great. "If I leave her alone—"

"You can't," Bill said, sighing. "Not unless you're willing to truly let her go. Now that Erin has initiated a bond with you, she needs to feed you. If you don't complete the bond and let her give you her blood...she will die."

ONE

Erin

I purposely got into work early the next evening so I could do some research on Mrs. Moore, the ninety-year-old patient who had succumbed to influenza. Her first name was, in fact, Irene, but her next of kin was not her first son but her husband, Clay Moore, an eighty-year-old man living in hospice care with advanced lung cancer. I couldn't help a slight smile. Mrs. Moore had been ninety—and a cougar. But then my heart broke a little. Mr. Moore might not even be aware his wife had died.

If I wanted to talk to him, I'd have to work quickly.

No mention anywhere of a son...

Wait! Her death certificate. Someone had to report the information to the state, and it was usually a relative. If Mr. Moore was in hospice, he wouldn't have done the reporting. The death cert wouldn't have been filed yet, but I could access the information. Up it popped.

Name of informant: Juan Mendez, Jr.

Relationship to deceased: Son

Yes! The Carlos Mendez in the news article I'd found was indeed Mrs. Moore's son.

I picked up the phone to dial the number listed for Juan Mendez but stopped just as quickly. I couldn't call the man at ten thirty in the evening. He was probably in his sixties, and he'd be in bed. I'd have to wait until I got off work.

Just as well, because in the distance, the sirens shrieked.

I wasn't officially on the clock yet, but I was here. I hurried out to the ER.

The first two gurneys were already coming in.

TWO

DANTE

hat?"

I hadn't heard Bill correctly. That was the only explanation.

"The bond has to be completed, Dante. Or she will die. You *need* each other now."

"I don't get it. This sure sounds like a fated mate thing to me."

"It's quite different. First, fated mates originate with the male. It's a bond of the heart and the soul, and though it's driven by the body, it's not a bond of the body. They can live without each other."

"I'm not understanding the difference."

"With a blood bond, the human, whether male or female, initiates the bond."

"Why would the prey create the bond with the predator?" River asked. "Not that we're predators in the true sense of the word, but we do require blood to live. They don't need anything from us."

"Instinct. Survival," Bill said. "They were weaker with less acute senses, so they instinctively exploited our need for them."

"You're positive this is coming from her," I said. "From Erin."

"Positive is a strong word for something that hasn't been documented in over a thousand years. But in theory, yes, that's what's happening."

I shook my head. "I don't believe it."

"How can you *not* believe it, Dante?" River asked. "You've been trying like hell to convince me this thing with Erin was something more than just your reaction to an amazing-smelling human. Bill is telling you that you're right. It *is* something more."

I sat down, dazed.

"I owe you a big apology," River continued. "I'm sorry I was so obtuse that I couldn't see what was really happening."

"Don't blame yourself, River," Bill said. "This hasn't been documented in ages. It's not even being taught in vampire history anymore. I'm lucky I found it."

"It still doesn't make sense," I said.

"No, not to us. But what other explanation is there for you losing your ability to scent anyone but Erin?"

"I don't know. Even now, I ache for her. I want to go to her, be with her." *Sink my dick into her while I bite into her jugular and suck her delicious blood.*

"Are you in love with her?" River asked.

"I have no idea, Riv. I don't know the first thing about love. I wasn't around to experience it. Have you ever been in love?"

"Once or twice." He smiled.

"What's it like?"

"It changes as the relationship grows, but when you first fall in love, it's amazing. It's like the other person consumes you. You think about her all the time, want to be with her all the time."

Sounded pretty familiar. "And how does it change?"

"The passion dies a little after you've been together for a while, but other things grow in its place."

"Like what?"

River shook his head. "I don't really know how to explain it."

Bill smiled. "What River can't explain is that love can't be defined, Dante. It's different for every person and every relationship."

"Then how will I ever know?"

"You'll know," Bill said. "And if what you're experiencing with Erin is truly a blood bond, it will lead to love."

"Then how is it different from having a fated mate?"

"Because it's a physical bond, not just an emotional one. Fated mates can live without each other, though they may never find true happiness. A blood bond between a human and a vampire is a physical bond, and I don't mean physical just in terms of a physical relationship. It's physical in that you require each other to live."

"You're seriously telling me that if I want Erin to live, I have to feed from her."

"Yes."

"How am I supposed to convince her of this? She'll think I'm mental. She's a nurse, for God's sake. She'll have the white coats after me before I can take the first taste."

"You could glamour her," River suggested.

I shook my head adamantly. "No. First of all, I can't. I tried once before, but she didn't go under."

"You're probably just not good at glamouring yet," Bill

said. "You haven't had enough practice."

"Maybe," I said. "But here's the thing. I don't *want* to glamour her. She means too much to me. I don't want to violate her in that way."

"Glamouring isn't a violation," Bill said. "It's for the human's own good so she won't remember what happened and be scarred by it."

"Bullshit. It's for *our* own good. To keep *us* safe. If they found out about us, we'd all be in danger. There aren't enough of us."

"He's got a good point, Bill," River agreed.

"Besides, if this is true, and Erin must feed me or die, I can't rely on glamouring. This is a life bond, apparently." And then something else struck me. "What if *I* die? And she can't feed me? What happens then?"

"Not likely," Bill said. "We have a longer life span than humans."

"Only by thirty or so years," I said. "And there are no guarantees. We're not immortal. We can get hit by cars just like anyone else."

"I don't know," Bill admitted. "From what I can tell, it's a lifelong bond."

"I still can't believe it," I said, shaking my head. "If it arose as a defense mechanism for humans, why do *they* die if they don't feed their vampire? Why wouldn't the vampire die?"

A brick landed in my gut. Bill hadn't said I *wouldn't* die. He'd only said that Erin would.

"If I had more information," Bill said, "I'd give it to you. This is all theory, but it makes sense given what you've described."

"Not the fact that the human dies," I said. "That doesn't make any sense at all if it's a defense for humans."

"He's right, Bill," River said.

"All I can tell you is the theory," Bill said. "I'll print all this stuff out so you can read it. Or do you still have an email account, Dante? I can just forward it to you and you can read it online."

An email account. Yeah, checking email had been the first thing on my mind after being tortured and held captive for years and then finding myself in a blood bond with a woman I hardly knew but couldn't stay away from.

"Just print it out, please." I sank my head into my hands. "Why me, of all people? Right after I come back?"

Bill sighed. "I don't know, Dante. I just don't. But nothing else can explain what happened to your nose."

"And the fact that you're so drawn to Erin," River said.

I stood and paced. Even now, I ached for Erin, wanted to go to her, kiss her, taste every part of her...especially the life force within her veins. But how could I explain all this to her when I couldn't even explain it to myself?

"What happens if I don't take Erin's blood? Does she get sick? Because the last time I saw her, she was perfectly healthy." Perfectly and beautifully healthy. I couldn't bear the thought of a world without her in it. If I had to take her blood for her to survive and live a long life, I'd figure out a way do it. I didn't have a choice.

Why? Why was this happening? I'd vowed to protect Erin from everything, including from me. How could I protect her from me when she needed me to survive?

"I don't know," Bill said. "I'll try to find more information."

I turned and stared at my grandfather and my cousin. "Do the two of you have any ideas how I'm supposed to tell this woman that I have to take her blood to save her life?"

Then a thought speared itself into my head. A thought that devastated me.

"What if it's not *me*? What if I'm not the one she's bonded to?"

"What do you mean?" Bill asked.

I crunched my hands into fists, rage overtaking me. "Someone has been feeding on her. I saw bite marks on her thigh."

THREE

Erin

After a long shift, I went home and took a quick shower. The number for Juan Mendez, Jr. had been a wrong number, probably entered incorrectly. I called Jay quickly and put him on it, and he said he'd call as soon as he found the correct number.

Now, I got dressed in a casual skirt and T-shirt. I was going to the hospice to talk to Mrs. Moore's husband.

I had no idea what kind of shape he'd be in, but I had to try.

The drive to the hospice was depressing. Oh, it was a gorgeous day, but hospices were horrible places—places where people went to die. I got my fill of death as an ER nurse, and I wasn't looking forward to staring it in the face today.

So why should I?

My neck chilled as I hung a U-turn in the middle of my drive. Why *was* I doing this, exactly? Why did I feel so strongly that Mrs. Moore had information for me?

Because of her association with Dr. Bonneville's mother—

or someone who might possibly be Dr. Bonneville's mother.

But why did I care?

So her mother was also a doctor. So Dr. Bonneville hadn't published anything in medical journals.

So what?

Why was this even any of my business? As long as Dr. Bonneville did her job well, even if she did make life miserable for those who worked with her, who was I to criticize? Or care?

I couldn't face the hospice today. Suddenly, learning more about Dr. Bonneville didn't seem all that important, and honestly, I wasn't sure why it ever had been. Lucy, Steve, and the rest of my friends just took her for what she was—a gifted physician who had no gift for dealing with people.

Still...she *had* asked me to have coffee after we'd lost Howard Dern, the heart attack. The conversation hadn't been anything memorable, but she'd reached out to me.

Not important. In fact, nothing was as important as where I stopped my car.

Right in front of the old Heartsong B and B.

Dante's house.

He was here. I could feel it—that familiar tug that drew me toward him.

How had I gotten here? I was thinking about Mrs. Moore and then Dr. Bonneville.

Highway hypnosis. All medical professionals were aware of how a person could drive to a certain location, respond to external events in a safe manner, without having any memory of consciously getting there.

Usually highway hypnosis was a response to driving to and from work or some other place a person went to regularly.

Me? I went to Dante Gabriel's.

I couldn't blame him for running out on me the last time. He'd gotten a text, and I'd convinced him to look at it. What had I been thinking? If he'd ignored the text, as he'd wanted to, I'd finally know what it felt like to make love with him.

Have sex, Erin. You would have had sex with him.

I closed my eyes and drew in a breath. I'd driven to his home without meaning to, without any conscious memory of doing so. Then I'd thought of the act as making love, not having sex or fucking, which it would have been.

Love.

I'd never been as drawn to a man as I was to Dante Gabriel, despite the fact that everything I knew about him was negative. I'd caught him in the act of vandalism. He'd left me hanging more than once.

Why was I chasing him? This wasn't me. Not at all. I didn't chase men, not even men as gorgeous and intriguing as Dante Gabriel.

I turned the key in the ignition, restarting the engine.

I was so out of here. I was exhausted after a long shift, and I didn't have the energy to deal with Dante.

As I put the car in gear, I looked up and gasped. Dante was standing by my car, looking in the window. I pressed the button to open it.

"Hey," he said. "What are you doing here?"

I wished I knew. "I'm not sure, actually."

"Do you...want to come in?"

I ached to reach out and touch him through the open window. He looked so gorgeous, his hair a tumbling mass, his eyes nearly black, his cheeks and chin covered in stubble, his full lips so...kissable.

My whole body was aware of his nearness, his closeness.

My skin was tight and prickly, and my pulse raced in my neck.

Thump. Thump. Thump.

Never had I been so aware of my heartbeat.

Put your foot on the gas, Erin. Just go. He didn't invite you here. Go.

"What's wrong?" Dante asked, his brows arched. "Are you feeling okay?"

I feel like I'll never be complete unless we finish what we started the other day. "Of course. I'm fine."

"Are you sure? You look a little pale."

"I always look pale."

His brow furrowed. He seemed genuinely concerned. "Please. Come in. Let me take care of you."

"Take care of me? I'm fine. Look. I'm a little embarrassed, Dante. I didn't come here on purpose." Yeah, that made me sound sane. "I mean... I don't know what I mean."

He opened the car door. "Come on. Come in. River's here. I want you to meet my grandfather."

"Oh!" *God, I'm so self-involved.* "How is your sister? Is everything all right?"

"Yeah, she's good. It was something else that River... needed."

"Oh." None of my business. That part was obvious. "Look. I don't know what I'm doing here. I had a long shift. I'm going to go home." I reached for the door.

But Dante caught my hand and pulled me out of my car. "Don't leave. Really. I want you to meet my grandfather. It's important."

"Why is it so important that I meet him?"

"I've told him all about you."

"You have?" I was slightly elated inside. Okay, majorly elated.

"Yeah. Come on. Please. I'll even make you breakfast."

"You will? Somehow you've never struck me as a guy who cooks."

"Well...I'll throw a piece of bread in the toaster." He smiled.

And I knew I was going into that house to meet his grandfather. I could not resist his smile.

I could not resist anything about him.

God help me.

I'd never felt anything like this. Maybe it *was* love. It was totally different from what I'd felt with Cory, totally different from anything I'd felt...ever. It was all-consuming, all-encompassing passion and desire and need for another person.

Could I really have fallen in love in a matter of weeks? With a man I still knew next to nothing about?

He took my hand, and sparks ignited through me.

We walked slowly up the cobblestone path leading to the ornate doorway. He opened the door and motioned for me to walk in ahead of him.

River sat in the living room next to a silver-haired man. No, *man* wasn't the right word. Gentleman was. He was handsome in a debonair way.

"Hi, Erin," River said. "Nice to see you." Though his tone was more, "what are you doing here?"

The older man didn't seem at all surprised to see me, which I found slightly odd.

Dante cleared his throat. "Bill, this is Erin Hamilton. Erin, my grandfather."

He called his grandfather Bill?

Mr. Gabriel—Bill—stood, holding out his hand. "It's nice to meet you, Erin. Dante has told us a lot about you."

My cheeks warmed. Dante didn't *know* much about me,

other than what I looked like naked. And ditto on my end. "It's nice to meet you."

He sat back down and patted the cushion next to him. "Won't you sit down?"

"I promised Erin a piece of toast," Dante said.

"Oh, it's okay. I'm not that hungry." Still, I stayed standing.

"Don't be silly," Bill said. "Let Dante bring you something. You must be hungry. You probably just got off work, right? Dante said you work the night shift."

I nodded. "Yeah."

"Then sit down, please."

I took a chair next to the sofa. For some reason, sitting right next to Dante's grandfather felt...strange somehow. I wasn't sure why.

I put my purse on the floor and twiddled my fingers.

"How's Jay?" River asked.

"He's fine. I'm sure you saw him more recently than I have."

"Actually, no," River said. "I took a few days off. But I have a *lot* to talk to him about."

River didn't look happy. Had he and Jay had a falling out? Not that I'd heard.

"How's Emilia doing?" I asked.

"She's fine," River said, his lips flattened into a line.

Okay, Jay and Emilia were obviously not good topics of conversation. I could bring up Lucy and the date River had with her this evening, but that would be awkward. Not that this whole thing wasn't already awkward.

I opened my mouth and then shut it, and—

Crash!

FOUR

DANTE

The glass slipped right out of my hand.

My nerves were frazzled.

Blood pooled on the ceramic tile floor. I'd only wanted a few sips. The need for Erin was consuming me, and I'd thought some steer blood might stave off the desire.

I'd been shaking. I still was. Now I had a mess to clean up. A mess that, if Erin saw it, would no doubt remind her of the mess she'd found the night we met.

River came running into the kitchen. His eyes widened when he saw the red puddle. "Shit, Dante."

"I know. The glass slipped out of my hands. You need to keep Erin out of here." I threw a towel over the mess and sopped up what I could. Then I threw the soiled rag into the trash. I'd gotten a lot of it, but there was still quite a bit of blood on the floor.

"She wouldn't go barging into someone else's kitchen."

"Yeah, she would. She's an ER nurse. Emergencies are her specialty. Keep her out—"

"What happened?" She stood in the doorway, her light-green eyes wide. "Did you cut yourself? Let me see."

"He's fine." River pushed her away, turning her back toward me.

"Let me be the judge of that."

Take a bite from your own flesh, and offer yourself to me.

Not now!

Quick as I could, I turned and ripped into the flesh of my forearm with my fangs. My head still turned, I said, "I just cut myself with the bread knife."

She yanked her arm away from River and turned back toward me. "That's a lot of blood, Dante. You'd better let me have a look."

"I told you, he's fine," River said. "We've got this under control."

"You're nuts." Erin walked toward me.

I clamped my mouth shut and willed my fangs to retract.

I didn't have much luck.

She touched my arm, igniting sparks in me. Every time her fingers grazed me, I felt the oceans of blood beneath her skin, the warmth of it, how it felt as it moved within her. Keeping the emotion coiled tightly in my gut zapped all of my strength.

"That doesn't look like a knife wound to me, Dante. Something bit you."

I said nothing.

"Do you have a dog?" she asked.

"Yeah, that's what it was," River said. "The neighbor's dog."

"Why didn't you just say so? Where's the dog? We need to make sure he's had all his shots. Trust me, you don't want to have rabies injections in the stomach."

"He went back over to the neighbor's house."

Erin couldn't possibly be buying any of this. Wouldn't they have heard a dog? And the dog just came in, bit me, and trotted back home?

She turned to me. "Why didn't you just say it was a dog? Why the lie about the bread knife?"

Seriously? She believed it? Then again...she had caught me vandalizing her blood bank, and she hadn't batted much of an eye. Part of the blood bond, maybe?

"I was...embarrassed," I said, keeping my lips as close to closed as possible.

"There's no reason for that. I could tell you some really embarrassing things that I've seen in the ER, and dog bites aren't among them. Let's just say some people come in with interesting things lodged in interesting places."

I couldn't help but laugh. Thankfully she was too interested in my arm to see my teeth.

"You've lost quite a bit of blood, Dante." She eyed the floor. "Are you feeling light-headed at all?"

"No. I feel fine." Since the blood on the floor wasn't my blood.

"That's good. You're obviously in great shape. Let me clean this up for you." She turned to River. "Do you have any bandages? And if not, just some rags will do. I just need to get pressure on this so the bleeding will stop."

River nodded and left the kitchen.

"I think we should take you to the hospital just in case," she said.

"No. I'm fine. I trust you to take care of it."

"Dante, I'm not a doctor. Plus, we need to find the dog and make sure you don't need any rabies protocol."

How had I gotten into this? She was fussing, and I could

already feel my blood coagulating. I didn't need a doctor.

River came back in with some bandages. "I just gave Daisy next door a quick call. The dog has had all her shots, and Daisy was completely apologetic. She said the dog just gets rowdy sometimes, but he's friendly. She's sorry he came over. I told her it was my fault. I'd left the back door open."

"Tell her I'm fine," Dante said.

"I did. She wanted to pay your medical bills, but I told her there wouldn't be any." He handed the bandages to Erin, who removed the kitchen towel she had been holding over my wound.

River wet a towel in the sink and began to wipe up the blood on the floor.

"That's a lot of blood, Dante," Erin said again. "I really think we need to take you to the hospital."

"All right. Fine. But River can take me. You need to go home and get some sleep."

As if on cue, her face split into a giant yawn. Good. She'd see I was right.

As she was closing her mouth, a chill swept across my neck. I turned to look behind me. Nothing.

We were inside. Where could the breeze have come from?

"Are you sure?" She looked to River. "I *am* tired, and I'm on tonight again. We'll be shorthanded, too, because Lucy's off."

River's lips trembled, as if he were trying to hold back a smile.

"I'm still worried about the amount of blood. How will I know if you're all right?"

"I'll call Jay, and he can let you know," River said.

"Okay. That will work." She looked at me intently. "You do *look* fine. No worse for wear. The blood loss obviously hasn't affected you." She turned to River. "I still think he should go in, though. Thanks for taking him." She yawned again.

"I'll be fine," I said. "Go ahead home and get some sleep."

⚜

"Take a bite from your own flesh, and offer yourself to me. I want you to feed me now."

"You've fed from me nearly every day since you brought me here."

"No. You will open your wrist for me, so I can drink from you."

"Rip it open yourself. Nothing has stopped you before."

"I can take what I want. I will always take what I want from you. I'm asking you to give it to me today. Give to me freely, Dante. Show me what I mean to you."

"You mean nothing to me!"

She gestured to her goon. Soon the cool steel of a sharp knife touched my cock.

"You're bluffing," I yelled. "You'd never let him hurt me there. He already told me you wouldn't."

"You're smart, Dante," she said. "Another reason why you're so important to me." She motioned to her goon.

The steel now cut into my ankle.

"True, you won't be as pretty without a foot, but I'll just cover that part of you up. It's not like you need feet anymore anyway. You will never leave here."

The blade sliced through my skin, and I felt my blood bubbling.

"Your choice, Dante. Do you lose a foot? We'll cauterize it quickly so we don't spill any of your precious blood. Or do you feed me of your own free will?"

Anger rose within me like a red rage. Nothing about any of this was of my own free will. To be forced to choose between my foot and opening a vein for her? I needed my feet to escape from here if I ever got the chance.

There was no choice. My fangs elongated in my madness, and I pulled the arm she'd unbound forward. With hate clouding my mind, I sank my teeth into my own wrist.

FIVE

Erin

I walked toward my car but then turned abruptly and headed toward their neighbor's house. The mansion was on a corner, so I didn't have to worry about getting the right neighbor. There was only one house next door.

I clanged the ornate knocker.

An elderly woman came to the door a few minutes later. "Yes? May I help you?"

"Are you Daisy?" I asked.

"Yes, I am."

"My name is Erin. I'm an emergency room nurse, and I'm also a friend of the Gabriels next door. I don't mean to intrude, but I think you'd better keep your dog either inside or fenced in. You could get into a lot of trouble with a dog that just goes into other peoples' houses and starts biting."

She narrowed her eyes, the wrinkles around them becoming more apparent. "My dog?"

"Yes, ma'am. Your dog that just bit Mr. Gabriel's grandson

who's staying with him. He lost quite a bit of blood."

"I'm sorry, but I don't know what you're talking about. I don't own a dog."

"But..." I sighed. She was elderly and maybe a little senile. "Just be careful, ma'am. Please. Sorry to have bothered you."

"No problem, honey." She smiled and closed the door.

I walked back to my car.

Senile? She couldn't be. She'd told River the dog had all its shots. Something else was going on here. I marched back toward Dante's house.

Only to see his grandfather walking out.

"May I speak to you a moment?" he said.

"I want to see Dante first. The woman next door just told me she doesn't have a dog."

"No, she doesn't have a dog." He looked into my eyes strangely, staring, and his irises... Were they moving? They looked like seawater—greenish-blue waves.

"Then who bit Dante? And don't give me that story about the bread knife. Those were bite marks from cuspid teeth. I'm a nurse. I know what I'm talking about."

"No one bit Dante. He cut himself with a bread knife, like he told you."

"No, he didn't, I told—"

"He cut himself with the bread knife, Erin." He stared into my eyes. "He cut himself with the bread knife."

My mind went fuzzy. His irises still swirled in teal currents. For a moment, I forgot where I was.

"Did River take him to the hospital yet?"

"No, he stopped bleeding. It was a minor cut. From the bread knife."

Yes, the cut from the bread knife. I remember now.

"I need to go home and get some rest," I said.

"Yes, that's a good idea," Bill said. "Go home and get some rest. It was great to meet you."

"Yeah, you too." I headed toward my car.

When I got to the hospital that evening for work, I found out Cynthia North had been discharged. She was staying with a friend, since she couldn't go home after her husband's girlfriend had shot her. So much for talking to her again, not that she'd had much information for me anyway.

Time to give Dr. Bonneville a rest. She was none of my business. Except, of course, when she was on duty, which she was not tonight. I said a thank you to the universe for the reprieve. The next time she came in, she'd be happy to see that the B positive supply had finally been restocked.

Seemed like we used a lot of B pos whenever Dr. Bonneville was on duty.

Probably just a coincidence. Or maybe she needed that blood type for her research.

B positive was my own blood type. Clearly, for whatever reason, they needed more of it here at the hospital. I made a mental note to donate soon. Two months had passed since I'd last donated, so I was eligible.

Out of curiosity, I typed in Cynthia North's name on my computer. *Blood Type: B positive.*

What about that other woman who'd gone missing from the free clinic? What was her name? I'd have to check with Jay. Our hospital wouldn't have any records on her anyway, and the clinic wouldn't release her blood type due to doctor/patient confidentiality.

Not that any of this mattered.

Still...it was strange.

Sirens blared. I'd have to think about this later.

❖

A rough night so far. I was getting ready to take a much-needed break, when the sirens bellowed again. The EMTs wheeled three patients in. I attended the first.

"Auto accident. Male, early thirties, multiple facial lacerations, unconscious. Possible concussion and internal bleeding. BP one ten over sixty. On O2 but he's breathing on his own."

"Broken bones?" I asked.

"Not that we can tell, but the x-ray will tell you if I'm wrong. I think this one got lucky."

I looked down.

Oh. My. God.

Beneath the oxygen mask was a face I recognized.

River Gabriel.

He was supposed to go on a date with Lucy tonight...

My mind raced.

"Lucy! Is Lucy with him?"

The EMT looked at me strangely. "He was alone in his car. The other two are from the other car."

I heaved a sigh of relief and looked at my watch. Two a.m. Their date must have already ended, thank God.

Still...River. He was Dante's cousin and Jay's partner. This was hitting way too close to home.

"River?" I said. "Can you hear me? It's Erin. I'm going to

take good care of you, okay?"

Should I call Lucy? She'd be up. Frankly, I couldn't believe they hadn't spent the night together.

Logan hurried up to the gurney. "The EMTs say the other two are in worse shape, so Dr. Anderson and the head resident are checking them out. What do we have here?"

"Male, thirties, facial lacerations. Possible internal bleeding and concussion. Nonresponsive, but vitals are okay. BP slightly low."

"All right. Let's get him into a room."

"There's something else," I said.

"What?"

"I know him. He's a police detective. He's my brother's partner." *And the cousin of the man I love.*

Did I really just think that?

Yes, I loved Dante.

Seeing his nearly identical cousin bleeding on a gurney had zapped it into my mind. It made no sense, but I loved him.

"We need to check for internal injuries," I said.

"I know that, Erin," Logan said. "I'm a doctor."

Even the nicest doctors looked down on the nursing staff sometimes. I'd tried to get used to it.

I'd failed.

Logan looked River over. "We'll need to x-ray for fractures."

"The EMT doesn't think he has any. He was probably wearing his seatbelt. He's a cop."

"I'm ordering x-rays anyway."

We wheeled him over to an exam room.

"Start an IV and type him," Logan said.

I was one step ahead of Dr. Crown. I found a good vein in the dorsum of his left hand and inserted the needle. I taped it down and began the trickle of Ringer's lactate solution. Then I drew some blood for his typing in case a transfusion was needed later. Right now, he looked okay.

Logan checked River's arms and legs and tried communicating with him. "No evidence of fracture, but the x-rays will tell for sure. He's got a concussion. Let's logroll him."

We rolled him, and Logan palpated his back to check for spinal injuries. "Looks good," he said. "I want an ultrasound of his chest and abdomen to check for internal bleeding."

I cut River's clothes off, and Logan checked his abdomen while I got the ultrasound ready. I spread the gel onto River's fair skin—so much like Dante's.

"It all looks good," Logan said, after viewing the ultrasound, "but let's get a CAT scan to be sure. He's clearly got a concussion. Get the CAT ordered, Erin, and then clean up the lacerations. Let's make him comfortable."

Logan left, and I prepared some antiseptic and antibacterial for River's cuts. Finally, when I was working on a fairly deep gash in his forehead, he winced.

"River? Can you hear me?"

"Where am I?"

"You're at the ER. You were in a car accident. You're going to be fine."

"You know me?"

"Yeah. It's me. Erin. Jay's sister."

"Oh." He squinted. "I can't see very well. Blurry."

"You've got a concussion," I said. "Your vision will clear. Are you in pain?"

"Kind of. Like achy. And my face hurts."

"Looks like your pretty face took the worst of it," I said, "but you'll recover. You might have a few tiny scars, but nothing that will detract from your looks. I'll check with the doctor to see what I can give you for pain."

"Lucy? Is Lucy okay?"

"Lucy wasn't in the car with you. You must have already taken her home."

"No. I don't remember..."

"That's okay. A few minutes of retrograde amnesia are common with a concussion. But Lucy's fine. She wasn't in the car."

"No. I hadn't taken her home yet..." He closed his eyes. "We were going to my place..."

"River, you must have been on your way back from taking her home. She wasn't in the car. I promise. Would you like me to call her?"

"Yeah, would you?"

"Of course."

I didn't have to. Lucy ran into the exam room.

"Luce! Where did you come from?"

"I just heard. Is he okay?"

"Yeah, he's going to be fine."

"And the people from the other car?"

"I don't know. I haven't checked on them. Wait. How did you know about the other car?"

"Steve told me when I came in." She touched River's cheek. "Hey, you."

He opened his eyes. "Thank God. You're okay."

"I'm fine. How are you?"

He suppressed a laugh. "Been better."

"You still look great to me." She smiled.

"Can you stay with him for a bit, Luce?" I asked. "I need to check with Logan about some pain meds for him. Plus, I need to call his family."

"Sure." She sat down next to the bed.

I checked with Logan on the pain meds and administered them, and then I looked through River's wallet for any contact information. Sure enough, there was Bill Gabriel's number. I hated calling people, but at least I didn't have the worst news this time.

I dialed the number.

"Hello?"

My heart skipped. Dante's voice. "Dante?"

"Yes. Erin?"

"Yeah, it's me."

"It's good to hear your voice."

"Good to hear yours too, but I'm calling because—"

"About today, and the dog bite..."

"What dog bite?"

"You know, the dog bite on my arm?"

What was he talking about? "You mean the cut from the bread knife?"

"What? No, I mean—"

"Listen, Dante, I don't have time to chat. River's here. He's okay, but he's been in an accident."

"No. What?" Tension laced his voice.

"He has a concussion and some facial lacerations. We don't think he has any internal bleeding, but we're going to do a CAT scan to be sure. It doesn't look like he has any broken bones, but we'll x-ray anyway. He's very lucky."

"Thank God. I'll get Bill, and we'll be right there."

"Okay. We'll probably keep him overnight for observation. Plus, he still needs the CAT."

"Erin?"

"Yeah?"

"Thanks."

"I'm just doing my job, Dante. I'll see you soon."

SIX

DANTE

I grabbed Bill and yanked him out of his bed. "You fucking glamoured her!"

He yawned and wiped sleep out of his eyes. "What are you talking about?" He disentangled himself from me. "And you're asking for an ass whooping, Dante. You're asking to be kicked right out of here. You know what happened the last time you got violent with me."

As much as I wanted to kick the shit out of my grandfather for daring to glamour Erin, I drew in a deep breath. River was at the hospital. That was more important right now.

"You need to get up. Riv's at the hospital."

His eyes widened. "Is he okay?"

"Yeah. Car accident, but he's going to be fine, according to Erin."

"She's with him?"

"Yeah, she is, and I hope you told him that you glamoured her, because if he starts talking about a dog bite—"

"Shit." Bill pulled on a pair of jeans over his pajama pants. "Let's go."

I called Em at work and told her I'd call again if she needed to come to the hospital. Then I seethed as I sat in the passenger seat of Bill's sedan. My own grandfather had violated my woman.

"A glamour isn't a violation, Dante. It's for the human's own protection."

"Oh, shut the fuck up!"

Bill turned to me. "Excuse me?"

"Why did you do it, Bill? Why did you fuck with Erin's mind?"

"Because she found out Daisy doesn't have a dog. Did you really want her asking a bunch of questions about what happened to you? What were you thinking, anyway, taking a bite out of your own wrist?"

Take a bite from your own flesh and offer yourself to me.

Damn it, not now!

"I was trying to cover up for the steer's blood all over the floor. I could hardly tell her the truth."

"If you've indeed formed a blood bond with her, you *have* to tell her the truth. You need her."

"How? How the hell am I supposed to do that, Bill?"

"We'll figure it out. But if you want my help, you're going to need to show some more respect and stop acting like an animal every time something happens that you don't like."

Stop acting like an animal? I'd been treated like an animal for the last ten years, penned up and kept for food.

I was *not* an animal.

I thought back to the night I'd escaped. I'd kept my sanity enough not to kill that night. I'd needed every ounce of strength and self-control I possessed, but I'd managed. If I'd been able to do it then—when I was starving and crazy—why not now?

The blood bond.

It wasn't just affecting Erin, it was affecting me. I needed her blood. Without it, would I go insane?

Damn.

There was no way to know.

Bill pulled into the hospital parking lot. I inhaled. Erin. She was here.

In the midst of a hospital full of people and full of blood, all I could smell was Erin.

My dick hardened.

Not now.

My gums itched.

Not fucking now.

"How do you do it, Bill?"

"Do what?"

"I can't smell anything but Erin, but what do *you* smell right now? All the people inside? All the bags of blood from others? Each bag has a scent to you. Some good, some bad. But you must be starving. How do you control yourself here?"

That night flashed in my memory. The moment I'd picked up the scents of the blood bank. How I could barely distinguish one scent from another. How I ran toward those scents, toward sustenance, how my mind had fixated on getting there no matter what the cost.

Then I'd gone into the hospital, had sneaked past the front desk. It had been the middle of the night, so it hadn't been difficult to whisk past the few unsuspecting people I encountered. Wearing the homeless man's clothes, I'd followed my nose to the large refrigeration unit. No one was there.

I yanked the door open and inhaled.

I closed my eyes and reached for the first blood bag I could find. I ripped it open with my teeth and poured it into my mouth.

Yes. Sustenance.

Another bag, and then another.

Images catapulted into my mind—a young blond woman who had never had children, an older bald man whose testosterone was waning, a younger man, probably an athlete, his blood full of oxygen...

The scents overwhelmed me, and I grabbed for bag after bag after bag of the red nourishment.

For years, I'd known only her blood. It had burned my tongue, clogging my throat and leaving a caustic trail. It gurgled in my stomach.

I never got used to it.

I ripped open one more bag, pouring the liquid down my throat, letting it trickle over my lips, down my cheeks and neck.

Then...Erin.

Her scream. My hand clamped over her mouth.

And...I inhaled.

All the other scents had ceased to exist, though I hadn't realized that at the time. Her fragrance overwhelmed me, made my dick harden, made my full stomach cry out for more.

"How do you do it, Bill?" I asked again.

"Through self-control," he said. "There's no magical formula, Dante. During young adulthood, vampires learn to control themselves when their senses of smell increase. They have guidance. You didn't have that guidance, and I'm sorry about that."

"It's all so overwhelming."

"I know it is."

"I mean... It *was*." I said. "I know there are thousands of scents here. But all I smell is her."

Bill inhaled. "Yes, she's here."

I stiffened. Bill had no interest in Erin, but I didn't want him smelling her. I didn't want anyone smelling her—no one but me.

"What am I going to tell her?"

"I don't know, son. We'll figure it out."

"I need you to promise me one thing."

"What's that?"

"Don't ever glamour her again."

"That was for her own good, Dante. You know that. I would never use glamouring as a weapon."

The Bill I'd known for the first eighteen years of my life would never use glamouring as a weapon. This Bill? I was no longer sure. Perhaps I was reading too much into the situation. Overanalyzing. Maybe Bill was the same as he'd always been.

But something inside me said he wasn't.

I couldn't help but feel something sinister lurking around Bill. Nothing I could put my finger on, but something wasn't right.

I inhaled. Erin's scent was growing stronger.

She walked toward us. "You can see River now. He's conscious, and he's doing well. He's got some lacerations on his face, and we're still waiting to get x-rays and a CAT scan, but the doctor doesn't think he has any broken bones or internal bleeding."

Bill and I stood and followed Erin back to an examination room. River was lying down, his face patched up with a few bandages. His eyes were heavy-lidded, but he was awake. Erin's friend Lucy Cyrus sat next to him. I quickly introduced her to Bill and then turned to River.

"Hey, Riv."

"Hey yourself."

"I can't lie. I've seen you looking better."

River chuckled. "Damn you, Dante. It hurts to laugh."

"What happened?" Bill asked.

"Car accident. I wasn't drunk or anything. I'd never do that. The other driver came out of nowhere."

"Erin says you're going to be fine," I said.

"Yeah, looks like you're stuck with me."

He turned to Lucy. "I can't remember taking you home."

"Retrograde amnesia," Lucy said. "It's very common with a concussion, especially if you lose consciousness."

"That's what I told him," Erin said.

"But it's weird. I don't remember taking you home, but I remember the accident."

Erin arched her eyebrows. "Really? That *is* odd."

"Oh, no, I've heard of that," Lucy said. "Sometimes the amnesia is fragmented. Anyway, the important thing is that you're okay."

"That's the truth of it," Bill said. "When can we take him home?" he asked Erin.

"He'll probably need to stay the rest of the night. He still needs the CAT and x-rays. He can probably go home sometime in the afternoon, though sometimes they keep concussions for a full twenty-four hours." She smiled. "If you all will excuse me, I need to get back to work."

A sense of profound loss enveloped me when she left the exam room.

"You two don't have to stay," I said. "I'll stay with him."

"All right," Bill said. "I'll go ahead home. Can I drop you off anywhere?" he asked Lucy.

"No, I have a car, but thank you." She touched River's face gently. "I'll check in with you tomorrow, okay?"

"Yeah, sure. I'd like that."

Bill and Lucy left, but before I could say anything to River, Jay Hamilton walked in.

Ice chilled the back of my neck. This was Erin's brother, the man who had gotten Em pregnant, if River was right, and I had no reason to believe he wasn't. Had River said anything to him yet? Probably not. How would he be able to explain knowing?

"Hey, partner," Jay said. "I just heard. How are you doing?"

"Been better," River said.

"Looked better too." Jay chuckled.

This time, River didn't laugh. Because it hurt? No. More likely he was pissed at Jay for fucking my sister.

I wasn't real thrilled with him either.

"Hey, I've been talking to the cop who took the report, and a witness said there was a big dog running away right after the accident. Looked like a German Shepherd or a Malamute. Do you remember that? Seeing a dog in the street? Maybe that's what caused the accident."

"No," he said. "I don't remember. All I remember is the crash. The other car came out of nowhere."

"They both survived, and from what we can tell so far, he'll be getting the blame for this one. You'll most likely be cleared of any wrongdoing."

"That's good, Riv," I said.

"Yeah, great. While I lie here in pain."

"You'll be up in no time," Jay said. "I talked to Erin on the way in. They're only keeping you to get a CAT scan and to observe the concussion. You'll be out of here soon."

"I wish I hadn't taken those couple days off now."

"Take more sick days if you need them. The boss is cool. You know that."

"Yeah," River said, wincing. "I'd rather be working than laid up though."

"You should rest," I said.

"I'll leave you alone," Jay said. "By the way, I got the information on where your car was towed. The department will pay for a rental until it's fixed. Get better soon, buddy." He left.

"Hey," I said when we were alone. "Did you know that Bill glamoured Erin? She thinks I got cut with a bread knife, not bitten by a dog." Just saying the words made me angry all over again.

"Oh?"

"I'm pissed as hell, but I wanted to let you know so you don't mention a dog bite to Erin."

"Okay. Though I've got to tell you, I may not remember any of this. My mind is totally fucked up right now."

"Try to get some sleep," I said. "I'll stay for a while."

I'd stay until morning. Until Erin got off her shift.

SEVEN

Erin

My heart sped up as I walked toward my car after work. Dante stood, leaning against it. Beautiful as ever, but his hair was mussed and he had bags under his eyes. He looked tired. Of course he was. He'd been up all night with River.

I'd checked on River before I left. He was getting wheeled away to a regular hospital room, and Bill had come back and was going with him.

That left Dante...here, propped up against my car.

"Hey," I said.

"Hi, Erin."

"What are you doing here?" Dumbass question, but I had to ask.

"I want to ask you something."

"Okay."

He showed me his bandaged forearm. "Do you remember this?"

Had he gone bonkers? "Of course I remember that. You

cut yourself with a bread knife. Are you okay? Do you want me to take a look?"

"No. And I'm fine."

I stared into his eyes. My heart sped up just looking at him. And not just my heart. My libido was doing a happy dance.

"What did you want to ask me?" I said.

"Do you want to have breakfast with me?"

"Uh...sure. I'd love that. But I look like shit."

"Are you kidding? You're beautiful. You're always beautiful, Erin."

My cheeks warmed. *So are you.* I didn't say the words, though.

"Sure. Let's have breakfast. Where do you want to go?"

"Wherever you usually go is fine."

"All right. Where are you parked?"

"I'm not. I drove with my grandfather."

"Then I'm driving, I guess." I unlocked the car. "Get in."

"Is your brother dating anyone?" Dante asked me after we'd ordered our meals.

My brow flew up. "What? Why do you care? Oh God." We'd been together how many times now and never consummated anything? "Please don't tell me you're gay."

He laughed loudly. "After everything, you can't possibly think that."

"We've never actually finished, Dante."

"That last time was your call. I wanted to ignore my text, remember?"

"Touché. And no, I don't think Jay is seeing anyone. Why do you care?"

"Just wondering."

Really? He was going to leave it at that? As much as I loved this man, I would never understand him.

"Why are you wondering?"

"What about you? Are you seeing anyone?"

"You're really asking me that? You think I'd have done all we've done together if I were seeing someone?"

"I did find you with that other guy, Erin."

"Oh." My cheeks warmed. I never had explained that. "And you've waited until now to ask me about it?"

He didn't respond.

"That was a onetime thing that didn't happen. I wasn't even that interested. I just wanted to..."

"Just wanted to what?"

I put down the bite of egg that was halfway to my mouth. "Honestly? I wanted to get you out of my mind. I don't really know you, and you don't know me either."

"No, I really don't," he agreed.

"Okay." I knew where this was headed, and I didn't like it one bit. "Logan was—"

"So that's his name? Logan?" Dante furrowed his brow and took a rather indignant bite of toast.

Thank God he and Logan hadn't crossed paths at the hospital earlier.

"Yeah. Would you please let me finish? What I was going to say is that Logan was a mistake. It's just as well that you interrupted us. I probably wouldn't have gone through with it anyway, but if I had, I know I'd be regretting it." I took a sip of decaf, gathering my courage. "I don't want to stop seeing you, Dante."

There, I'd said it. Put myself out there. I steeled myself

for rejection, even though the thought of never seeing Dante again made me sick to my stomach. That pull, that desire—how would I get over it?

"I'd like to get to know you, Erin."

Thank God. I stifled my sigh of relief.

He continued, "I want to take you out. On a date."

A date! What a novel concept. Odd that it hadn't occurred to me. For some weird reason, what Dante and I had shared so far seemed almost...normal to me. Seemed like what I'd been put on the planet for—to be with him.

"Sure," I said. "I'd love to go out with you."

"Are you sure?"

Seriously? "I think it's pretty obvious that I'm attracted to you. But you're right. We don't really know each other. So let's get to know each other. A date would be a good start."

"What do you like to do?"

"All kinds of things. I love going to a nice dinner. A movie. A show. Live music. Dancing. What do you like to do?"

He arched his eyebrows, his forehead creasing. "I don't know."

"You don't know what you like to do?"

He cleared his throat quickly. "I mean, it's been a while since I've dated."

"Yeah, me too."

"How about dinner?" he said. "We both have to eat. When is your next night off?"

"Tonight, actually." God bless the luck!

"Okay, great. Tonight it is, then. I'll pick you up around seven."

"Perfect." I couldn't stop smiling.

❧

After I'd driven Dante to Bill's, I stopped for a few groceries. When I got back out to my car, it wouldn't start.

"Damn!" I said aloud.

"Anything wrong?" A handsome older man wearing jeans and a T-shirt approached me. He had dark hair with some silver at the temples.

"The engine won't start," I said.

"You want me to take a look?"

"Do you know anything about cars?"

"A few things."

He smiled, and I was automatically at ease. A nice man who meant no harm.

He got in the driver's seat and tried the ignition. "It could be the battery or the alternator. I'll check it out." He popped the hood button.

I followed him to look at the engine even though I had no idea what I was looking at.

"Let's see." He poked around a little. "Does your husband know anything about cars?"

"I'm not married."

"Oh. Dating anyone?"

Was he really going to try to pick me up? "Yes." I cleared my throat. "I have a date tonight."

"That's nice. Have a wonderful time." He fiddled with a few wires. "May I make a suggestion?"

"Well...I guess so."

"Keep an open mind. A *very* open mind."

"Oh, I thought you were going to suggest something about my car."

"Try it now." He smiled.

I got in the driver's seat and turned the key. Sure enough, the engine started. I got out of the car to thank him, but he was gone.

EIGHT

DANTE

Nerves.

Nerves in a different way than I thought possible.

Tonight was the night. I'd finally make love with Erin. And after that...

The truth.

River wasn't here. Bill was, but I didn't want to talk to him. Not since he'd glamoured Erin.

I couldn't shake the fear that Bill might be wrong. What if someone else had already formed a blood bond with Erin, was feeding from her, and she'd die if I stopped it?

I couldn't be responsible for Erin's demise.

My skin tightened around me like cellophane as rage filled me. *No one will feed from her but me, damn it!*

I'd find whoever was doing it, and I'd destroy him.

She was mine. All mine. Body, heart, soul, blood.

Mine.

My gums itched and prickled.

I went to the kitchen and downed a pint of blood. I had to

keep myself under control tonight, at least until...

What if she ran from me screaming?

Who wouldn't? Any sane person would get as far away from me as she possibly could.

I had to try, though.

Had to try to find life and happiness for us both.

That meant I needed a contingency plan. I didn't want to glamour her, and I wasn't even sure I could. So if she screamed... What could I do? Tie her down to make her stay and listen to me?

Tie her down.

The thought both disgusted and aroused me. How could I even think of binding someone, when I'd been held captive for a decade? But a beautiful image emerged in my mind—Erin, a feast on a platter, bound, ready and willing for me to take whatever I wanted, whatever I needed...

I showered and got ready to shave but then decided to keep the couple days' worth of stubble. She seemed to like it. I dressed quickly and ran a comb loosely through my hair. Maybe time for a haircut? The waves hit my shoulders. River wore his shorter.

No. This was me. The me I'd only seen so recently. I was still getting used to the mature face in the mirror. I couldn't change anything. Not yet.

I walked downstairs and stopped at the door to Bill's office. He'd glamoured Erin, and I was pissed. Still, he was all I had at the moment. He was busy tapping on his computer. I reached toward the doorknob and then decided against seeing him before my date.

He hadn't dated in forever. What advice would he have? I wished Riv were here. I didn't want to add to the stress of his concussion by asking him about dating and blood bonding and all that jazz. Still, I found myself calling him, hoping he was awake and would take my call.

"Hey, Dante," he said.

"Riv. How are you feeling?"

"I'm fine. I want to get the hell out of here, but they're insisting on keeping me another night even though my CAT scan and x-rays were fine."

"It's better to make sure everything's okay." I cleared my throat. "I have a...date with Erin tonight."

"Yeah? That's great."

"Yeah...great. I'm scared out of my mind."

"It's just a date."

"A date with the woman who needs to feed me, and when she finds out, she's going to come unglued."

"Give her a little credit, Dante. Everything will be fine."

"Easy for you to say."

"It *is* easy for me to say. If she's formed this bond, she will understand. Maybe not at first, but you can *make* her understand. Just go with it."

Just go with it. I said goodbye, drew in a couple deep breaths, and left.

I drove to Erin's and parked, my nerves a mess of jitters as I walked to her door. I was tempted to check if the door was unlocked, but I didn't. I knocked.

"Just a minute," she called through the door.

I swallowed the nausea erupting within me.

Tonight was the night.

The first night of the rest of my life.

Please let it work out. Please don't let her run away from me.

The door opened.

And in front of me stood pure beauty.

Erin's dark hair fell in soft waves around her bare shoulders. She wore a soft-green camisole dress—perfectly matching her eyes—that flowed midway down her thighs. Her nipples protruded through the silky fabric. God, those legs. Long and luscious.

With bite wounds on them...

No! Don't go there.

Her toes were painted light pink, and her feet were clad in strappy silver sandals.

"You okay?" she asked.

My mouth was hanging open. I shut it quickly. "Yeah. You look amazing."

She blushed adorably. "Thank you. So do you. You want to come in?"

"Later." If I went in, I might not be able to leave without getting her naked. "I want to have our date."

"Okay. Let me just get my wrap."

The drive to the restaurant didn't take long. We were seated, and she looked at the menu.

I looked at *her*.

She bit her bottom lip.

My gums tightened and tingled.

Not now.

I flagged down a waiter. "Could I get a cup of coffee please?"

"Oh, sure. And for the lady?"

She arched her eyebrows at me. "Coffee?"

"Make it Irish coffee." I needed the coffee to stave off the blood lust. Not that I thought it would actually do any good.

"What do you want, Erin?"

"I'll have a mar— No. Make that a cosmopolitan." She smiled. "The last time I had a martini—well, two martinis—I got pretty hammered."

I smiled. Had she been hammered? All I remembered was the music, the sweet taste of her blood...

I'd been hammered.

Then River had tried to tell me I was hearing things because of the booze.

No reason to think about that now. I had Erin here, looking ravishing, at a nice restaurant, and I was going to make this date work. I had to. For both our sakes.

The waiter brought our drinks. I inhaled the robust scent of the Irish coffee. It still didn't take Erin's fragrance out of the air.

Did I even like Irish coffee? Time to find out. I took a sip. Not bad.

"How is River doing?" Erin asked.

"He's good. Still at the hospital."

"Oh?"

"Yeah. He's fine though. That's what he tells me anyway."

"They probably want to keep him a second night because of his concussion. It's standard procedure. No reason to worry."

"I'm not worried." River was the least of my worries, although I'd wondered more than once what had led to the accident. Vampires had amazing reflexes. They were almost never in car accidents—or accidents of any kind.

But I couldn't think about that now.

"Tell me about yourself," I said. "Everything."

She laughed. "Everything? That could take a while."

"We have all the time in the world," I said.

"Okay. Well, you know I'm a nurse. I originally wanted to be a doctor, but my parents couldn't help with college or med school, and I didn't want to go any deeper in debt than I had to, so I chose to be an RN instead."

"Do you enjoy it?"

"I do." She nodded. "It's very rewarding work, though it can be heartbreaking sometimes."

"Yeah, especially in the emergency room."

"Exactly. Losing patients is hard, but it's hard no matter what department you're in." She took a sip of her drink. "What about you? I never found out what you do for a living."

Okay, I hadn't thought this through. Questions about her would invite questions about me. What could I tell her? That I'd been held captive and abused for the last ten years wasn't going to cut it. Presently I did nothing for a living, but that would have to change. Funny how I hadn't considered it until now.

I had to keep her focused on her own life.

"We'll get to that." When I could figure out what to say. "Tell me about your childhood."

"It was modest. Small house in a suburb of Columbus, Ohio. Just Jay and me and our parents. My mom still works as a cashier in a local supermarket, and my dad does construction."

"Were you happy?"

She smiled. "Yeah, I was. My parents stayed married, which was uncommon back then. Probably even more so now. They're still married. Still live in the same house."

"How did you and Jay end up here?"

"Jay went to school here and then stayed. I ended up here because..." She reddened.

"Because...why?"

"For a... This is kind of embarrassing. I actually moved here for a guy."

An anvil of jealousy hit my gut. "Oh?"

"He's history now. It didn't work out, but I decided to stay anyway. I found work at University and met Lucy, who became one of the best friends I've ever had. And Jay was here. Plus, there's just something about New Orleans. It's a special place. I feel like I belong here. I suppose that sounds stupid."

"Not at all. My family feels that way too. It just seems like our place."

"That's exactly what I mean!" Her green eyes gleamed. "I think you get it."

Yeah, I got it. Our kind were accepted here. Jay and Erin were descended from vampires somewhere in their line. Plus they both worked night shifts. No wonder they felt at home here.

Problem was...I no longer felt at home here. But that had nothing to do with the city.

Home was—

It hit me like a brick in the chest. Home was the woman sitting across from me.

Blood bond or not, I needed her. I wanted her.

Damn. I'd fallen in love.

River had been right. There was no mistaking it. I knew it in the depths of my heart. Erin Hamilton was the first thing I thought about when I woke up and the last thing I thought of when I went to bed. She mingled in my mind all during my time awake, and she was clustered in my dreams as well. I wanted to see her, touch her, kiss her, all the time. Being with her was euphoric, and I felt passion and desire I'd never known. Being without her left me hopeless, nauseated, counting the minutes until I could be in her presence once more.

And the jealousy, the obsession... When I'd found her with that other man, I'd wanted to kill him, to wipe him out of existence. Then when I'd found that someone had fed on her...

My gums tingled. I took a sip of my Irish coffee.

Just the thought had rage overtaking me. A chill hit the back of my neck.

No one would ever touch what was mine again.

Never.

Somehow, I had to make her understand what I was—what she was to me and what I could be to her.

All of that without having her run screaming away from me.

The waiter came to take our orders.

"I think I'll start with a garden salad with balsamic vinaigrette, and then I'll have the Cajun catfish," Erin said.

Sounded good, but I needed some red meat. "I'll have the same salad and then the twelve-ounce strip, very rare."

Erin scrunched up her nose. "*Very* rare?"

"The only way to eat a good steak."

"Nah. Medium-rare is the best. Very rare is way too bloody."

Not a good sign. "Way too bloody? You're an ER nurse. You're around blood all the time."

"That doesn't mean I want to eat it." She laughed as the waiter took her menu.

Really not a good sign. How the hell was I going to convince her that she and I shared a blood bond?

I looked her over. She was in good health, was acting fine. Thank God. Maybe there was no hurry.

Though there was certainly a hurry on my part. I needed

her blood. I'd only had a drop, but it had been the most luscious concoction I'd ever tasted, as if she'd been created to feed me.

Apparently, if Bill's theory was correct, she *had* been.

"Taste my steak when it gets here," I said. "I bet I can turn you."

"No thanks." She laughed.

"Come on. For me?"

She narrowed her eyes slightly. "If it means that much to you, I'll try it."

That had gone easier than I expected.

Now, what had we been talking about? Oh yeah, she'd come here for a guy.

"So what happened with the guy?"

"What guy?"

"The guy you moved here for?"

"Oh. Cory. We broke up."

"Were you in love with him?"

She smiled. "I thought I was. I know now that I wasn't."

"Really? How do you know?"

"Because what I felt for him is nothing like—" She pressed her lips together for a few seconds. "I just know, that's all."

"How do you know?"

"Because...I just know. Love can't be explained, Dante. It's either there or it isn't, and you know it somehow."

Did I ever. I smiled at her, and her eyes lit up. She was so beautiful.

I hoped our dinners would get here soon.

NINE

Erin

The bite of Dante's steak melted in my mouth. How had I not known rare beef could be so delicious?

His grin was a mile wide. I wasn't sure why he was so happy that I'd enjoyed his steak, but that didn't matter. I wanted him happy.

Dante kept the conversation going smoothly from one topic to the next throughout dinner. It didn't escape my notice that we never got back to what he did for a living, but he guided the conversation so seamlessly that I didn't want to poke at him. I wanted to enjoy tonight. More importantly, I wanted *him* to enjoy tonight.

If things progressed as I hoped, we'd be spending the night together. I'd waited long enough.

Just looking at him made me sigh. His nearly black hair framed his perfectly sculpted face and jawline. His dark eyes, heavily fringed with ebony lashes, smoldered. His deep-violet shirt worked perfectly with his fair complexion, and the few chest hairs peeking out made me want to strip off the fabric and let the buttons go flying as I'd done before in my bathroom.

The time he'd run away when I'd tried to sink down on him.

Would this evening end up just like all the other times?

No. I wouldn't—*couldn't*—let it. I was in love with this man, this man who I knew next to nothing about.

Didn't make sense. None of this made sense. How could I be in love with someone I didn't even know?

But I was. As sure I was about anything else in my life, I was in love with Dante Gabriel.

It didn't matter what he did for a living, where he'd gone to school, whether he'd vandalized a blood bank. I was truly and completely in love with him.

I'd even briefly fantasized about him tying me up and spanking me, something I'd never found appealing in the past. When Cory had suggested it, I'd said "Oh, hell no!" and then hadn't spoken to him for a week.

But the idea of being bound and laid out for Dante Gabriel? *Oh, yeah.*

I squirmed as the tickle between my legs intensified.

I really wanted to go back to my place and fuck Dante's brains out. That was where tonight was headed. I was determined not to take no for an answer.

When the waiter came to ask for dessert, we both said, "No thank you," in unison.

Good. He was on the same page.

After he paid the bill, he said, "Would you like to go to a movie? Or maybe check out a club?"

How could I tell him no without looking like a bitch in heat?

"Whatever you want is fine with me." *Please suggest going to my place. Please.*

"I'm not much for crowds," he said, "so if you don't mind, I'd prefer not to go to a club."

"I'm not much for crowds either," I said. "Why do you think I work nights?"

He smiled. God, he was so freaking gorgeous.

"In fact, I'm kind of tired," I said. "Maybe you should just take me home."

"Oh." His lips curved downward. "Sure."

"No, I don't mean..." I was sending him all kinds of mixed signals. First I told him I'd do whatever he wanted, and then I told him to take me home. Oh, hell. I'd just let him take me home, and I'd make my intentions clear when we got there. "I think I'd like to go home."

"Of course." He came to my side of the table and pulled out my chair. Such a gentleman.

He didn't say much while we drove home. I knew he was thinking this was a rebuff, but he'd find out it wasn't when I grabbed him and pulled him into my townhome.

I did so when he left me at the door.

"I thought you said you were tired?"

"That was just an excuse to get you here, so I could do this." I pulled him to me and smashed our lips together.

He opened immediately, and our tongues began the swirling dance I'd come to love. The kiss spoke of passion, of desire, of pure, raw need and ache.

He pushed me up against the wall and cupped one of my breasts. My hard nipple tightened further at his touch. His erection pushed into my abdomen, and I arched my back, the throbbing between my legs becoming unbearable in its intensity.

I love you, I said inside my mind. *I love you so much, Dante.*

He broke the kiss with a loud smack and inhaled. He pushed some stray hairs off my face. "You're so fucking beautiful, Erin."

I sighed, moaning. "So are you. So beautiful."

He resumed the kiss, our tongues tangling. He put one of his thighs between my legs, and I rubbed against it, soothing my aching clit.

More. I wanted more.

I threaded my fingers through his hair, pulling him closer, closer to me. No space. Needed to be inside his skin, one with him.

He inhaled. "I smell you, baby. I smell your arousal." He trailed wet kisses over my cheeks and neck.

I smelled it too, that earthy female musk. I was sopping wet from kissing and rubbing up against his thigh. My thong was no doubt soaked. My whole body throbbed with hypersensitivity.

"I want you, Dante. Please. I need you to make love to me."

The words were raw and truthful, words that had never come from my mouth. But they felt right, so very right.

"I want you too, Erin," he said, his breath hot against my neck. "God, I want you so fucking badly."

"Take me to my bedroom."

Then out of the corner of my eye—

I gasped. A man stood against the wall in my living room, watching us.

"What? What is it?" Dante asked.

But he was gone. He'd looked like... No, couldn't be.

"I'm sorry. I thought I saw... Never mind." My heart was still pounding from fright.

"Thought you saw what, Erin? Something got you spooked."

"I must actually be tired. For a minute, I thought I saw a guy standing over in that corner." I pointed.

He turned, following my finger, and then walked over to the space. He rubbed the back of his neck.

"Are you okay?"

"Yeah. I just felt a chill on my neck. Probably just a draft. There's a vent right here." He returned to me. "Do you want me to leave? If you're truly tired, I can—"

"Are you kidding? If you don't take me to bed right now, Dante Gabriel, I'll never speak to you again."

He smiled. Oh, God, that smile.

Then he scooped me into his arms and carried me up the stairs to my bedroom.

TEN

DANTE

God, her fragrance. All that dark chocolate, the earthy truffles, and then the sweet musk between her legs. Tonight I'd taste her no matter what bite marks I found.

No. Don't go there. My fangs threatened to descend. I'd managed to keep them at bay while I was kissing her. I was determined to do so now.

She felt so right in my arms, against my body.

I was so completely in love with her.

Tonight, I would tell her. I would make love to her, tell her how much she meant to me, and then—

Please let her understand...

First things first. I needed to get her naked, needed to kiss every inch of her succulent skin, needed to taste that delicious pussy, and then...

My cock throbbed.

We'd been so close that time. So close.

Tonight, *she* would not interfere.

You're mine, Dante.

No, not tonight. Stay out of my head!

Even now, I'm watching you.

No!

I stopped and dropped Erin onto her bed.

I squeezed my eyes tightly shut.

"Dante?" she said timidly.

I opened them. Her hair was mussed, her lips red and swollen, her skin flushed.

Nothing would come between us tonight.

Nothing and no one.

I had control. Total control.

"I want to undress you," I said. "I want to peel every layer of clothing off you and watch as each new inch of skin is exposed. I want to go slowly. I want to savor this night, Erin. I want to savor *you.*"

"Yes," she said, closing her eyes. "*Please.*"

"No running away," I promised. "No answering texts. This *will* happen for us tonight, Erin."

"Please," she said again.

I sat down on the edge of her bed and pulled her into a sitting position. I brushed the straps of her dress over her shoulders and let them fall down. When she pulled her arms out, her bountiful breasts fell free.

All those tits that night. That hellish night. So many...and none compared to Erin's. They were perfect. I cupped them both in my palms, thumbing her hard nipples.

She moaned. "Feels so good, Dante."

"So beautiful," I said on a sigh. "So perfect." I leaned down and flicked my tongue over one.

She jolted. "God. More. Suck them. Please."

I clamped my lips around a nipple.

She moaned again. "So good."

So good. Yes. The texture was like silk under my tongue. I sucked harder while I rolled the other nipple between my thumb and forefinger. "You're amazing," I said against her fair skin.

She groaned. "Yes, harder, Dante. Suck my nipples harder."

I complied. I was her slave right now. I'd do whatever she asked. She owned me.

I *own you, Dante.*

I forced *her* out of my head.

I deserved this one shot at happiness with Erin, and I would have it. She owned me, and I owned her.

And somehow, I'd make her understand.

I had to, for both our sakes.

I sucked her nipple harder, pinched the other between my fingers.

"I want you so much," she said. "I'm so wet for you."

I let go of her nipple and trailed my hand down her smooth skin to her hip, pushing the dress as I went. Then I let the other nipple drop from my lips. "Let's get this off you."

She slid up, and I released her from her dress. Then I quickly unbuckled her sandals and set her feet free.

Only a lacy white thong covered her now. Her scent was dense in the air. My gums tingled, but I fought off the sensation. I'd have her first, have her in every way a man could have a woman. Then I'd worry about the rest.

I spread her legs and held back a rush of contempt when I saw the puncture wounds.

Easy, Dante. This isn't her fault.

In my mind, I knew that, but my body reacted differently. Again, I swallowed down the release my fangs craved. I drew in a deep breath and exhaled. Then I lowered my head.

I inhaled her earthy sweet musk. Mmm. With one finger, I ripped the lacy thong off her. She gasped, but I tossed it aside and dived into her treasure.

I swiped my tongue across her silky wet folds. So smooth and creamy. I suppressed the itching in my gums with all the strength I possessed. I couldn't nick her down here. Couldn't mar this beauty.

"Dante, oh my God!"

Her voice fueled my passion. I sucked at her, pulled her labia between my teeth, and then went to work on the hard nub of her clitoris. It was swollen and engorged, beautifully dark pink. I flicked it with my tongue and then clamped my lips around it and sucked.

She arched beneath me, grinding into my face, her juices slathering over me. I lapped her up as if I were dying of thirst.

And I was. Dying of thirst for her, for her sweetness.

For her blood.

The tingling, the salivation...

No, not yet.

Control. Needed control.

She bucked beneath me, grinding her pussy into my lips, my chin. "I'm going to come, Dante. Oh my God!"

I thrust two fingers into her heat, and she exploded around me, her pussy pulsing against my hand.

"Good. That's good, love. Come for me. Only for me." I clamped my lips onto her clit once more and her pulsing increased.

She moaned, arching her back, grinding into my fingers as I moved them inside her. Her whole body flushed a light rose.

I kissed the inside of her thigh, such sweet succulent flesh.

And then...

The puncture wounds.

My fangs descended despite my will.

Mark her. Take what is yours.

I turned my head and closed my eyes, her pussy still pulsing around my fingers.

Easy. Let it go. Easy.

How could I want her like this? Want to take her this way? After all I'd been through? How could I need to bite her and make her mine?

Just go with it.

River's words.

Just go with it. Yes. If Bill's theory was right, Erin and I belonged together. It was up to me to make her understand that.

When her climax finally subsided, I moved forward and found her lips with mine, kissing her deeply, letting the flavor of her arousal mingle with the flavor of her mouth. A heady concoction.

She moaned into me, and I felt more than heard it as it vibrated into my mouth. Into me. A part of me. Yes, the moans were coming from me as well.

Hot, beautiful Erin. Erin with the sweetest pussy. Though I had nothing to compare her to, I already knew in my heart, my soul, that hers was the sweetest.

When I broke the kiss to inhale, she smiled at me, her eyes heavy-lidded and glazed over.

"Mmm," she said. "You have *way* too many clothes on."

My cock was diamond-hard inside my pants. She reached down and gripped me, and I closed my eyes and moaned.

"I want this. I want *you*, Dante. Please. Now. Don't make me wait again."

I left the bed, unbuttoned my shirt as quickly as I could, and threw it on the carpet.

"You're so magnificent," she said. "As if you were carved by the greatest artist."

My cock throbbed. "I'm glad you find my appearance... pleasing. Because God, Erin, you are the most beautiful thing I've ever seen."

And she was. Her body was flushed, her pussy swollen and dark between her legs. Her nipples were hard and ruddy, and her lips... God, her lips—the most kissable lips ever, full and pink and soft, her blood flowing beneath them.

"Pleasing?" She laughed softly. "You go so far beyond pleasing, Dante. You're glorious. Your muscles, your hair, your amazing face and eyes... I can't imagine another man in the universe who is as amazing looking as you are."

My cock throbbed harder. I unbuckled my belt and kicked off my shoes. My nerves jumped. She'd seen me before, but this was the real thing. Tonight, we'd sanction our blood bond.

The itching in my gums tortured me, but I held my ground. *No. Not yet.*

I pushed my pants and boxer briefs over my hips and stepped out of them.

Erin gawked at me.

I couldn't help a prideful smile.

So beautiful. And all mine...

Fucking not now!

Erin sat up in bed and inched to the edge. She caressed my thigh, the globe of my ass. Her touch was like fire, each fingertip prickling me with the pop of her capillaries.

"Perfect. Your muscles. Oh my God. You're incredible, Dante."

She trailed fire over my body, skimmed the sides of my thighs, abdomen, my flanks and shoulders.

My cock stuck out hard and ready, but she left it alone. Sheer torture.

"I have to have you, Erin. I have to. Now."

"Don't you want me to—"

"Now," I said through gritted teeth. "You *will* obey me."

I closed my eyes. Had those words left my lips?

You will *obey, Dante.*

No. No. No.

I compartmentalized. Stuck it in a hidden place in my mind. Nothing would ruin this night.

When I opened my eyes, Erin was staring at me, her light-green eyes wide and circled. "Yes, Dante. I will obey you."

Tingles of arousal shot through every cell in my body.

Yes, Dante, I will obey you.

I nearly climaxed then, so powerful were her words.

Did I want her obedience?

Yes. The word shot into my head as if it had always been there. No matter that I'd been forced to obey someone I hated. Erin didn't hate me, and I *loved* her.

I wanted Erin's obedience in bed. In blood. In life and in soul. I was her slave and she was mine. I'd give her what she wanted in the bedroom, and right now, she'd give me what I wanted.

Her obedience.

She opened the drawer on her bedside table and pulled out a condom. Damn. I hadn't thought of that. I was glad she had. I needed to get tested. God only knew what taking *her* blood might have left in my body.

No. No. No.

She *will not ruin this moment.*

Erin ripped open the foil packet and touched the rubber to my cockhead. I closed my eyes and inhaled. How I wanted to be inside her with no barrier, to feel every millimeter of her pussy as she sucked me up, took me into her body.

She smoothed the condom over me with her hands this time. "You're amazing, Dante. So big and beautiful."

I opened my eyes and looked into hers, her face shining with emotion.

"Take me now," she said. "I want you inside me."

"Lie down," I said. "Spread your legs for me."

She complied, no questions asked. Obedience. What a fucking turn-on.

She lay on top of her rose-colored comforter, her own body flushed a paler hue. A platter of gourmet delicacies couldn't have been more enticing. A full *blood bank* couldn't have been more enticing.

I willed my fangs down and got on the bed, hovering over her, letting the head of my cock tease her swollen pussy.

If only I could go in without the condom...

Not yet. I'd take care of that first thing tomorrow.

I closed my eyes and groaned. I couldn't take her blood tonight after all. Not when I couldn't enter her without a barrier.

Damn.

Then I thrust into her heat.

ELEVEN

Erin

I gasped, grabbing his shoulders and clawing my nails into his skin.

So full. So complete.

He stretched me exquisitely, such a good burn.

"Damn, Erin. Damn," he said through clenched teeth. "I want to make this last."

"God, yes. Make it last all night. I've wanted this for so long. An eternity." I closed my eyes, relishing the exquisite fullness. Had anything ever felt so amazing? So empowering?

He pulled out and then pushed back into me, bumping my clit.

I gasped, the feeling so intense.

I caressed the smooth skin of his shoulders, the hard muscle underneath. I lifted my head and pressed my lips to the pulse point on his neck, kissing him there, opening my mouth and trailing my tongue over his salty skin. I rained tiny kisses over his neck and shoulders as he continued to fuck me.

In. Out. In. Out.

And with each thrust, I became more and more his.

This man. This emotion.

Love.

How I loved Dante Gabriel.

"You feel so good, Erin. So tight. God."

Sweat dripped from his brow onto my face. Locks of hair stuck to his forehead. Still he pumped into me, until—

"Fuck, Erin. I'm going to— Fuck!" He thrust into me so deep, I swore we became one body.

I felt him then. I felt every pulse in his penis as he emptied himself, and then I began to soar as a climax crept up on me.

Higher, higher, higher still...

And then the music. The soft jazz. It floated around us in a hazy mist.

When we both finished climaxing, he stayed on top of me, embedded inside me.

"Don't want to let you go," he said, his voice muffled against the pillow.

"Then don't," I said. "Take a rest, and we can start again."

He didn't turn to face me, and suddenly, all I wanted in the world was to look into those smoldering dark eyes.

"Look at me, Dante."

He didn't move.

"Please, look at me."

He rolled off me and turned to face the other way.

I wasn't about to stand for this. We'd just had the best sex of my life, and I was going to look into his dark eyes and tell him so. I sat up and pulled him over.

And I screamed.

Teeth. His teeth.

Did you see him?

See who?

The vampire.

"Erin, please. Let me explain."

I hopped off the bed and ran downstairs, still naked. My heart raced as pure fear blinded me. What to do? Call 911? Get out of here? I was naked. I grabbed a throw off of my couch and wrapped it around myself.

Don't come down here. Don't come down here.

Then—

I screamed again.

The man in the room. The man who had helped me with my car. The back of my neck prickled with a sudden chill.

"Easy, Erin," he said.

"How do you know my name?" I said, my voice cracking.

"I mean you no harm."

My mind went fuzzy, along with my vision. Who was he? How had he gotten in my home? Again, the chill on my neck.

"It will all be okay," he said, his voice soothing.

Calmness settled over me, warming me. My mind muddled further.

"I told you to keep an open mind."

"But his teeth..." He had fangs. He was still beautiful...but he had *fangs.*

"His teeth are perfectly normal. Go to him. Love him."

"I *do* love him." But I couldn't. Not now.

He smiled. "I believe that you do. *Tell* him."

"But I—"

"You came down here to get something to drink. Some wine, maybe. Take it to him. I wasn't here."

Wine. Wine sounds good. Dante would like some wine.

"Yes, I came down to get some wine."

I went to the kitchen and pulled a bottle of Pinot Noir from my wine rack. I uncorked it, filled two glasses, and went back upstairs to Dante.

He had gotten dressed and was standing next to my bed. No. I wasn't ready for him to be dressed yet. I wanted more of naked Dante.

He turned, his face paler than usual.

"I brought us some wine. Perfect for the afterglow, don't you think?" I smiled.

He looked at me, his eyebrows arched. "You don't want me to...leave?"

I laughed. "Why would I want you to leave? That was amazing. The best sex I've ever had, actually. But don't get a big head." I glanced at his crotch. "I don't mean *that* head. It's already enormous."

He furrowed his brow.

"What's the matter with you? Don't you want to stay?" I handed him a glass of wine.

He took it timidly. "Don't you want me to explain?"

"Explain what? How you just made me feel something I've never felt before?" I smiled. "I doubt you *could* explain that. We'll chalk it up to intense physical chemistry."

Tell him.

Where had that thought come from?

Intense physical chemistry. We had that, no lie. But we—at least *I*—had something so much more profound.

Love.

Tell him.

I'd never said *I love you* first. Ever.

But right now, the words were lodged in the back of my

throat, threatening to tumble free.

I took a sip of my wine for courage.

"Dante. I love you."

TWELVE

DANTE

"Dante. I love you."

My mouth dropped open. When she'd run away screaming, my fangs had retracted almost instantly. Her fear had done it. Something new to me.

And now she loved me?

How? Did she not remember?

"Erin, you screamed when you left the bedroom."

She widened her eyes. "Dante, did you hear what I just told you?"

"Yes."

"And you have nothing to say?"

Confusion swept over me. What was going on? "I don't understand."

"Oh, God." She bit her lip and her cheeks turned crimson. "I'm such an idiot. Just forget I said anything. It's okay. It's too soon. I understand if you don't feel the same way. I don't expect anything from you." She turned around.

"Hey." I turned her back to face me. "I'm just a little

confused. You ran downstairs screaming, and then—"

"No, I didn't. I went downstairs to get us some wine. I came right back up."

"What?" How could she not remember? Who could have—

"Look. I spoke out of turn. Don't worry about me."

Bill. Bill was here somehow, and he'd glamoured her again. Damn him! That was the only explanation.

But I couldn't succumb to anger in this precious moment. Erin was here—not running away, not screaming.

And she loved me.

I touched her cheek, thumbing the apple, the blood underneath her skin warming my fingertips. "Your skin is so soft."

Her lips trembled.

She thought I didn't love her. Thought so many things.

I couldn't allow it. Couldn't allow her to think I didn't return her feelings, could I? But there was so much she didn't know, so much she had to know before we took that crucial step of love.

You love her.

God, yes, I did love her. And right now she was doubting that. I couldn't bear the thought of her aching over something that wasn't even close to true.

"I love you, Erin. So much."

A dazzling smile split her beautiful face, but a second later it had morphed into a frown. "You don't have to say that just because I—"

I placed my fingers over her lips. "I'm not. I wouldn't do that. I love you. I feel like I've always loved you, though I know that doesn't make any sense."

Her smile returned. "It does. It makes perfect sense."

"You're all I think about," I said.

"Ditto. You're never out of my mind. It's like I'm being pulled to you. And no matter what, I *have* to be with you. I've never felt anything like this before. It's so...*powerful*."

"There's so much you don't know."

This time she placed her fingers over my mouth. "I know that. There's a lot you don't know about me too. But this feels so...right. Just so right."

"It does." I knew why.

But she didn't.

The blood bond. Somehow, I had to make her understand.

"Are you feeling okay, Erin?"

"Are you kidding? I feel better than I ever have before. Amazing sex can do that to a person. And being in love." She walked into my arms. "It's the best."

She was right about that. I'd never felt so at peace.

Yet so at war.

I couldn't lose this. Couldn't lose *her*.

Somehow, I had to make her understand what she must do.

My fangs itched to descend.

No.

First, I'd get tested. I'd make sure I could keep her safe.

Lord, what if I couldn't? What if *she* had diseased me somehow? What if...

You're mine, Dante. Always and for eternity. I've made sure of it.

No!

As much as I wanted to, I couldn't make love to Erin again. Not until I could do it without a condom.

"Baby," I said, "I don't want to use condoms with you."

"I'm on the pill and I'm clean. We're encouraged to get tested regularly at work," she said. "And if you say you're fine, I trust you."

"I'm sure I am," I said, though I wasn't sure at all. "But I want to be positive. I'll get tested first thing tomorrow."

"In the meantime," she said, "I have a drawer full of condoms."

No. Couldn't. I wouldn't be able to keep my teeth from descending. Not now. Not when I knew she loved me.

I needed to be with her without a barrier. I'd get tested. If the test found something, I'd find a way to counteract whatever *she* had done to me. I had to. Erin's life depended on it.

But no more lovemaking tonight.

I had no more self-control left. I had to get out of here now. I needed some blood.

I needed Erin's blood, but that would have to wait until the next time we were together. I would find a way to make her understand...without Bill's interference.

I kissed her lightly on the lips. Any more than that, and I wouldn't be able to stop myself. "I have to go. I'm sorry."

"No. Please stay. If we love each other, we should sleep together. Wake up together."

"I want that more than you know, but I can't tonight. Next time." I cupped her cheek. "I promise."

It was a promise I hoped I could keep.

I barged into Bill's office when I got home. "How *dare* you?"

He stood. "Excuse me?"

"You were at Erin's apartment. You fucking glamoured her again!" I raced forward and grabbed him by the collar.

With seemingly little effort, he broke my hold and then pushed me against the wall, grabbing me by the throat. "You don't walk in here and talk to me like that, boy. We've had this discussion."

This was the first time Bill had used his considerable strength against me. I gritted my teeth. "You're not denying it."

"I shouldn't have to. I'd glamour the whole damned world if I thought it would help you. I'd do it gladly. But I didn't glamour her again. I only did it once after the 'dog bite' issue."

"You're lying," I said, my voice hoarse from his hold.

He let me go. I steadied myself.

"I'm not lying. I would never lie to you."

I would never lie to you. The words seemed false to me. The Bill before I'd been taken wouldn't have lied to me. This one? I wasn't sure. "Somehow you got into her townhome tonight and glamoured her after she saw my teeth."

"I swear to you. I did not. Now get the hell out of my office."

Could he be telling the truth? River couldn't have done it. He was still at the hospital. And Emilia was at work. Or so I'd assumed. She probably didn't even know I was at Erin's. Would my grandfather really break into Erin's apartment and hang out like a creep while we were making love?

I stood my ground. No way was he chasing me out of his office again. "Someone did. I was with her, and my fangs..." I shook my head. "She screamed, and then about fifteen minutes later, she returned and didn't seem to remember what had happened."

"I won't deny the strangeness of what you're saying, but I've been here all evening," Bill said. "And I'm done tolerating this volatility. Get a grip on yourself, Dante. You can't use what happened to you as an excuse for acting out. You're a grown man. It's beneath you."

"Beneath me? I've lost ten years of my life. I've lost my father. My uncle. I've met a woman who has consumed me so much that I haven't been able to deal with anything else."

"Yes, beneath you. If you need to mourn Julian and Braedon, do so. Deal with what happened to you. I will find someone to help you, because I have obviously failed. But stop using it all as an excuse."

Darkness settled over me. He was right. I hadn't yet mourned my father and my uncle—two men who had meant everything to me. I hadn't dealt with my time in captivity, only with fragmented memories that came to me at the worst possible times.

I would mourn my father and uncle...and then I would avenge them.

But before I could do either of those things, I had to somehow complete the blood bond with Erin. I'd go mad if I didn't.

"If you didn't glamour Erin, who did?" I asked, forcefully unclenching my teeth.

"Maybe it has something to do with the blood bond. I need to do more research. Though there's precious little information about the phenomenon."

Only that I'd go mad if I didn't take her blood. Perhaps madness was my destiny. Maybe it would help me avenge my father and uncle. Maybe it would draw me back to *her* so I could inflict punishment for my own redemption.

I closed my eyes. I could *not* let myself descend into hysteria. Erin was my priority. I couldn't protect her if I wasn't in my right mind. I drew in what I hoped would be three calming breaths and then opened my eyes and faced my grandfather.

"What if you're wrong about the bond, Bill? Erin looks fine. She's perfectly healthy. What if nothing will happen to her if she doesn't feed me? What if I bring her into my fucked-up life for no reason at all? I can't live with that. I can't."

"You have feelings for her," he said.

I had to force myself not to grab two fistfuls of my hair and yank them out of my scalp. "Of course I have feelings for her! I've told you about the pull I feel when I'm near her. Even when I'm not near her."

"Those are physical feelings. But you're concerned for her well-being. Your emotions have gotten involved." He paced around the office. "It's all part of the bond. It happens on every level."

I didn't respond. I couldn't. He was right. I was in love with her. Completely and hopelessly in love with her.

"You're in love with her," he said.

Damn! Reading my mind again.

"I don't have to read your mind to know that, Dante."

Bill was slowly making me crazy. His statement could have been purely intuitive. Hell, I had no idea. Besides, I had other things to worry about. "I need to have a blood test."

"What for?"

"To make sure I don't have any diseases."

"How could you—"

"She made me take her blood into my body. I have no idea what it could have done to me. A lot of horrific diseases are passed through blood."

Bill cleared his throat. "Dante, blood doesn't harm a vampire. It's our sustenance."

"But it was *her* blood. Vampire blood. We're not supposed to..." I sighed. No use spelling it all out again. "I can't take the chance of harming Erin with anything she might have put into me with her blood."

"All right. You're most likely fine, but I understand your concern. You can see the doctor who is taking care of Emilia. He's an old friend. He delivered you, River, and Emilia. You might have seen him when you were a kid."

"Would he be able to expedite the exam and any tests?"

"Probably. He runs his own lab and has techs working all the time. You shouldn't have any trouble getting a twenty-four-hour turnaround." He handed me a business card. "Give him a call."

"Thank you." I left Bill's office.

I'd get a physical. Blood tests if I had to. I was probably fine, but I didn't feel any better.

I still didn't know who had glamoured Erin.

THIRTEEN

Erin

I awoke with a huge smile on my face.

I was in love!

Better yet...he loved me back!

I lay in bed for a few precious moments, reliving my amazing time with Dante. How our bodies had fit together like perfect puzzle pieces, how he'd filled me so completely that I hadn't realized how empty I'd been, how we'd professed our love for each other, and the warmth I still felt remembering his words.

I love you, Erin. So much.

I hugged myself, imagining his arms wrapped around me, his lips at my ear, whispering.

I love you, Erin. So much.

By the time I got into work, River had been discharged. I checked his chart. The CAT indicated no internal bleeding, thank goodness. Lucy rushed in a few minutes later.

"Hey," I said. "You look a little...ragged."

"Thanks," she said sarcastically. "I didn't get any sleep. I was here with River most of the time."

"Oh?"

"Yeah. I mean, I didn't want him to be alone. Especially since— I just didn't want him to be alone."

"I didn't realize the two of you had gotten that close. Didn't you only have the one date?"

"Yeah. But it was a great date."

"But you didn't..."

"Fuck him?" She laughed nervously. "No. I know. That's not like me."

"I didn't say that."

"You were thinking it."

I was. But I still didn't say it. "Did the date not go well?"

"It went great. I am actually capable of having a good time and not winding up in a man's bed, Er."

"I didn't mean—"

"Yeah, you did. But it's okay. I am who I am. A horny little bitch." She laughed.

There went the epithet again. It was kind of Lucy's lingo, but today for some reason it bothered me more than usual. Lucy was a great person and an amazing nurse. "You shouldn't think of yourself that way, Luce."

"Why not? It's true."

"Having a healthy sex drive doesn't make you a bitch. You're my best friend. I don't like you putting yourself down."

"Who says I'm putting myself down?"

"I do. You're not a—"

"Incoming!" Steve rushed past us as the sirens wailed.

Time to go to work.

"Tell me about your date with River," I said to Lucy the next morning over breakfast.

She reddened a little, which wasn't like Lucy at all. Usually she couldn't wait to spill all the gory details.

"It was nice. We went to dinner and then went dancing. I guess I just wasn't in the mood for anything more."

Something didn't add up. Lucy was *always* in the mood. Except with Logan Crown, and he didn't inspire the mood in me either. But River Gabriel? He could inspire lust in the most frigid woman on the planet.

"Is this your way of saying you don't want to talk about it?" I took a sip of my O.J.

She sighed. "It's not that. It just...didn't go the way I expected."

"You just said it was great."

"It was. I know this isn't making sense."

"It's okay. If you weren't feeling it, you weren't feeling it."

"Yeah, I guess. I just wasn't feeling it."

Still, I didn't buy it. If she hadn't felt anything, she wouldn't have stayed by River's side at the hospital. I'd get her to spill her guts eventually. Maybe I was just so enfolded in a thick cloak of love that I wanted everyone else to be feeling such wonderment too.

I signaled for the check, and we counted out money on the table.

"Do you think you'll see River again?" That was an innocuous enough question.

"I don't know," she said. "I think that's up to him."

Again, totally weird. If Lucy wanted a guy, she normally

went after him, and there wasn't a man alive who could resist Lucy's charms. At least not that I'd seen, Logan Crown excepted, though I'd always assumed that had been Lucy's decision, not his.

My phone buzzed on the table.

A text.

From Dr. Bonneville?

I need to see you right away.
Meet me at the ER.

FOURTEEN

DANTE

D r. Jacques Hebert was nearly as old as Bill and had been practicing medicine for fifty years. Or so he told me.

"I see human patients as well," he said. "There aren't enough vampires around for me to make a living solely in vampire medicine. It's amazing how similar our physiology is. Our DNA is nearly indistinguishable. Most human scientists call the deviations 'anomalous DNA.'"

"Anomalous DNA?"

"Anomalies are found all the time in science. Certain anomalies are found in Native American DNA, for example." He laughed. "That's science for you. When they can't explain something, they call it an anomaly."

"But aren't *you* a scientist? As a medical doctor, I mean?"

He nodded. "But I know that the slight differences in vampire DNA aren't anomalies. I just can't tell any of my human colleagues."

"I used to want to be a doctor," I said.

"Really? We could use another vampire doctor. I'm not

going to be around forever, and I'm the only one in Louisiana. Most vampires go to regular human doctors."

"It's no longer in the cards for me."

"Why not? It's never too late. You can still go to med school."

But I never graduated from high school.

I'd have to get a GED and then an undergrad degree. Med school was definitely off the table. I did, though, need to find some way to make a living. I couldn't live off Bill forever, especially when I'd been getting really strange vibes from him since I'd returned.

"I'm taking a different path now," I said.

"I'm sorry to hear that. Let me know if you change your mind. I have a lot of connections in the medical field." He checked my chart. "So you're in today for a physical and possible blood work."

"Yeah, I..." Hell, what could I say?

"I'm not here to judge you, but I do need to know what your concerns are if I'm going to help you."

"You won't tell anyone what I tell you?"

"Of course not. I take doctor/patient confidentiality very seriously, as do most physicians."

I looked at the ceiling. "I was held against my will for ten years. By a female vampire." I reluctantly returned my gaze to Dr. Hebert.

He widened his eyes until they were nearly circular. I had to give him credit, though. He didn't gasp or say anything.

"She made me drink her...blood. That's why she kept me."

He cleared his throat. "I see. Any side effects?"

"No. She said she'd found a way to treat them."

"Any side effects for her?"

Really? "How the hell should I know? Or care? I hope my blood killed her."

"I'm sorry. Of course. It's just that...as you said, I'm a scientist, and it would be fascinating... Never mind."

He wanted to study me. And he wanted all the information I had on *her*. I couldn't blame him for being curious, but I wasn't going to be anyone's lab rat. Not today. Or any day, for that matter.

"It's unlikely that her blood infected you with anything, but I can run some labs just in case."

"Just run everything," I said dryly. "I need to know I'm clean."

"I see. You're in a relationship then?"

"The beginning of one, yes. In fact..." He wanted a study? I'd give him a study.

"What?"

"This is going to sound ridiculous to you, but have you ever heard of a human forming a blood bond with a vampire? Meaning a human develops a need to feed a particular vampire?"

"No, I have— Wait a minute." He rubbed his chin. "About fifteen years ago, I attended a seminar on vampire medicine. We had to keep it very quiet, of course, but something about what you're describing sounds vaguely familiar. Tell me what you know."

He listened intently as I told him everything that had happened between Erin and me and explained the research Bill had done.

"Doc, I need to know. How do I deal with this? Will she really die if she doesn't give me her blood?"

"I don't know, honestly. This is mostly new to me. Does

she seem okay to you?"

"She seems fine. Not ill at all."

"Then perhaps she won't die, but can *you* live without taking her blood?"

God, no. She was all I thought about. All I could smell. All I wanted. My need for her went so far beyond the need for her blood. "I can try."

"You can."

"But I need my sense of smell back. I'm vulnerable without it."

"You're not overly vulnerable. These days, a vampire doesn't need an acute sense of smell for protection. There are other ways to protect ourselves. Your life won't be cut short because of a failing nose."

"A *failed* nose. Except for the scent of one particular person."

"Make a fist for me," the doctor said. He tightened a band around my upper arm and punctured my vein.

I shut my eyes against the stick. "Can you get me any information you have on blood bonding?"

"I'll see what I can find out." He filled the clear tube with my blood and then bandaged the tiny wound. "I assume you want these results as quickly as possible?"

"Yes, please. How soon can you get them?"

"Probably in the next few hours. My staff does all the work right here. I'll give you a call when I know something. Otherwise, all your vitals are perfect. You're in excellent health."

"All right. Thanks, Doctor."

"Call me Jack. Everyone does. I've known your family for years."

"How's my sister doing?"

"I can't discuss my other patients, but since you're her brother, I'll tell you that the pregnancy is progressing normally. I don't foresee any problems."

I breathed a sigh of relief. "Good. Thank you. She won't tell any of us anything."

He smiled. "Emilia's her own person. That's for sure."

I nodded and left the exam room.

Now...what to do for the few hours before I could be with Erin again?

If I could be with Erin again.

No, it *would* work out. Jack had said it was unlikely *she* could have diseased me with anything.

I clung to that thought as I drove back to Bill's, remembering the night I'd escaped.

She *hadn't come to me in a few days, though the goons had come to drain me so* she *could drink. At least I assumed that was why they took my blood.*

They hadn't tortured me.

Three times a day, they came to unbind me and feed me.

I'd learned to pass the time.

I lived in my own head, dreaming up adventures, thinking about home. About what might be going on with my father, Emilia, River.

Most often I dreamed of the severed human heads feeding me what I craved most. Human blood. I hadn't tasted a drop of human blood in... Had I ever? We'd drunk animal blood from the butcher at home. I'd been taught that vampires didn't feed on humans unless the need was dire. It was morally wrong.

But oh, how I craved it.

The bitch's blood was thick and acidic, as if it left talon marks in my throat as it oozed down to my stomach.

Did my blood taste as repugnant to her *as hers did to me?*

I hoped so.

I slept off and on, never knowing whether it was night or day.

I relished the time when I was unbound, could allow my muscles a tiny bit of freedom. Oddly, they never atrophied. She said it was from the vampire blood she *coerced me to drink from* her. *The repugnant ooze that clawed at me constantly as* she *forced it into me.*

Maybe it was. I didn't know.

Her blood...

The goons had drained from me, but she *hadn't fed me her blood in a couple days. At least I thought it had been a couple of days.*

I'd long since stopped pulling against my bindings. It was no use, and the leather had cut into and scarred my wrists and ankles from trying.

But what if...

I pulled against the binding on my left wrist. Nothing. Then my left foot.

No again. My right foot.

I sighed. Wishful thinking.

Then my right hand.

I gasped.

It pulled free! Though I couldn't see because of the darkness, and it required quite a stretch, I worked the binding on my left wrist with my freed right hand.

I struggled, sweat pouring from my brow into my eyes and

stinging them. Still I kept at it, until—

Yes! The binding unfastened, and my hands were free.

I sat up. How glorious to sit up alone! I leaned forward, aching a bit at the stretch, and again, without the benefit of sight, unfastened the bindings at my ankles.

I was tempted to go into the small room that housed a toilet and sink to check out how I looked in the light, but no. I had to act quickly. Who knew when someone would be back in to check on me?

Of course, there was no way I could get out of this room. It had no window, and the door would be sealed shut for sure.

I walked slowly forward, so as to keep steady on my wobbly legs, and tried the doorknob.

What? It turned in my hand, and I pulled the door open.

More darkness, but small slivers of light illuminated a dark path before me. I inched forward, wishing I had eyes in the back of my head. My vision adjusted to the tiny bit of light, and it was like the sun was shining on me compared to the pure darkness I'd been in for so long.

I walked, naked, along the tiny pathway for...an hour maybe? Two? Time had ceased to exist for me. It might have been four hours. It might have been ten minutes. I didn't know.

Finally, I came to a narrow flight of stairs. I climbed up, stopping at what appeared, from this side, to be a manhole cover.

I sighed. It would be bolted down of course.

But I nudged it upward, and it loosened. I pushed it away, amazed at my own strength, and peeked out into the world.

The world.

The world that had been denied me for so long.

My eyes adjusted once again. It was nighttime, and I was in a dark alleyway.

But noise. Noises I hadn't heard in so long. Noises that conjured images of Bourbon Street. The scents of people.

Of blood.

I gathered all my strength, climbed out of the manhole, and ran.

I pulled into Bill's driveway.

I hadn't thought about it at the time because I was so eager and thrilled to finally escape.

But it all added up now.

One of my bindings had been loosened. The door had been unlocked. The dark path had been illuminated just so. The manhole cover had been loosened.

Coincidence? Never.

She had *let* me go.

FIFTEEN

Erin

Ugh. My head was pounding. I'd never been prone to headaches, but this one was a doozy. I took a few ibuprofen when I got home from my meeting with Dr. Bonneville. She had wanted my help with a research project. At the time, I'd meant to ask her why she hadn't published any of her so-called research—at least not that I could find online—but then the thought had fled my mind. Strange. Why she couldn't have asked someone on duty to help her, I didn't know. She gave me some BS about my being the most qualified for this particular project, but I wasn't buying it. She wanted me to research blood types in pale-skinned women with dark hair. Since I was a pale-skinned woman with dark hair, apparently I was qualified.

She'd given me some ridiculous reason why she needed the information—something about genetics and blood types. Everyone knew that blood types were hereditary from either the mother or the father. They had nothing to do with hair color or skin color. But I knew better than to argue with Dr. Bonneville, especially since she'd agreed to pay me fifty dollars an hour for my work.

I promised her I'd work on it during my next night off. Right now, all I wanted was a hot bath and a good night's—or rather day's—sleep. The perfect combination to help me shake the headache.

I went upstairs and started the bath water running, pausing for a moment to inhale the steam floating off the water. I added a few drops of lavender essential oil—no bath bomb this time—and shed my clothing. I didn't even bother aiming for my hamper. Everything ended up on the bathroom floor.

Right now, I needed relaxation.

I let my hair out of its ponytail, brushed it quickly, and then piled it on top of my head in a messy bun.

I lifted one leg to step in the tub, when—

"What is that?" I said out loud.

On my inner thigh, oddly close to my vulva, were two pink marks. I palpated them gently. They were slightly raised. They didn't seem to itch, but they looked a lot like bug bites. A lot like...

I turned and looked into the mirror.

A lot like that mosquito bite that Dante had nicked on my neck the night we were dancing...to no music.

A lot like the same type of marks I'd seen on my brother's neck at breakfast a few weeks before.

A lot like the marks on Abe Lincoln's neck in the ER...

Did you see him?

See who?

The vampire.

He'd told me about vampires, how he let them feed from

him in exchange for a hot meal...

I stared in the mirror. The mark from Dante's nick was nearly gone.

How would a bug bite me on my inner thigh, though? That part of me was almost always covered except when I was here at home, and I hadn't noticed any mosquitoes flying around lately.

Abe Lincoln had said—

I laughed out loud. This headache was doing a number on me. A really big number. I was exhausted and achy, and I needed this bath and some deep sleep to get my mind back in order.

I was a nurse. A scientist. I knew what was real and what wasn't, and here I was letting my imagination run wild over bug bites.

I rolled my eyes.

I turned back to the tub and turned off the faucet. The water had run deep, and I stepped in and immersed myself, breathing in the relaxing aroma, letting the heat soothe my tired body, my aching neck and head.

I closed my eyes and inhaled again.

No more worry about bug bites.

Just a hot bath.

SIXTEEN

DANTE

*S*he had let me go.

Bill had told me I was safe in this house, that she wouldn't find me.

How could he guarantee that?

He *couldn't* guarantee that...unless he knew.

He knew I had been let go.

I raced to his office and entered without knocking. "We need to talk, Bill."

"How did the tests go?" he asked.

"I don't know yet. Jack said it would take a few hours for him to run the results. But I need some answers."

"You'll have them in a few hours."

"No, that's not what I'm talking about. You said I was safe here. That no one would find me under this roof. Maybe you're right. I don't know. But I've been out and about since I returned. I haven't been thinking about my own safety because this pull I have with Erin pervades my mind and pushes everything else out. But I should have been concerned about my safety, concerned that the person who kept me prisoner would come after me. I should have been concerned for River, for Em, especially in light of her pregnancy. Their blood is the same as mine. If not for Erin, all of that would have been foremost in my mind."

"Yes. I understand that."

"But *you* never seemed concerned. River was concerned. Emilia was concerned. But not you."

"That's not true, I—"

"She let me go, Bill. It hadn't occurred to me because I was so happy to get away, and then I was so preoccupied with Erin and the pull...but today I thought about it. I relived it. She fucking *let* me go."

"And that's a bad thing?"

I curled my hands into fists. "No, *that's* not a bad thing. What's bad is that you knew, didn't you? You *knew* she let me go."

"How would I know that, Dante? You're just worried right now. Worried about the tests. Your mind is—"

"My mind is fucking fine, damn it. Yeah, it shouldn't be. She messed with it for ten years. But I lived. I survived. I gritted my teeth and I bore it all. Because I was the son of Julian Gabriel, the grandson of Guillaume Gabriel, part of one of the most powerful and respected vampire lines still in existence. I made it through, and yeah, I should be majorly fucked up, but I'm not. I won't deny that there are times when I feel like I'm on the brink of madness, but I still know what reality is, Bill."

"Dante, with all respect, no, you don't. You're overreacting and you're projecting your anger for your captor onto me. I've been patient—"

"Patient? That's a laugh. You kicked me out of your house, Bill."

"I acted irrationally when you got violent. You know you'll always have a home here."

"A home where I'm safe, right? A home where *she* can't find me. That's bullshit. You know something, Bill. You know she let me go, and that's why you think I'm safe here."

"Dante"—he advanced toward me—"listen to reason. I don't know anything about your abduction. If I did, don't you think I would have found you long before now? Don't you think I would have moved heaven and earth to free you?"

No. I didn't think that. Ten years ago, I would've thought that. I knew my grandfather—and my father and uncle—would do anything to protect me. Now? I wasn't so sure.

"You've been reading my mind since I got back."

"I don't have that gift. You know that."

"I know it's not common among vampires. It's not common among humans either. But a select few can do it."

"I'm not one of those select few. If you think I know what you're thinking sometimes, it's because I do. You're my grandchild. I'm intuitive when it comes to all three of you."

"That makes no sense. You don't even know me anymore. I was gone for a decade."

"That doesn't change the blood between us, Dante."

I sighed. Was it possible I was making this up in my head? I felt normal, felt like I had a grasp on reality, but I could not deny what I'd been through. I also couldn't deny that many of those memories were fuzzy and I didn't know if they were real or nightmares. And the whole thing with Erin had wreaked havoc on my mind.

Was Bill truly on my side? He had been in the past. I was sure of it.

"How do you know I'm safe here, Bill?"

"I just do."

"Damn it!" I brought my fist down on his desk. "Can't you be honest?"

"All right. You want honesty? Fine. Here is honesty. This house is safe—*you* are safe—because you have a ghost watching over you."

A ghost. I scoffed. "I haven't lost my mind. *You* have."

I walked out of the office.

I drove around for a few hours, trying to work off my head of steam, until my phone buzzed with a text.

From Jack.

I closed my eyes for a moment, breathing in, before I looked at his words.

All tests negative. Congratulations.

SEVENTEEN

Erin

"Erin!"

I jerked upward, water sloshing over the sides of my tub. A chill swept over me. The water was lukewarm, even cold in places. Why hadn't I gotten out?

Dante stood above me, holding a towel.

"You were asleep, Erin. You fell asleep in the tub. Do you have any idea how dangerous that was? You could have drowned!"

I shivered, rubbing my arms as I stood and stepped into the towel he was holding. "How did you get in here?"

"Your door was—"

"Unlocked? Again? I could have sworn..." I shook my head. "Oh, never mind. What has gotten into me lately?"

I'd come upstairs with that horrible headache. I could easily have forgotten to lock my door. Still, though, this was happening a lot lately. What was going on with my mind?

My headache seemed to be gone, thank goodness. I was

still tired though. It was the middle of the night...er...day.

My body throbbed just being near Dante. He looked wonderful, as usual, his dark hair mussed and his coffee-colored eyes blazing as he gazed upon me.

So gorgeous.

My nipples were hard. From the roughness of the terry towel? Maybe. More likely because Dante was doing the rubbing of the fabric against my skin.

"Erin, you *have* to lock your door. I know it's the middle of the day, but—"

"I *do* lock my door. At least I think I do." My mind flew back to the time I had made myself remember the actual turning of the deadbolt. All the other times? I was on autopilot. I'd never neglected to lock my door in the past, even on autopilot.

Not since I'd met Dante...

But he was here, taking care of me. The man I loved, who miraculously loved me in return.

I leaned into him and inhaled his woodsy fragrance. Cinnamon, wood, and man. Dante.

"Mmm...not that it matters," I said, closing my eyes as I melted into him. "But why are you here?"

He chuckled against the top of my head. "Because no matter what happens in my life, I always feel like I should be here. With you."

"I know the feeling."

He pushed me slightly away. "Erin, seriously, you need to—" He stopped abruptly.

When I looked at him, his eyes were wide, his eyebrows arched.

"What?"

"Have you always kept your door unlocked?"

"No. Of course not. Not on purpose anyway."

"Have you ever fallen asleep in the tub before?"

"No. But—"

"Oh my God. You're not going to get sick."

"What? Of course not. Why would you want me to get sick?"

"I don't. I mean..." He shook his head.

"Dante, what are you talking about?"

"I had it all wrong." He walked out of the bathroom, his hands on either side of his head. "It's all making sense now."

"I hardly ever get sick," I said. "I've been around sick people for so long that I've grown immune to most common illnesses."

"I'm glad. I don't want you to get sick. Of course. I just thought..." He sighed. "Never mind what I thought. Please don't ever fall asleep in the tub again."

"I don't make a habit of it." I smiled.

"Damn it, Erin. This isn't funny." He grabbed me and pulled me close, only the towel between my naked body and his fully clothed one. "If anything ever happened to you, I don't know what I'd do. I can't lose you, Erin."

"Nothing will happen to me."

"It will if you keep leaving your door unlocked and falling asleep in the bathtub."

"Dante—"

He slammed his lips down on mine. His kiss was full of the passion I'd come to know, but this one held something more.

Fear.

He truly was afraid of losing me.

I gave to him with my kiss, tried to convey how much he meant to me and that there was no need for concern. I was a grown woman, and nothing would happen to me.

Then he broke the kiss, suddenly, his eyes laced with a faraway look. Almost a look of...

I'd seen it before.

That look of madness.

He'd had that same look in his eyes when he looked between my legs and—

Oh. My. God.

The marks. The bug bites.

Were they something else?

Who tasted you?

I'd thought, then, that he was referring to Logan. That he thought Logan had gone down on me. But we'd still been fully clothed...

Did you see him?

Who?

The vampire.

He was here. In the hospital.

I stepped backward slowly.

No. I was making things up. I was tired. That was all. I'd had that headache after meeting with Dr. Bonneville, and I'd taken some medication and run the bath to...

"Erin," Dante said, "I have to leave you for a little while."

"Why? Can't you stay with me?"

"I have to take care of something, but you'll be safe. I will stand outside and make sure you lock your door, okay? And no more baths until I return."

"I won't need another bath until tomorrow, at least," I said.

"Good. Where are your pajamas?"

"I usually just sleep in a tank top and undies." I went to my drawer and put them on.

Dante eyed me lasciviously.

"You like?" I teased.

"Yes, but I don't have time right now. Soon. I promise. And with nothing between us. I had a blood test and I'm clean."

He smiled, and he was as gloriously gorgeous as ever, but something was missing in that smile.

Something I couldn't quite put my finger on.

Still, I was thrilled at the prospect of making love with him sans condom. My nipples hardened against the soft cotton of my tank, and the tickle between my legs intensified.

"When will you be back?" I asked.

"Get some sleep. Do you work tonight?"

"Yeah, unfortunately."

"Okay. I'll meet you here after your shift." He brushed his lips gently over mine. "Let's go downstairs, and I'm going to make sure you lock your door."

I smiled and followed him downstairs. He kissed me quickly again. "I love you, Erin."

"I love you too, Dante."

He left and I shut the door, turning the deadbolt into place.

Marking it in my mind.

EIGHTEEN

DANTE

I had more questions, but I wasn't going to Bill this time. I no longer trusted him. I still couldn't believe he'd tried to placate me with some stupid ghost story. Vampires didn't believe in ghosts. We were taught from a young age—

Why don't you believe him?

The words popped into my thoughts so quickly that I almost didn't believe they'd come from me. "Because it's nonsense," I said out loud.

But what *was* nonsense, anyway? A few days ago, I'd never have believed there could be such a thing as a blood bond between a vampire and a human. Now I had no doubt. Erin had formed a blood bond with me. I was sure of it.

I'd been so afraid that Erin would fall ill, but she always seemed so healthy. Now I realized the threat wasn't illness. It was something else. She was deliberately putting herself in harm's way, and she didn't even realize it. Erin was intelligent, a medical professional. She knew better than to leave her door unlocked or let herself fall asleep in a full tub.

She would die not of disease but from an accident or a seemingly random act of violence. Something in her brain chemistry had changed, making her do these things, put herself in danger.

Only giving me her blood could save her, according to theory—a theory that seemed more real by the second.

Only her blood could save both of us.

My phone buzzed against my thigh. I retrieved it. River.

"Hey, Riv. How are you feeling?"

"Good. My headache is pretty much all gone now. I think the doctors made a mountain out of a molehill keeping me in the hospital for so long."

"You back at work already?"

"No. They're making me take a few sick days. I'm fine, but department policy and all that. So I thought we could get together and start working on your case."

I sighed. River wanted to find who had taken me. So did I, but I'd been so focused on Erin that I hadn't cooperated with him much. Normally I'd be champing at the bit to bring *her* to justice.

But this Erin thing. This blood bond thing.

It had taken me over.

I was still focused on Erin, but I did need to talk to my cousin. I had to talk to someone because I was no longer going to talk to Bill. I'd meet him under the guise of working on my case, but then steer the conversation where I needed it to go.

"Okay," I said. "Where are you?"

"I'm at my place. Where are you?"

"Just coming back from Erin's. I'll meet you at your apartment."

"Sounds good. Pick up some burgers or something, will

you? I'm starving. The hospital food sucked balls."

River had set out two glasses of blood, and I placed the bag of fast food down on his table.

He inhaled. "Man, that smells great."

Interesting. I could still smell food, flowers, whatever. Just not people—other than Erin, of course.

Unfortunately, I could also smell River. "When was the last time you had a shower?"

"Sorry. Before the accident. I decided to go out on a run before I showered."

"You went out on a run. When you're recovering from a concussion."

"I just couldn't stay still any longer, man. Being trapped in the hospital about did me in."

"I don't mind waiting while you take a quick one."

"The food'll get cold."

I laughed. "All right. Right now, I wish my sense of smell didn't work on regular things as well."

He pulled the food out of the bag and set it in front of us while I drained my glass of blood and then asked for another. Being with Erin always made my blood lust go crazy.

River set another glass for me on the table and then sat down. "I've been thinking. I need you to tell me exactly where you were when you realized you had escaped."

"I was in a back alley near Bourbon Street. I came out of a manhole. The cover had been loosened."

"Okay. Do you know which alleyway?"

"Not really. I was desperate, scared she'd come after me,

and hungry. So fucking hungry. My mind wasn't working quite right."

"If we went back there, do you think you could find the manhole?"

"Man, Riv. I don't think I want to go back there."

"That's a victim's mentality, cuz. And yes, you *are* a victim, but I need you to be strong. You don't want this to happen to anyone else, do you?"

"Of course not."

"Then you have to do this. You have to testify."

"I have no idea who to testify against."

"I know that. We'll find out who did this to you, and I will personally make the arrest and see to it that whoever did this to you is brought to justice. You can count on that."

"It was a vampire, Riv. She'll just glamour everyone into believing she's innocent."

"Not if *I'm* on the case."

River was a good cop. He believed in what he was doing, and it meant a lot to him. I could see it in his eyes. I still didn't know why he'd opted out of business school for the police academy. I still didn't know a lot of things.

But that wasn't what I needed to talk about right now.

"Riv?"

"Yeah?"

"Has Bill seemed a little...*off* to you lately?"

"No, not really. Why?"

That made sense. River hadn't been gone for ten years, and if Bill had slowly changed during that time, he probably hadn't noticed.

"He told me something ridiculous."

"What?"

"He said there was a ghost protecting me."

River laughed. "He said what?"

"I'm serious. He said there was a ghost protecting me. That the woman who kept me couldn't come after me because of that."

"That doesn't sound like Bill. He's always so logical."

"I know. But for the sake of argument, if it's true, and there really is a ghost protecting me, where the hell was that damn phantom for the last ten years?"

"Are you sure that's what he said? Maybe you misunderstood."

"My mind is working just fine. You all think I've gone mental after being held captive for so long. I could have, believe me. But I didn't. I'm in my right mind. I'd think the blood bond theory would have convinced you of that."

"What do you mean?"

"I *was* starting to doubt my mind," I said. "I was so obsessed with Erin, and it didn't make any sense. I mean, she's beautiful and I was attracted to her. Big time. But why the obsession so quickly? The blood bond makes sense. It's starting to make a lot of sense."

"How so?"

"Erin. I kept thinking she was going to get sick if she didn't feed me, but she's perfectly healthy. So maybe the blood bond is nonsense, right? But it isn't happening that way. Something has gone haywire in her brain. She's been putting herself in dangerous situations without realizing it, like leaving her door unlocked when she's sleeping. Something like that is going to do her in, not illness." Just saying the words sent a chill of fear through me. "I can't let her die, Riv. I can't."

"Then you have to take her blood. If you're not ready to tell her yet, glamour her."

"We've been through this. I don't want to. Even if I did, I tried it once before and it didn't work— Wait. Here's another thing. Erin saw my teeth the other day. She ran away screaming and then came back as if nothing had happened. Someone had glamoured her. You were still in the hospital, and Em doesn't even know about any of this. Bill is the only one who could have, and he denied it. He outright lied to me."

"That doesn't sound like Bill."

"Who else could have done it?"

River shook his head. "I honestly don't know. Unless she did it herself. Maybe the blood bond messed with her brain somehow."

"I don't think so. You didn't see her face when she ran away."

"There's a lot we don't know about what's happening to the two of you. A lot we may never know."

"There's something else," I said.

"What?"

I cleared my throat. "She loves me. And I love her."

"And that's bad?"

"No. It's just..." I sighed. "What if it isn't real? What if it's this blood bond thing?"

"That doesn't mean the love isn't real even if the blood bond *is* real. And it sure seems like it is."

"It does," I agreed. "I do love her. She's consumed me since the moment I met her. I always wondered why she didn't turn me in when she found me in the blood bank, why she let me go."

"The blood bond," he said. "In a way, you're lucky. You might be rotting in jail right now if she had turned you in."

"You would have pulled some strings."

"I would have tried. But I don't glamour on the job. Not even for you. It's unethical."

I chuckled. "Then I guess I'm really grateful for the bond. I'm seeing her tomorrow morning after she gets off work. I'll take her blood then. I'll figure out a way somehow. I can't have her in danger."

I arrived at Erin's before she got home the next morning and turned the doorknob.

Damn! Unlocked again.

I had to take care of this. Now. I had to keep her from running, and I knew only one way to do that.

I'd have to tie her down, just as I'd thought before. I had the rope in my jacket pocket.

My groin tightened.

I closed my eyes, an image appearing in my mind. Erin, naked, tied to her bed, her body flushed warm pink, her nipples taut and tight, the scent of her earthy arousal thick in the air.

No doubt about it, I liked the idea, despite having been tied down myself and violated for so long.

Maybe something *was* wrong with my mind.

I wasn't completely naïve. I'd known a lot when I was eighteen. I knew some people enjoyed sexual bondage. I just never thought *I* would. Especially considering my history.

I hoped to God Erin would, because I didn't know how else to keep her from running. She'd already said she would obey me. Tying her up would require a whole new level of obedience, though. Would she trust me? She loved me. I had to believe that would lead to trust.

Whatever happened, I had to be strong. I had to go through with this, for both our sakes.

I stalked around her townhome, making sure nothing was out of place. No one had been here, at least not that I could tell.

Good. Thank God.

I turned when she bustled through the door.

"Dante!" Her eyes widened. "Oh my God. Don't tell me."

"Unlocked again, Erin. You have to be more careful."

She set her purse on the table. "I honestly don't know what's wrong with me. I assure you this is completely new. I never did this before..."

"Before what?"

"Huh." She let out a huff. "Before I met you, actually."

NINETEEN

Erin

Dante grabbed me and kissed me hard.

What had I been saying? All thoughts fled from my mind. I parted my lips and met his tongue—his rough yet velvety tongue—and surrendered to the moment.

I'd left my door unlocked again? Who cared? Right now I was kissing the beautiful man I loved.

We'd be together soon, our bodies joined with no barrier.

My nipples tightened into such firm little knobs that I was sure he could feel them poking him through my bra and both our shirts. His cock was hard against my belly, and my pussy was already pulsing, moistening, getting ready to take him into my body.

I broke the kiss quickly. Saying nothing, I grabbed his hand and led him upstairs to my bedroom.

I began undressing. "Take off your clothes," I said.

I didn't want to take the time to undress each other, to savor the moment.

No. I wanted him inside me. Now.

Soon I stood before him naked.

But he was still dressed.

"What's wrong? Why didn't you take off your clothes?"

He stared at me, his eyes full of fire. "I don't obey you, Erin. You obey *me*."

Oh, God. Never had I imagined I'd be so turned on by a dominant man. But I was. I was so wet right now, he could slide into me and I wasn't sure I'd feel it at all.

"Lie on the bed."

I complied, watching him as he pulled a length of rope out of his coat pocket.

Please. Tie me up. Blindfold me. Whip me.

I'd dreamed about this. The idea had surprised me. Surprised me in that it hadn't disturbed me. No, it had aroused me. Made me want things I never knew I wanted.

"What's that for?" I asked, willing my voice not to shake.

"I'm going to bind your wrists to the bed, love."

I moaned. "Oh my God."

"Do you like that idea, Erin?"

I closed my eyes and swallowed, embarrassed to tell him yes.

"Do you? Answer me?"

I opened my eyes and met his fiery gaze. "Yes."

He smiled. "Good. So do I. Grab a rung of your headboard with each hand."

I did as I was told. He tied my wrists gently. "Let me know if it's too tight."

I pulled. I was secure, but the rope didn't rub or burn. "It's fine."

"Good. Good. Do you have any idea how beautiful you

look right now, Erin? Naked, bound. All for me."

I sighed.

"But I'm not the only one who is going to experience pleasure today. I'm going to give you gratification unlike you've ever known. I'm going to sink my cock into that beautiful sweet pussy. No condom. Just *me* taking *you*."

He sat down on the edge of the bed and trailed a long finger over my cheek, my lips, down my neck and over my breasts, stopping and circling a nipple. "Do you like that?"

I closed my eyes. "God, yes."

"Tell me what you want me to do to your nipples, Erin."

"Kiss them."

He lightly kissed each one. My pussy gushed.

"Suck them."

He took one between his full lips and lightly tugged.

I squirmed. "B-Bite them."

He smiled against my breast. "I *like* to bite." He gave my nipple a quick nip.

I arched my back, searching for more. Something more.

I knew what I wanted.

I tugged at my bindings, wanting desperately to touch Dante, to curl my fingers through his thick dark hair.

But I couldn't.

And I found, suddenly, that I was thrilled.

I was at his mercy, couldn't touch him though I longed to. I whimpered.

"What is it, love?"

"I want to touch you, Dante. To feel you."

"I know you do. You will. In good time." He smiled. "Would you like me to get undressed?"

"Please. I want to feel your skin against mine."

He stood and slowly undressed. Achingly slowly. With each new inch of fair skin exposed, my pussy quivered.

Finally he was naked, his gorgeous cock jutting straight out, a drop of fluid glistening at the tip. I wanted so badly to lick it off, to take him to the back of my throat.

But no. Not before he was embedded in my hot pussy.

"Please, Dante. Please come into my body. Come into me. We've waited so long for this."

"Yes, my love."

He sat down on the bed and then hovered over me, teasing my labia with his hard cock.

"I feel how wet you are for me, Erin. So wet." He inhaled. "I smell you. I smell how much you want me. I wish you could smell how much I want you."

I inhaled his salty cinnamon scent. Maybe I couldn't smell his arousal as I smelled my own, but I knew. In my heart I knew he wanted me as much as I wanted him. In his eyes, I saw it. I saw what I knew he was seeing in my own.

That fire. That passion.

That true love.

He groaned as he thrust inside me.

Such sweet intrusion.

"My God, Erin. I feel your warmth. I feel every ridge inside you, your walls closing around me. You were made for me."

I hadn't been able to find the words, but he'd said them perfectly. "Yes. Exactly. I feel it, too."

He stayed inside me for a moment, and I relished the sweet fullness, as if I'd never been filled before.

And never would be again by anyone else.

Only by this man.

Then he gritted his teeth, pulled out, and thrust back in.

I arched into him, tugging at my bindings, wanting so much to touch his smooth skin.

"I love you, Dante. I love you."

He thrust back in. "I love you too, Erin. My only love."

Thrust.

Thrust.

Thrust.

His pubic hair and bone nudged my clit with each thrust, tickling it, making it flutter.

So close.

So close.

Until I erupted, the orgasm taking me with a force I hadn't yet known.

My whole body vibrated, every cell humming the jazzy tune that drifted to my ears.

"Dante, I'm coming. I'm coming so hard."

"Yes, love. Come. Come for me." He thrust once more, filling me. Each contraction of his cock in rhythm with my own pulsing.

"Ah, God!" he cried out, embedding himself into me.

We climaxed together, each of us moaning, our bodies sliding together from the perspiration.

Savor this moment. Savor it.

Again I tugged at my bindings. I lifted my head, trying to reach his lips. Sweat from his brow dripped onto my face, from his chest onto mine.

And then, as the pulsing finally began to subside, he opened his eyes.

They were blazing and full of fire.

"Come, my love, and I will bring you to true completion."

THE QUEEN

Y ou're mine, Dante.

Even now, I'm watching you in my mind. Remembering you, the taste of your blood, the intense feeling when you sank your teeth into my flesh.

I own you, and you *will* obey.

When the time is right, I'll come for you.

You're mine, Dante.

Always and for eternity.

I've made sure of it.

***This story continues in* Unhinged**
Blood Bond Saga: Volume Two!

MESSAGE FROM HELEN HARDT

Dear Reader,

Thank you for reading *Unchained*. If you want to find out about my current backlist and future releases, please like my Facebook page and join my mailing list. I often do giveaways. If you're a fan and would like to join my street team to help spread the word about my books. I regularly do awesome giveaways for my street team members.

If you enjoyed the story, please take the time to leave a review on a site like Amazon or Goodreads. I welcome all feedback.

I wish you all the best!
Helen

Facebook
Facebook.com/HelenHardt

Newsletter
HelenHardt.com/Sign-Up

Street Team
Facebook.com/Groups/HardtAndSoul/

ALSO BY HELEN HARDT

Blood Bond Saga:
Unchained: Volume One

Unhinged: Volume Two
(October 30, 2018)

Undaunted: Volume Three
(Coming Soon)

Unmasked: Volume Four
(Coming Soon)

Undefeated: Volume Five
(Coming Soon)

The Steel Brothers Saga:
Craving
Obsession
Possession
Melt
Burn
Surrender
Shattered
Twisted
Unraveled

Misadventures Series:
Misadventures of a Good Wife
Misadventures with a Rock Star

The Temptation Saga:
Tempting Dusty
Teasing Annie
Taking Catie
Taming Angelina
Treasuring Amber
Trusting Sydney
Tantalizing Maria

The Sex and the Season Series:
Lily and the Duke
Rose in Bloom
Lady Alexandra's Lover
Sophie's Voice
The Perils of Patricia
(Coming Soon)

Daughters of the Prairie:
The Outlaw's Angel
Lessons of the Heart
Song of the Raven

ACKNOWLEDGMENTS

Beginning a new series is always a bit daunting for an author. This time, though, not only did I have to equal the Steel phenomenon, I had to do so in a different romance genre. Venturing into paranormal was an easy decision creatively. I love everything about the paranormal, and I especially love vampires. But would my readers follow me?

To those of you who have followed me, thank you! And to those who are picking up a Helen Hardt book for the first time, thank you as well! Please stick around as exciting things are coming.

As I got to know Dante and Erin, I became confident that readers would love them as much as they loved the Steel Brothers. Perhaps even more. Dante is the ultimate dark and tortured hero whose love for his heroine is all-consuming and passionate. Erin is feisty, smart, and strong-willed. Exploring the paranormal with two such interesting characters has been a lot of fun, and there's much more to do!

Writing the emergency room scenes presented a challenge. Massive thanks to Brian Archer, MD, and Tina Jaworski, RN, for helping me with medical procedure and terminology. I've taken creative license here and there, so any errors belong to me alone.

Of course my work wouldn't shine without my amazing editorial team. Thank you to my editor, Celina

Summers, my line editor, Scott Saunders, and my proofreaders, Amy Grishman, Michele Moore, Michele Lehmann, and Rebecca Jacobs. You each added your own special touch to this story, and I'm forever grateful.

Thanks as always to the team at Waterhouse Press— Meredith, Jon, David, Dave, Robyn, Haley, Jennifer, Jeanne, Kurt, Amber, Yvonne, and Jesse. Your support as I leap into a new genre means the world.

To the ladies of my street team, Hardt and Soul—you rock! The love and support you give me lifts me to new heights. Thank you for spreading the word about the Blood Bond Saga and for your wonderful reviews and general good vibes. Special thanks to Amy Denim for your always amazing help.

Thank you to my family and friends and to my two local RWA chapters, Colorado Romance Writers and Heart of Denver Romance Writers.

Most of all, thank you to all my readers. None of this would be possible without each one of you!

ABOUT THE AUTHOR

#1 *New York Times*, #1 *USA Today*, and #1 *Wall Street Journal* bestselling author Helen Hardt's passion for the written word began with the books her mother read to her at bedtime. She wrote her first story at age six and hasn't stopped since. In addition to being an award-winning author of contemporary and historical romance and erotica, she's a mother, an attorney, a black belt in Taekwondo, a grammar geek, an appreciator of fine red wine, and a lover of Ben and Jerry's ice cream. She writes from her home in Colorado, where she lives with her family. Helen loves to hear from readers.

Visit her at HelenHardt.com